D1498173

AMITABHA BAGCHI

FOURTH ESTATE • *New Delhi*

First published in India in 2013 by Fourth Estate
An imprint of HarperCollins *Publishers* India

Copyright © Amitabha Bagchi 2013

ISBN: 978-93-5116-018-2

2 4 6 8 10 9 7 5 3 1

Amitabha Bagchi asserts the moral right to be identified as
the author of this work.

HarperCollins *Publishers*
A-53, Sector 57, Noida, Uttar Pradesh 201301, India
77-85 Fulham Palace Road, London W6 8JB, United Kingdom
Hazelton Lanes, 55 Avenue Road, Suite 2900, Toronto, Ontario M5R 3L2
and 1995 Markham Road, Scarborough, Ontario M1B 5M8, Canada
25 Ryde Road, Pymble, Sydney, NSW 2073, Australia
31 View Road, Glenfield, Auckland 10, New Zealand
10 East 53rd Street, New York NY 10022, USA

Typeset in 10.5/14.5 Galliard BT at
SÜRYA

Printed and bound at
Replika Press Pvt. Ltd.

For my traveling companion,
Ratika Kapur

'Ghulaamii ko barkat samajhne lagen
asiiron ko aisi rihaaii na de'

'Don't give your prisoners such release
that they start thinking of servitude as a blessing'

– Bashir Badr

⊰∞⊱

'Where the bookstore used to be
A pharmacy is going up.
I have read too many books.
What is the medicine for that?'

– 'Charles and 25th Street', Robert Schreur,
Citypaper, 15 March 2000

1

'JEEVAN,' CALLED HENRY, PUSHING HIS WALKER UP THE SIDEWALK. 'Orioles won yesterday.'

'Did Cal play?' Jeevan asked.

Henry laughed. 'Oh, for five,' he said. 'Struck out three times. He played.'

Cal had played; he had been playing every day of every season for the last fourteen or fifteen years. And although Jeevan had little interest in baseball, he always checked the paper in the morning during the season. When he found that the Orioles had the previous day off, he would make a point of asking Henry how last night's game had gone. 'Os were traveling,' Henry would say, to which Jeevan would respond, 'Did Cal play?'

Oscar, whose leash was tied to one of the legs of Henry's walker, had a daily ritual too. It involved first examining Jeevan's stoop with his nose and then turning around to raise his leg and make up for the fading of his scent on this outpost of his domain. He pulled at his leash now, anxious to get on with the day's work. One of the forelegs of the walker got stuck in a broad crack in the concrete paving. The metal frame began to tip over.

'Oscar!'

That one word, his name, was enough to remind the dog that he was not free to do as he pleased. In the meantime, one of the two old tennis balls that protected the plastic cups at the bottom of the walker's forelegs and, according to Henry, made it easier for him to push the walker up the grainy pavement, had come loose. Jeevan got up and retrieved it. The lower half of it was worn out, almost all the way through.

'We'll need a new tennis ball,' Jeevan said.

'When I hear it squeak,' Henry replied and, turning around, sat down on the lowest step, a few inches away from Oscar's target. The dog whimpered in protest, but thought better of taking the matter any further. As Henry laid the walker on its side, a beautiful note came quivering out of Ms Lucy's organ from next door and wrapped both men and the dog in its arms.

They looked up at the house from where the music was coming. Crowning the façade was a plaster trim that ran the length of the three houses of this short block, adorned with a bas-relief procession of steam engines of varying vintage, lined up as if for a parade. Below this trim and above the tiled awning that covered the porch was a workmanlike but pleasing red brick front with two white rectangular windows cut into it. Behind one of these windows sat the organ that was the source of the music, and its player.

The sound vibrated through the summer morning; it felt like it was pouring down from the brilliant blue sky. It seemed to be entering everything: the asphalt with its cracks, the empty parking lot across the street, the deserted factory building next to the alley and the traffic passing by on Howard Street beyond. There was a yellow truck waiting to turn on to the street. The music had distracted Jeevan so much, he forgot to notice it was a moving truck.

'That sweet chariot's not swinging low enough for me,' grumbled Henry. The ball would not stay on the foot of the walker. The hole he had made in it was too large.

'I'll get you something for it,' Jeevan said.

The sun was slanting into the living room, falling on the empty mantelpiece. Below it sat an electric fireplace log left behind by a previous tenant, eternally suspended halfway between wood and cinders. Jeevan had not thrown it out all these years, but he had never felt the urge to switch it on either, not even in winter. On one side of the room sat the foldout couch that had never been folded out, at least not since he had found it in an alley and brought it home a few days after he had moved to this house. At right angles to it sat the overstuffed chair where the paper was read in the mornings. Jeevan looked around the room and for a moment it felt like he was visiting himself, Jeevan Sharma, an old acquaintance. He felt a twinge of curiosity, as if he had known this Jeevan Sharma when they were both much younger and was eager to see what his life was like now and how he kept his house.

To Jeevan's right, under the staircase, was the cupboard he was headed to. There among the brooms and mops and pieces of old vacuum cleaners was a cardboard box that contained the tube he was looking for.

When he returned to the stoop, Jeevan found the yellow truck parked outside the house next door. The organ had stopped playing. The cars whooshing up and down Howard Street were audible again.

'Shabbir say anything about this to you?' asked Henry, taking the adhesive from him.

The house Jeevan lived in had been the first property Shabbir had bought in America. The neighboring house had been the second. Once he had bought the second house, a long sequence of cousins and nephews from Pakistan had passed through it. Each one of them drove a cab Shabbir owned and paid him rent on both the house and the taxi. A few days after Shabbir bought a new taxi, one of his many relatives would decide – sheer coincidence, he always said – that he wanted to leave Lahore and come to Baltimore. And with each new relative's arrival, the time that elapsed till the next cab was bought reduced. But then, a few years ago, after his son got a scholarship to UMD, Shabbir slowed down. Nowadays he sat at Food Point, two blocks from here, where he served every kabab that a hungry Pakistani might want, as well as various kinds of biryanis, curries, sandwiches and fries.

Food Point had begun as a common kitchen for his extended taxi-driving family. But many of them had moved on to other things or other places. This second phase of Food Point's life saw a steady clientele of various kinds of people not related to Shabbir: African cabbies, students from India or Pakistan, black neighbors; all people Shabbir could now charge for food without the occasional pinpricks of conscience that used to trouble him when he took money

4

from a sleep-deprived cousin who was also paying him for a rundown cab and shabby living quarters.

As Food Point flourished, the two houses he had first bought had fallen into disuse, Shabbir having bought another house right next to the restaurant for himself and his wife. He had offered one to Jeevan. At first, he had asked for rent, and initially Jeevan had paid. But a few weeks after becoming Shabbir's accountant, Jeevan had stopped paying rent, telling Shabbir he would pay only if Shabbir paid him as much as someone who knew everything about his finances should be paid. Shabbir didn't ask again. The other house had remained empty and it had become one of Jeevan's duties to open it from time to time and make sure that everything was okay.

'He had mentioned some people were interested,' Jeevan told Henry. 'I didn't know they were moving in.'

Jeevan's new neighbors were Matthew and Kay. Matthew was tall and thin, in the manner of a person who ate fewer meals than he should. His old frayed T-shirt with the name of a band and the dates and venues of their 1989 tour was layered over a white cotton inner that was longer than the outer. He wore glasses and a two-day stubble that seemed to be a mark of inward contemplation rather than laziness or affectation. Kay carried her body with the kind of ease that sometimes comes with playing sports competitively, but her face, even at rest, bore a faintly surprised expression. It was a pale and freckled face, with a roundness that might have come from a Native American ancestor somewhere up the family tree. She was shorter than her husband, but filled out in a way that made the difference irrelevant.

They were holding up the ends of a large couch. He brought it around to the stairs and started climbing them backwards. She was going to take the weight of it, Jeevan realized, so he stepped forward to help. 'I got it,' she grunted, and heaved upward. Matthew tripped on the last step and almost fell over, but recovered in time and managed to bring the large piece of furniture softly down to the floor. They appeared even younger than Jeevan would later discover they were; he was just past thirty and she was twenty-seven. There was something about them, or perhaps there was something about their carrying heavy furniture into a rented house together without any help, that made them appear young.

An hour later, everything had been moved in. Henry stayed through the hour, occasionally offering advice on how to lift this or that item, or how to carry a box so that it didn't feel as heavy. 'Drove a delivery truck into my sixties, didn't miss a single day,' was his claim to authority. 'On one bum leg.'

Jeevan brought some cold water out and two glasses.

Henry asked Matthew if he liked baseball and, without waiting for an answer, began his monologue: 'I could have played in the major leagues. Even as a boy I was better than the men. My daddy wasn't keen on it. Study and be an engineer like myself, he would say, there's no future in playing ball. He had managed the machines in that big mill down off Falls Road when he was a young man, but that was all over since I can remember. He talked about it an awful lot though. It kept him going while he shifted from one job to another, trying to keep food on the table. They'll come back, he'd say about the mills, there's no better place to make cotton than here. There'll be new mills, you'll see. Study well, he told us boys, and you could work the new machines one day. But I didn't care about that. I could hit the ball far, and that's all I

6

cared about. We had real balls back then, not like the ones they have nowadays. If you hit a homer in my time, that was something. Maybe someone hit one every two or three games. Not like today. Some runt steps to the box and waves his bat, and see you later. What we used to hit back then were real homers. They called me Herman, like the Babe. I had a couple of offers, some scouts saw me play and offered me a salary. I even played a couple of seasons with a team out of Hagerstown, got to send money back to my ma and all. But then the war started. Came out of it with this limp. Wasn't a bullet or anything, just fell out of the back when the truck hit a pothole one morning in Germany. They probably should have fixed it up better than they did. But anyway, that took care of that. No more Herman, just plain old Henry.'

'Babe Ruth was a great player,' said Matthew, not sure how to respond. 'They love him up in New York.'

'Are you a Yankee fan?' asked Henry, looking Matthew up and down.

'No sir,' said Matthew. 'I grew up on Long Island. We follow the Mets.'

'Well, you're in Baltimore now, boy.'

Matthew said nothing, which was the right thing to do. If he had taken up for the Mets, Henry would have turned belligerent. Agreeing to switch loyalties or downplaying his love of his home team would have lost him Henry's respect, and Jeevan's.

'I'm from Watsonville, California,' said Kay, melting the awkwardness with the warmth of her voice. 'And as far as I'm concerned, baseball-shmaseball.'

~∞~

Jeevan Sharma was born in Delhi, India, in June 1960, two months before Cal Ripken Jr. was born in Havre de Grace, Maryland. His father was a bus driver who saved money for years and finally, Jeevan must have been ten or eleven at the time, bought himself an autorickshaw. For the first few months of this new phase in his family's life, Jeevan rode the auto with his father on weekends and holidays. A small corner of the driver's seat would be his. Jeevan would sit with his back resting against his father's side, watching the city slip by, thinking there was nothing better he could do in the world than drive an autorickshaw. At first his father laughed when he said so, flattered the way every father is flattered when his son says he wants to grow up to be like him. But Jeevan didn't stop talking about growing up and driving a rickshaw. So his father started discouraging the boy. You won't go hungry if you drive an autorickshaw, he would say, but you will never make any progress in this world either. And soon he stopped letting Jeevan come along with him when he went out. Do your homework, he would say.

Of all the subjects Jeevan had to study, mathematics came easiest to him. In class ten he decided to get all the math textbooks up to class twelve. He waited outside school the day of the final exam and asked the boys coming out to give him their books rather than tear them up in celebration. Through the summer he studied on his own. By the first day of class eleven he had decided he would study mathematics in college. It was just a matter of waiting through two years of school and making sure he didn't fail in the other subjects.

Around the time Jeevan was preparing for his school-leaving exam, his father was diagnosed with diabetes. Long hours spent driving the autorickshaw around the city would leave him exhausted. The doctor advised against it. But his medication had driven their expenses up. One day Jeevan's mother came to him and said, Beta, you have to help your father. He will never ask you for help, so I am asking you. The next morning Jeevan got up early, bathed and ate his breakfast, then went to the table near the door, where the keys to the autorickshaw were kept. His father was sitting there, right across from the door, but Jeevan didn't turn to look at him. He just picked up the keys and left the house.

Jeevan did his B.Sc. in mathematics by correspondence. It was a disappointment. He would sit down to study after a full day of driving a rickshaw and he would find himself falling asleep. The textbooks felt dry, the problems repetitive. After the final exams he found himself feeling like he had wasted his time. He passed the exams without a problem, but that didn't mean anything. Just a B.Sc. would not get him a job. Some kind of advanced degree was necessary. But he didn't have the time to attend lectures and there was no distance-learning program of any repute. So he was left driving the rickshaw full time, realizing as the days passed that the nighttime studying for his B.Sc. – a drudgery when he was doing it – had been a way of escaping for a few hours what he went through during the day.

A few months after the B.Sc. exams, a distant relative came to Jeevan's house and suggested they move to Trilokpuri. Many new houses were being built in the area, he said, and those people would need provisions. He had acquired some space for a shop. If Jeevan and his parents were willing to move to that area and set up the shop, he said, they could run it. They could keep a part of the profits and he would charge very little rent. Jeevan thought it was a good opportunity. His father could run the shop once it was set up. It would give him something to do, make him feel like he was earning. And Jeevan could do his M.Sc. in mathematics and then find a job that paid enough to take care of his parents. His talent for mathematics could make their lives better. So he sold the autorickshaw and they moved to Trilokpuri.

The first year in Trilokpuri was good. Jeevan was doing well in his M.Sc. The shop had started slowly but the profits were rising steadily as more and more of the housing societies in the area got completed and people moved in. Jeevan's father sat in the shop and handled the cash. He chatted with the customers and his neighbors through the day. Jeevan's mother had begun talking about finding a girl for him. And then there was Harpreet, the daughter of one of the neighbors. She would smile at Jeevan whenever he passed by her veranda.

Jeevan started his search for a job with great vigor the day after the M.Sc. results were declared. It would take a while to find the right job, that he was aware of, but when many months passed, he began to worry. The disappointments sprang from ordinary reasons: some jobs were reserved for relatives, some for those who could pay the largest bribe, and some for people who came recommended by important people. Jeevan was told to learn some computer skills, but he didn't have the money to spare, nor did he feel his qualifications were lacking. Someone suggested he try to clear the chartered accountancy exam but he refused, saying that he didn't want to spend his life adding and subtracting numbers. He began to dislike spending time in the shop. Sometimes when he went into the storeroom he would feel claustrophobic and start gasping for air. There were times when he slept for hours during the day. He began to miss interviews or show up for them in crumpled clothes. Then, one day, somebody told his parents that they knew a person who could arrange for him to go to Canada. There was a significant amount of money to be paid but his father said they should go ahead. His mother wept, but she didn't oppose the suggestion. Jeevan must have said yes at some point, but later, he didn't remember actually doing so. All he could remember was sitting in a small whitewashed room with a squeaky ceiling fan turning above his head and someone handing him a passport with this name in it: Jeevan Sharma. And then some airports, some aeroplanes, some vomiting and finally, Canada.

It was not in Jeevan's nature to look back with regret. But there were days when he thought about his parents. He sometimes thought that he could have sent them some money, but the shop was probably doing well enough to keep them fed and clothed and to pay for medicines and hospitals. He could have called them on the phone but he didn't know what he could say to them except that he was all right and that he was eating well. He could have visited them, but he had been told that it was better not to put his papers to the test once he'd got into North America. He never regretted not doing the things he didn't do, but there were days when he wondered why he never felt the urge to meet his parents again.

'Your vine is beautiful,' said Kay.

Jeevan looked up, startled, to see that she was sitting on the fire escape next door. Her knees were folded under her, her elbows resting on them. Behind her was the red brick of the abandoned pickle factory's rear wall, its trim of ivy a soft green frame for her gentle face. She was holding a lit cigarette. 'Trumpet honeysuckle,' Jeevan said. 'It grows well here.'

They both looked at the plant draped over the fence that ran between their yards, its oblong red flowers opening downward in bunches. The light was fading into dusk, making the creeper look like a large hairy animal at rest.

'We have it in California too,' she said. 'Not as much of it, but it's there. What's that small white flower?'

'Straw lily,' Jeevan said.

'And you have blueberries as well.'

'Just one bush.'

'You know, right,' she said, half-smiling, 'that blueberries give much better yields if there's another variety growing nearby.'

'This one flourishes on its own,' said Jeevan. 'It's bluecrop. Ms Lucy gave it to me.'

'The organist?'

'Yes.'

She dragged on her cigarette and, stubbing it against the side of the staircase, got up. It struck Jeevan that although he had known that having another bush nearby would help the plant,

12

he had never considered the possibility that Ms Lucy's blueberries – just across the fence on the other side, just a few feet away – could have anything to do with his bluecrop.

'I haven't had a garden since I moved away from home,' Kay said. 'Mom loves to grow things – flowers, vegetables, fruit. When I was a little girl, I used to love helping her in the backyard. It was like a special treat.'

'You miss it?' asked Jeevan.

Kay had missed gardening since she had moved to Southern California. Irvine has a great pharmacy program, her mother Emily had said. People will always need pharmacists – I've spent my whole life working for a doctor, I should know. So Kay had gone to Irvine and started living in a dorm, still tending the garden with her mother when she came home on holidays and for the summer. But whenever she returned from college, she would find a bush gone or a new hedge being grown. At first she was annoyed; she would argue with Emily over the addition or get upset over something that had been removed without asking her. She would complain to her father, but John would say, You girls keep me out of this. It took a while but she began to accept that the garden was now no longer hers, it was her mother's. She began to give up her claim to it. Sometimes when she visited home she felt like trimming something or turning up the soil in the vegetable patch, but she did nothing about it and said nothing. She listened without rancor when her mother told her about all she had done between Kay's last visit and this one, and all she was planning to do.

'Does she live alone?' Kay asked.

'Who?'

'Miss Lucy.'

'Yes,' Jeevan said.

'I saw her on her porch earlier, she looks quite old.'

Kay had walked down the stairs now and was standing across the fence from where Jeevan stood. Her face and her hair, black and unruly and wavy, were the only parts of her that Jeevan could see.

'How old is she?' Kay asked.

'Maybe seventy, maybe a little older.'

'Who looks after her?'

'She looks after herself,' Jeevan said.

'She appeared to be hobbling.'

'She has a little trouble with walking.'

'Then how does she look after herself?' Kay asked.

There was a challenge in her voice. Jeevan turned away and began to finger the leaves of the straw lily. From Howard Street, a block away, the angry sound of a car's horn rose and fell.

'I'm sorry,' Kay said. 'I didn't mean to pry.'

'She has a daughter who lives in North Carolina,' Jeevan said. 'She visits sometimes. Every time she asks Miss Lucy to come live with her, every time she refuses.'

When Emily visited Kay in the first few months of college, she would bring placemats or a potted plant or paintings of dolphins frolicking in the water. Make sure you crumple some paper and put it in the toes of your good shoes, she would say, it increases their life. Or, I saw a really nice pair of blinds, one with an ocean sunset painted on the slats and one with a sunrise, you can put one on the western window and the other on the eastern one. Kay would ask her how

14

John was and she would complain about how he was always going fishing and leaving work around the house undone, and how Victor was working him really hard and bossing him around. Why didn't you bring him with you? Kay would say to herself. But her mother would already have started talking of the plans she was making for this year's holiday: a package tour of Italy or France or Spain with her friends.

'I guess it's difficult to move at her age,' said Kay. 'But what about groceries and stuff?'

'She goes to the store herself most of the time. Sometimes I get her a few things.'

'Matthew wasn't so keen on moving either,' she said. 'But it was the right thing to do. I was done with New Jersey, I can't be a pharmacist anymore.'

'You're a pharmacist?' Jeevan asked.

Soon after Kay met Daniel, Emily's trips to Irvine became infrequent. What a nice boy, she had said at first. His parents lived in a large house on Sunset Boulevard and he had studied at an expensive private school in West LA. And he was good-looking and loved to surf, both attributes that ranked high in Emily's reckoning. But Daniel hadn't welcomed or reciprocated Emily's affections, choosing to leave town whenever she came to visit. He's so smart, she would say, he probably thinks I'm a hayseed. Kay would laughingly shake her head no, and try harder the next time to convince Daniel to stay when her mother visited.

'Was. I was a pharmacist. For years. But it wasn't what I really wanted to do. Tell me, um, I'm sorry I forgot your name ...'

'Jeevan.'

'Tell me, Jeevan, what little girl dreams of growing up to be a pharmacist? I mean, how does it happen that when you're in second grade you want to be an astronaut or a movie star and by the time you're graduating, the counselor and your mother have convinced you that the best thing you could do with your life is sit behind a counter in a white coat putting pills into bottles?'

Out of college, Kay had begun working as a pharmacist in Costa Mesa. Daniel got his MBA and got a job in a bottled water company based out of Newport Beach. He would come home in the evening, having visited the gym on his way back, then go for a swim and, immediately after dinner, be ready to party. Three or four nights a week, Kay would find herself at trendy clubs in LA or San Diego, crossing the velvet rope with Daniel's friends, all of whom seemed to be acquainted with bouncers and club owners at the most expensive nightspots in Southern California. The women were warm enough with her, but she didn't have much to contribute to their discussions of holidays they had taken and clothes they had bought, and she found herself being subtly excluded from their conversations. The jokes about her job – 'Hey, maybe you can fill my prescription' – went from being funny to being cutting. Sometimes she felt like they were shaking their heads and wondering what a great guy like Daniel was doing with a girl like her.

'What does it mean, Jeevan?'

'Umm …' Jeevan began, not sure what question he was being asked, 'parents just want their children to have secure jobs.'

'No, I meant your name, Jeevan. Does it mean something?'

'Life.'

'That's nice,' she said. 'I did it for years, you know, pharmacy. In California, right out of college, then I moved to Providence, thinking I'll work and take some pre-med classes, and I did try, but then I met Matthew and we got married and we moved to Jersey and I didn't feel like just sitting at home and taking classes, so I went back to work, and it was okay for a while, but then it was like, Where am I going with all this? So, when this thing came up at Hopkins, I told Matthew, Let's do this. I need to do this.'

Kay wasn't surprised by Daniel finally breaking up with her. What did surprise her was her own reaction to it. She missed work several days in a row, sitting at home on the couch in front of the TV, flipping channels. Her mother kept calling her but she ignored her calls. When Emily left a message on her machine saying she was coming down, Kay called her back and told her not to come. Emily came anyway, and was surprised and hurt to find that Kay's anger was directed not so much at Daniel as at her, that rather than wanting to talk about Daniel's shallowness, Kay wanted to talk about her own frustrated aspirations and Emily's role in frustrating them. Two days later, an hour after Emily drove away, Kay packed her things, loaded them into her car and drove east. She called the pharmacy from a payphone in Phoenix and told them she wouldn't be coming back.

'You're studying at Hopkins?' Jeevan asked.

'It's a job as a technical assistant at a lab in the biomedical engineering department,' she said. 'But I get to take one class a semester for free and I can pay and take another one if I want. If I do it for three semesters I can get all my pre-med requirements done. Then I'm good to apply for medical school.'

It was dark now and the alley's streetlight had come on behind her. Jeevan couldn't see her face clearly enough to make out if she was waiting for him to ask her why she wanted to be a doctor.

'Sorry, I'm boring you with all this,' she said.

'No, no,' Jeevan said.

'I haven't asked you anything about yourself,' she said. 'It's all me, me, me, me.'

There was something about the way she said me, me, me, me that made it seem like there could be nothing more delightful in the world than to hear her talk about herself. 'Have you always wanted to be a doctor?' Jeevan asked.

'Since I was little, my mom has worked at a doctor's office. And it was always, Dr Ross said this and Dr Ross said that and Dr Ross bought a boat and Dr Ross is skiing in the Alps this weekend and blah blah blah. And I would be like, Mom, you've worked for this guy for twenty years, why can't you call him Mike? At least at home, for heaven's sake. But she can't even think of him as anything but Dr Ross. Even in her dreams she calls him Dr Ross. Once, when I was seven, I called him Mike at the office picnic and my mother was really mad. She yelled at me and we had to leave early. And I thought back then that one day I should be a doctor too, so that I could go to Dr Ross's office and when he called me Kay, I would call him Mike, right to his face, right in front of my mom. It's the kind of thing a seven-year-old would think, right? But that's how these things begin sometimes, I guess.'

Two physically and emotionally draining weeks later, Kay reached Providence. It felt far enough from California for her to stop. She found an apartment and a job as a waitress. Her life settled into a routine as she waited for her head to clear. But before that could happen – how would she know when it happened? – she met Matthew. He was sad, struggling, trying hard to be something that was perhaps a little more than he could be. He listened. A few months later, they were married. She encouraged him to quit graduate school. It's making you miserable, Matt, you need to move on. I'm with you, let's get the hell out of here. But in Jersey Matthew's frame of mind became darker and darker. They liked him at work, they thought he was smart, and this made him feel worse about himself. She was sympathetic in the beginning, but slowly this began to anger her. You don't realize sometimes, she told him, that you're much more successful than a lot of other people, much more than me, for example. Staying at home became harder and harder for her to bear. She started working again, at first enjoying being at work but soon beginning to feel imprisoned behind the counter in her white coat. Matthew thought it was a good idea she was working. You need to get out of the house, he said. But what she needed was more than just to get out of the house. Matthew didn't understand what she needed, or how badly she needed it. Then, one evening, when he was away to Houston on work, she cheated on him.

'You coming in?' called a voice from inside her house. 'Dinner's done.'

'In a minute,' she called back. 'I'll talk to you later,' she whispered across the fence. 'He gets grumpy if he has to reheat dinner.'

Jeevan often met people from India or Pakistan or Kenya or the Ukraine or Somalia. Some of them were clients. He helped them with their taxes, filled out their loan applications, looked over their property purchase papers when they got to the point that they could buy something. These people either talked a lot about the moment when they left home and came here or they never talked about it, but either way Jeevan could see that in their minds their lives were divided into two parts. In the early days they felt that it could perhaps be undone, something like the feeling that comes when a person dies. He will wake again, he will live again. How can this unnatural state be the truth of his life, of my life? But as the days passed and the documents accumulated – social security card, driver's license, grocery store discount card – the possibility of reversal began to recede. The people who returned home within a few months made it back successfully. The rest stayed. The realization that they were never going to return came one day when they woke up and it occurred to them that it had been weeks since they had thought of what their life would have been like if they had never left home. On that morning they would try hard to rekindle the reverie but they wouldn't be able to, and they would recall how it used to come to them all the time in the early days to the point where they wished it didn't and drank too much to make it go away. Finally they would stop thinking about it because they were late for work.

Later in the day, standing near the dumpster behind the store on their cigarette break, these same people would realize that they didn't know anymore – that they would never know again – what their life would have been like if they had stayed on in Karachi or Delhi. The thread is broken, they would think. Some people would be disturbed when this happened, they would start planning short trips home or they would think of going to the temple or mosque more often, or they would feel like listening to Hindi film songs and think that they should buy a few new cassettes of old movie soundtracks. The rest of them would just stub out their cigarettes and return to work.

A few months after Jeevan left India, he found himself in New York. He had traveled across the border with a man who told him that there were plenty of jobs for taxi drivers in New York and that he could get Jeevan one. The man had asked for two hundred dollars. And because Jeevan had worked in a restaurant in Toronto where he ate leftovers and slept in the kitchen at night, he had the money to give.

In New York Jeevan found that everyone around him was working towards something. They tried to save money so they could get married or, if they were already married, they saved money so that their wives and children could come over to the US. Those whose wives and children were already here worked hard so they could move from where they were to a better place, maybe out to New Jersey.

There were days when Jeevan tried to want the things that they wanted. If nothing else, he thought, it would give him something to contribute to the conversation. But whenever he tried, he failed, so he stopped trying.

At first the thing Jeevan liked best about New York was that he could work all night and all day if he wanted. He turned to his cab when he found his mind growing empty and quiet. The lives and conversations of the people who rode with him diverted him. He drove to all corners of the city, picked up all kinds of people. It never bothered him that some areas were more dangerous than others or that some people were more likely to tip well and others weren't. Guns were pointed at him and knives held at his neck, and he gave the money that he had. And he gave it as calmly as anyone can when death is that close. He was still afraid of dying, but he did not fear losing money. What he earned was a lot more than what he needed for rent and food and for the few shirts and socks, some underwear, one pair of pants and one pair of shoes he bought himself every year. So, when he got mugged, he made a report of it to the police because that was a civic duty, then just shrugged it off and went back to the streets.

Finally the very thing that kept him driving cabs for long hours on the streets of New York drove him off them. Thinking about it later, he couldn't remember when or for what reason he had begun feeling that more and more of his fares were unhappy with their lives. There would be a week when everyone was going to the hospital. Some weekends he would find one person after another coming into his cab high on something, either animated beyond reason or with their eyes unfocused, the whites showing. Many of those rides also ended in the hospital. There would be couples who screamed at each other, or looked away from each other as he drove. There would be women who rode with besotted men they did not love, and men who got in with women they were probably going to use. The prostitutes – from all the various price ranges – and their johns also traveled by cab. And then there were people who were simply, without any label to label them with, in despair. He began dreading taking fares. Sometimes a person would wave him down and Jeevan would speed past after one look at their face. But after a while even the happy people appeared to be deceiving themselves, and Jeevan began to feel that the problem did not lie in his fares; it lay in him.

Jeevan left New York for Baltimore. When the bus had rolled over the bridges and through the tunnels, he turned back and saw the island of Manhattan shining in the bright light of day, and he realized that he had always thought of this place as a way-station, that he would never want to return.

An acquaintance had given Jeevan the name and address of a cousin of his, Shabbir Ahmad. He owns a few houses there, he had said, he'll find you a place to live. Shabbir rented Jeevan the place on 26th Street. He offered to rent him a taxi as well and, out of politeness rather than necessity, Jeevan accepted. But his taxi-driving days were effectively over and he realized this a few weeks into his stay in Baltimore.

It happened one evening in early fall. Jeevan picked up two men near Patterson Park. They gave him an address up on Harford Road. A baseball game was playing on the radio, the Orioles seemed to be beating the Yankees. It was the fifth inning and darkness had fallen by the time the cab reached Clifton Park. The Orioles had put two big innings on the board.

'Yankees going to lose bad tonight,' Jeevan said.

'Pull up over here, man,' one of them replied.

'Already?'

'Just pull up,' said the other.

Jeevan felt something cold on his neck. This was where he was supposed to say, slowly and clearly, I'll give you all the money I have, please don't hurt me. But Jeevan didn't say anything. Every sense within him seemed to be focused on the cool feeling on his neck. He swallowed and the sharp edge nicked his skin. Drops of blood oozed out. The pain tingled down to his chest and up to his jaw. And suddenly he felt himself silently urging the knife on, as if it were a person, urging it to slash into him.

'Where's the money, man?'

And the feeling passed.

Later, when the men had left, Jeevan felt fear. He started up the car and drove straight home, speeding as he went, scared that if someone else mugged him he would die, he would make himself die. It was the last time he drove a taxi.

Shabbir suggested Jeevan buy a couple of taxis and rent them out. He also offered Jeevan a job looking after his accounts and maintaining the house next to the one Jeevan was living in. Word had already got around that Jeevan could help with taxes and other financial matters. Shabbir said he should charge for these services, and so Jeevan started a little business of his own.

The days were long and more or less empty once Jeevan

stopped driving a cab. It was busy enough near tax time, but the rest of the year, clients came only occasionally. In the evenings he would walk over to Food Point and spend some time working on Shabbir's accounts, then linger for dinner and to chat with Shabbir and his wife. But the mornings were empty once Henry had walked by with his dog. Miss Lucy on the other side didn't say much. She sat on her porch quietly while Jeevan sat on his. He never quite knew what to say to her on the days when the weather or his latest trip to the grocery store didn't give him something to talk about.

Perhaps to give them something to talk about, one day Miss Lucy gave Jeevan a cutting of a blueberry bush. It was a good specimen. Just planting it and tending it for a few days made it come to life with fruit. Jeevan had never eaten blueberries before that day, he hadn't even noticed them in the grocery store. But after that first crop, he began to seek them out in the fruit aisles and compare the size and color with the ones he grew. Flowers came next. He started planting tulips in the park near 29th Street. Let the City take care of the Dell, Henry would say. What are you wasting your money for? There's more space there than in my backyard, Jeevan would tell him.

One evening in early fall, the year after he planted his first blueberry bush, Jeevan climbed up the slope of the Dell, having inspected the locations where his tulip bulbs lay buried. Early evening traffic was rolling up Charles Street. At the corner two girls stood under a cherry tree's yellowing leaves, talking animatedly as they waited to cross the road. Dusk's muted light sat quietly on the sienna brick-work of the elegant rowhouses that lined Charles opposite the Dell. Michael, the young black man who gave blow jobs for a living, sat at the bus stop, as always, his headphones plugged into his ears, his shy effeminate smile on his face, waiting for the later watch when his business would begin. He waved hello to Jeevan, and Jeevan smiled and waved back.

Standing there on the street that evening, Jeevan found himself thinking that he had never in his life asked himself if he was happy. He wouldn't know how to answer that question if he had. But he felt something like contentment here in Baltimore. He felt like he could stay in this place for a long time.

Shabbir emerged from the kitchen carrying two Styrofoam cups of tea. He put one down in front of Jeevan and, nursing the other, sat down on the chair not across the table from Jeevan but to his left.

'Sorry for keeping you waiting, Jeevan bhai,' he said. 'There were one or two late orders.'

Near the door, two African cabbies were emptying their trays. One of them raised his hand to Shabbir.

'Allah hafiz, brother,' Shabbir said.

'Allah hafiz,' the African said. Then, to Jeevan: 'Good night, Sharma.'

Shabbir watched the door swing shut behind them. 'Are you sure you won't eat something? The nihari is really good today.'

'No, no,' Jeevan said. 'It's too late. If I eat now, I won't be able to sleep till three.'

'Arre Jeevan bhai,' said Shabbir, smiling, putting his hand out. 'When do you sleep before three anyway?'

'The new people moved in yesterday,' Jeevan said, ignoring the outstretched hand. 'Matthew and Kay.'

'Yes,' Shabbir said. 'He works in a big company. Their office is in Towson. Eighty thousand dollars a year, Jeevan! He's a programmer. That's why I told Kamran, study computers, that's where the money is. But he won't listen, that boy is as stubborn as his father.'

'Come on, Shabbir mian,' Jeevan said, well prepared for the habitual diversion of the conversation towards the life and choices of Kamran Ahmad, son of Shabbir Ahmad. 'You have earned enough for him to live his life comfortably without working.'

'It's all for the children, Jeevan,' said Shabbir, and today he said it somberly rather than playfully. 'All our sins we commit for our children.'

'Mir says: Don't worry about the black ink that the angels put in your record, the merciful Prophet will vouch for your deliverance.'

Shabbir came out of his reverie and sighed. 'That's true, Jeevan. Peace be upon him.'

Jeevan wondered for a moment whether Shabbir was wishing peace on the Prophet or the poet, then said: 'I asked him, Matthew, why he wanted to live here.'

'Who am I to ask him?' said Shabbir. 'He said he wants to stay on 26th Street, so I said, you want to stay, you can stay.'

'No, Shabbir bhai, I asked him,' Jeevan said. 'She needs to be near Hopkins. She is working in some lab there.'

'You have got all the information, Jeevan bhai,' said Shabbir, a question in his tone.

27

'I was outside when they came,' Jeevan said.

Shabbir looked at him for a long moment. He was a funny man, this Jeevan Sharma, who often didn't look up the first time his name was called, who always looked like there was something within him that had never been spoken and never would. White was beginning to show in his sideburns, and noticing it again today, Shabbir realized that quite a few years had passed since the time this man had come to him from New York, given him a cousin's name, and asked for a job in return. Over these years he had been neither a brother to him, nor a son to his wife, but he had helped them build their business, he had suggested expansion into new areas, he had looked after Food Point when the two of them had to go to Pakistan after Shabbir's father died, he had taken Rashida to the hospital when she had impaled her thigh on a knife after falling awkwardly in the kitchen one evening while Shabbir was away to DC. He was not an uncle to their son but he had played cricket in the backyard with Kamran, when he was still young enough to want to play cricket in the backyard, driven him to school magazine meetings when he was in high school and traveled with him to various campuses when he was applying to college. Despite all this, Shabbir could never think of him the way he thought of his own siblings or cousins or the various people from the village that came to America dependent on him. They spoke to Shabbir, all those people; they told him what they wanted and what they feared, they laughed when they were happy and cried when they were sad. Perhaps Jeevan did those things too, but he never did them in front of Shabbir. There had only been one time

Shabbir had seen something like a tear in Jeevan's eye: the day Kamran went to college. From inside the minivan, through the pile of bags and suitcases, Shabbir had seen Jeevan embrace the boy. Be happy, Beta, Jeevan had said, and his voice had thickened perceptibly when he said 'Beta', a word Shabbir could not recall hearing him use ever before for Kamran.

Shabbir knew Jeevan handled the finances honestly. He gave Jeevan the impression that the accounts were a mystery to him, but he knew enough to know that Jeevan had never stolen from him, not a single cent. Shabbir checked routinely in the first few years, but slowly his native caution faded. There was something about this man who never talked about his parents or relatives, who showed no interest in women or drink, who never even mentioned the city or village he grew up in, that told Shabbir instinctively that money meant nothing to him. But although Shabbir trusted him implicitly with his money, there were times when he felt unsure around Jeevan. There were times when Shabbir sensed disapproval, at tax time every year when he gave Jeevan bills they both knew were fake, or the time when Shabbir forced a sickly cousin to go back to Pakistan. He can't work hard enough to pay his rent, Shabbir had said. How long can I support him? Someday he will have to support himself. Jeevan hadn't disagreed, but he hadn't agreed either.

And then there had been the time Kamran had come home from college and declared that he would major in journalism. Shabbir had been very upset. With his intelligence the boy could easily have become a computer programmer or a doctor. All these years he had seen him grow and slowly a hope had risen within him that Kamran would earn enough for his father and mother to stop working. Shabbir had eased his own father's burden, sending him enough money for him to live comfortably until the day he died. At the same time, he had saved so that Kamran could go to the best university that would take him. Shabbir had worked all his capable years to pay off the debts of his childhood and ensure that his old age was comfortable. And now the boy wanted to join a profession where he would struggle for years before making a good living. By the time he reached that stage, he would have his own family. And if the girl Kamran married was not generous of spirit, Shabbir thought, then he and Rashida would have to work till they died. So Shabbir ranted at his selfish son, and wept and refused to talk to him. For several days there was sullen silence in the house till, one day, Jeevan came over for dinner and said: If you let the boy do what he wants to now, he will not blame you for what he becomes later. Shabbir had not understood what he meant at first, and then, when he understood, had not agreed. But Jeevan did not speak after that, just listening to everything Shabbir had to say. Finally Shabbir began to find that the logic of what Jeevan had said was slowly unraveling the logic of his own arguments, and he shut up. When Jeevan left, he went to his son's room and told him that if his heart was set on journalism, he should do it. While your father is alive, Shabbir said, you will not have to worry about money. Rashida had wept with happiness and told him how her respect for him had increased manifold. Shabbir didn't tell her about his conversation with Jeevan.

Jeevan had been right, he had been wise. This troubled Shabbir; he felt like he didn't know anything about this man who knew so much about him. In his mind gratitude for Jeevan's intervention mixed with something else, not quite suspicion, not quite fear. It was just a thought that came to Shabbir again and again: A man without a past is unpredictable.

And so Shabbir hid some things from Jeevan. He hadn't told Jeevan, for example, that he owned the house Ms Lucy lived in. It was technically collateral, her husband Chester had given it to him a year before he died. Chester's illness had eaten up the money he needed to pay his mortgage. An old black man that no one wanted to lend to and with too much pride to ask his daughter, he had asked Shabbir for money and offered the deed to the house as surety. A year later, the old man was gone and with him went any chance of Shabbir getting his money back. There had been times when he had needed one more house for one more cousin to stay in, but Shabbir did not evict Ms Lucy. He had thought that she would die sooner or later, and the house would come to him anyway. Till that time she could stay there, still thinking she owned the house. He got no rent from her in this world, Shabbir thought, but in the next world he would make sure the angels knew the exact amount of money he had lost so that one old woman could live out her last days in peace. But despite having assured himself that he was doing something that deserved merit, he didn't tell Jeevan about it, because he had seen Jeevan buying things for her from the grocery store, sometimes going over to her house to fix the wiring or a broken chair, or paint over a few cracks; he had seen the blueberry bushes she had given Jeevan and, more telling than all those things, he had seen the calm that descended on Jeevan's face when she began to play her organ. So he didn't tell Jeevan that Miss Lucy effectively no longer owned her home, that she was a rent-free tenant in a house she and her husband had spent most of their lives paying for.

'They are friendly people, Matthew and Kay,' Jeevan said. 'Especially the girl.'

'That's good,' Shabbir said. Then, glancing around the room as if to check if there was someone else in it apart from the two of them, he lowered his voice and said: 'I had an idea.'

It wasn't the first time Shabbir had opened with that line. Sometimes it was possible to dispatch his ideas, like the time Jeevan spent a long evening convincing Shabbir that the numbers didn't add up for opening a Pakistani restaurant in Towson – the cabbies there were mainly Ukrainians with no stomach for chappali kababs, and white yuppies were unlikely to develop a taste for nihari that came with a thick layer of oil. These conversations normally ended when Shabbir's wife, Rashida, came out of the kitchen. Jeevan bhai, she would say, tell him I am not going to let him waste our precious money. Allah has given us enough, we don't want more. Till then Jeevan had to wheedle and coax, support and undercut, contradict and agree, while Shabbir expounded his latest plan.

On other occasions, it was a possibly workable scheme that someone of Shabbir's drive could make happen, like the time when he felt that a weekend mandir-masjid shuttle could be started to ferry people to their religious destinations

32

once a week for a small annual subscription. In such cases Jeevan discussed the modalities with him and tried to see if it could work. When they had finished, Rashida would ask: What do you think, Jeevan bhai, can we do this? Sometimes Jeevan would say yes, sometimes he would say no. When he said no, the scheme was, more often than not, put away.

And then there were the times when Shabbir brought something fully formed, like the time he explained why it made sense for him to buy rundown houses in dangerous neighborhoods. Sooner or later, Jeevan, he would say, it will get so bad that the City or someone else will have to come in. They'll buy whole blocks at a time, and they'll have to pay well. Right now I'm spending one or two thousand dollars. I don't have to do anything to the house, just spend another fifty-sixty dollars to have it boarded up. Once it's boarded up, all I have to do is wait. At such times, both Rashida and Jeevan sat and listened.

'Bhabhi!' Jeevan called out, turning to the kitchen. 'Bhabhi, Shabbir bhai has an idea!'

'No, no, yaar,' said Shabbir. 'It's not that kind of idea.' Then, his eyes flitting towards the kitchen, he said: 'In fact, this is her idea.'

Jeevan turned to look at the doorway, but neither Shabbir's wife nor a reason for this turnabout was forthcoming.

'Your bhabhi met Rukhsana at the masjid last week. Rukhsana said there was this woman who had come to her recently, the wife of someone her husband knows. She might be about thirty or so. Poor girl, she has had a hard time. Rukhsana says she's very soft spoken.'

Jeevan was about to interrupt this narration when Shabbir

33

lowered his voice further, bent towards him and said: 'And she's good to look at.'

'What's the idea, Shabbir bhai?' Jeevan asked, although he had begun to get the idea.

'She's Hindu, Jeevan bhai,' said Shabbir and leaned back as if he had won the argument.

'Just like me.'

'Exactly! Her husband is a bastard, threw her out of the house. There's some other woman. It's better this way, he used to beat her anyway. Who knows if their marriage was even official, god knows how he got her into this country. But she's here now and she has no one in this world, Jeevan bhai.'

'Just like me.'

'Exactly!' said Shabbir. 'When Rukhsana told my wife, her first thought was: She would be perfect for Jeevan bhai. I told her, twenty-five years we have been married, this is the first time a good idea has come from you and not me.'

The door swung open and three Pakistani men walked in.

'Shabbir mian, salaam aleikum!'

While the last order of the night was consolidated, Jeevan went to the bathroom. Street lights had tinted the frosted window orange. As he waited for his bladder to open, he found himself imagining the view outside the bathroom: an empty lot behind a gas station, a warehouse changed into a children's theater company's studio, a hairdresser, a basement bar with Korean lettering on its door. And, across the street, the alley that led to his apartment four blocks north of here. Staring into the distorted translucence of the bathroom window, Jeevan could see himself walking up the alley towards his house. Then he saw another figure walking with

34

him, a woman of about thirty, wearing a burkha although both Jeevan and she knew she was Hindu. The splash of urine against water dissolved the image. Jeevan finished, washed his hands and face and walked back out into the restaurant.

Shabbir's wife was collecting the Urdu newspapers and putting them on top of the fridge.

'Jeevan bhai,' she said. 'What do you think of my idea?'

'Waleikum assalaam,' Jeevan said.

Behind the counter, Shabbir snorted with laughter as he counted his cash.

'Hmmph,' said Shabbir's wife. 'Always joking. Never a moment for a serious thought.' But her smile undercut her feigned annoyance.

'Bhabhi,' Jeevan said. 'This cannot happen.'

'Why? Why can it not happen? Is it because you haven't met her? Okay, meet her, I'll ask Rukhsana to bring her here next time she comes.'

'It's not that, Bhabhi,' Jeevan said.

'Are you afraid she's too old? Look at you, you must be forty now, all this gray hair. She's at least ten years younger. Any younger and she could be your daughter.'

'It's not that, Bhabhi.'

'So you don't want a woman who has been with another man, is that it? Arre, it was her bad luck that she got stuck with that bastard. Otherwise, with her looks she could have got any man. Even now, she is beautiful.'

'It's not that, Bhabhi.'

'Then what is it? Why don't you tell me what's wrong with Su ....'

'No,' Jeevan said, then, realizing he had shouted, lowered his voice to a whisper. 'I don't want to know her name.'

Rashida looked at Jeevan, then at her husband. Shabbir motioned with his right hand for her to calm down.

'Okay, Jeevan bhai,' she said, coming to the table. 'You tell us, what is it?'

'Bhabhi,' Jeevan said. 'I'm sorry.'

Shabbir's wife said nothing. She sat down at the table and fixed Jeevan with her gaze. He would have to earn her forgiveness.

Loneliness burns like a slow fire in the morning. Pores begin to smolder, hair crackles in the flame. Something within burns each morning. Its glow lights up the room like a newly risen sun filtered through heavy blinds. The room is all ceiling. A plaster trim runs along the top of one wall to its end, then turns onto another. For a long waking moment the eye rests on that corner, then its lids fall again and the darkness that lies within is restored.

Coffee is best drunk on the porch, even in winter. Across the street, tufts of grass break through cracks in the asphalt of a vacant parking lot. Chain-link fencing has begun to peel from its frame. Near the corner stands a metal stump, probably the bracket for a long vanished traffic barrier, its jagged head brown with rust. Below the surface, the railway tunnels through the city.

Sneakers hang from phone lines, their laces tied together, irretrievable. In the quiet afternoon, their shadows move slowly across the empty street. A light breeze makes them swing like pendulums. The time they mark passes gently, unobserved.

Around the corner, at the senior care center on Charles Street, wheelchairs come out on to the cemented backyard overlooking the street as the sun begins its descent. Soon it will be time to walk dogs. The street will begin to fill with cars. Lights will come on inside buses as they trundle from one end of the city to the other.

Orangeness forces its way into the room through gaps in the blinds. It spreads across the wall facing the bed, cutting it in two. Somewhere a train whistles. As it comes closer, the rumble accompanying it gets louder. It approaches the entrance to the tunnel, just across Howard Street; another, longer whistle. The rumble becomes a muffled, prolonged shudder as it makes its way under the streets and empty lots. The windows rattle. A shadow quivers on its chosen wall. There is another whistle, moving away this time, and the earthquake is over.

Covers lie heavy on the legs. A puddle of sweat forms in the crook of a knee. Kicking off the sheets doesn't help. The table fan convects hot air continuously but offers no release. Embers cannot be extinguished by blowing on them. Turning from one side to another makes no difference. The water on the nightstand is lukewarm now. Finally there is an acceptance of defeat, a surrender to an enemy of surpassing power. And with this acceptance comes sleep, and it feels like an immolation in this slow fire that burns at night.

2

'SUNIYE! SUNIYE!' A WOMAN'S VOICE TORE AT THE FRAGILE NET of Jeevan's sleep. His eyes struggled open. The room was dark in its yellow-tinged way, the clock showed three thirty-five in large red figures. For a moment everything was quiet, the room soothed by the electric hum of the night, and then a fist banged on the door and the silence was broken.

'Suniye! Open the door!'

Jeevan's torpor formed itself around the thought that the person hammering on the door was not using his name to address him. She hadn't ever – the realization slowly unfolded in his mind – since he had first met her at Food Point two weeks ago. Sunita, the Hindu girl, is how he had thought of her when Rashida introduced her to him. She will stay with us, help us in the restaurant, Shabbir had said. But barely a week later Rashida had come to Jeevan and said: Jeevan bhaiyya, where is the space in our house? When Kamran visits, he will have to sleep in the living room. I don't have a problem with that, but she herself feels she is getting in our way all the time. He wants her to stay in your house. The order, Jeevan understood, had come from the man Rashida referred to as 'he'; she was merely relaying it. Besides, she had called Jeevan 'bhaiyya', something she did rarely because she knew he was susceptible to it. So Jeevan had agreed, to the extent that he could agree to something he didn't have the option of refusing, and Sunita had come to stay in his house. The few exchanges that had passed between them so far had not required her to address him; perhaps by chance, perhaps by design. Nor had she referred to him as 'he' in conversation with anyone else in the few days since she had moved in, Jeevan thought, at least in front of him she hadn't done it yet. And that 'yet' woke him up faster than all the banging on the door.

'There's someone in the house,' she said from the other side of the door. 'Please wake up.'

When he opened the door, Jeevan saw Sunita standing outside his room wearing a long flowing nightgown, with a paisley pattern on it that took on a peculiar life in the attenuated light. Her hair was tied back in a braid as always but some strands had lost their habitual neatness.

'There's someone in the house,' she whispered on seeing Jeevan, a dark form in the doorway.

'How do you know?' he said. Then, realizing he had spoken brusquely, he asked more gently: 'Did you hear something?'

'From the basement,' she said. 'There were noises.'

Jeevan's stomach fluttered. His ears began, unbidden, to listen more carefully: a slight rustle of leaves outside, a distant muffled whoosh of a car passing by, but the house seemed quiet. 'Let me see,' he said.

The stairs creaked as he walked down them, then creaked again and he turned to see she was walking down behind him. 'Go to your room,' he said. 'I'll see.'

But as he walked further down, the creaking above him continued. In one corner of the kitchen, two trapdoors set at an angle to the floor led into the basement. Jeevan turned towards them. He took his keys out.

'Be careful,' Sunita whispered.

The doors were opened and a steep flight of stairs leading down came into view. Like a stepwell fed by a subterranean spring, the basement stood stagnant and black. Jeevan hesitated. 'Hello,' he said. 'Is anybody there?'

'Where is the light switch?' Sunita asked.

'Ssh,' said Jeevan. He pointed down into the darkness.

'What should we do?' she mouthed silently, miming with her hands.

Jeevan gestured to her to wait. He pointed to himself, then into the basement. It didn't make sense, he thought, as he took the first step down. He should just shut these doors, go up and lock himself in his room and wait. But with her standing there he had to keep going, forcing one leg after another down the stairs. Getting to the bottom, he reached for the light switch. Something grazed the back of his hand. He pulled it back with a jerk and it hit the ceiling. There was a rattling of cans, a sound of small feet hurrying.

'Come up! Come back!' came Sunita's muffled voice from upstairs. But Jeevan relaxed. He found the switch and flicked it on.

'It's nothing,' he said. 'Just a rat. There's no one here.'

Sunita came down. Jeevan picked up empty pesticide cans

and stacked them against the wall next to bags of fertilizer. On one side sat an old couch and some broken chairs next to a set of shelves stacked with gardening implements and tools. Behind the stairs was the electric board – red and green lights, solid and undisturbed – and the boiler, its aluminum-covered pipe tunneling through the ceiling. Otherwise the basement was bare.

'Why is that window broken?' asked Sunita, pointing at the skylight that looked out onto the street.

'Go up,' said Jeevan. 'Go up right now.'

He followed her up and locked the basement doors, pulling on the handles to make sure they were shut.

'What happened?'

'Whoever it was has gone now,' said Jeevan. 'They won't come back.'

'There was someone in the house?'

'Do you want some tea?' asked Jeevan.

'Was there someone in the house?'

'Yes,' said Jeevan. 'But they have gone now.'

'How do you know they won't come back?' Sunita asked.

'They didn't find anything. Why will they come back?'

'What should we do?'

'Nothing. I'll fix the window tomorrow,' said Jeevan. 'Do you want some tea?'

'Tea?' said Sunita. 'Aren't you going to call the police?'

'No,' said Jeevan, going to the stove. He emptied a saucepan into the sink, then filled it again with water and put it on the burner. When he turned to get the milk from the fridge, he saw that Sunita had her face in her hands. The tips of her fingers were massaging her forehead.

'I had told my mother,' she said finally, her face still covered, 'don't marry me into a foreign country, don't marry me into a foreign country, I told her again and again. What's wrong with Meerut? Aren't there boys here? Do girls not marry these boys? But she didn't listen. He is from a good family, she said. He has his own house, his own car, she said. He will keep you like a queen. This is how a queen lives, I should tell her. The car you thought was such a great thing is old and dirty. The house has musty walls and is full of rats. And even in that third-class house and that third-class life, this man from a good family cannot keep your daughter happy.'

She was rocking back and forth in her chair, sobbing and wiping her tears as they rolled down her face. Jeevan stood looking at her, then suddenly aware that he was still holding the milk, turned to the stove and hurriedly added some tea and milk to the boiling water.

'See,' he said, turning to face her, 'whoever broke in has gone now. It's okay.'

'But someone else will come tomorrow,' she said, looking straight at Jeevan. 'Or the day after that. Outside, on the street, someone will point a gun or show a knife. What then? What will you do then?'

His weak attempt at comforting her had helped deflect her anger towards him, away from the two absent people that had caused it: the burglar and her husband. Anger cools faster when its object is present, thought Jeevan, so he turned again to the stove where the tea was frothing over. Adding some sugar, he lowered the flame. 'Do you like cardamom in your tea?' he asked.

Sunita rose from her chair. 'Should I make the tea?' she asked, her back straightening with an ungrudging sense of duty. She looked complete, compact, standing there in her paisley nightgown, her hair pulled back from her forehead, her face unwrinkled, her lips parted slightly in the aftermath of the words she had spoken, her eyes honest.

'It's made,' said Jeevan. 'Cardamom?'

'Yes,' she said, sniffling and wiping her nose with the back of her hand.

They sat at the round plastic table in the kitchen, holding their mugs of tea. Sunita talked about her family in Meerut. Her father had been cheated out of property by his brothers and so had to work for a meager salary in a government office all his life. She talked about her mother, who had taken her to the kitchen when she was six and said, Start with chapatis, the rest will follow. Her brother had studied hard in school but never seemed to be able to pass his exams. Finally their father begged and pleaded with a local politician to have him appointed to a menial position in a public health project, and immediately got him married. Then her sister-in-law had arrived, friendly and loving, but also determined to take over the household from the women who had run it so far. Sunita told him every detail of the various things all these people had gone through, each narration ending with the words 'and then I came here'. As she spoke, Jeevan could see that despite the small and big trials she and her family had gone through, Sunita was essentially not used to being unhappy. It didn't fit her well, this new cloak of misery that her life in America had been these last couple of years. And so, while he nodded in sympathy at the appropriate moments, Jeevan felt a lightness descending on him as she talked.

'It's morning,' she said finally, when she had run out of things to say.

'Yes,' said Jeevan. 'We have been talking for some time.'

'We?' said Sunita. 'You didn't say anything. You heard my whole Ramayana and didn't say one word about yourself.'

'There's not much to say.'

She gave Jeevan a searching look. Her brow furrowed, first in puzzlement, then in thought. She sat back in her chair and put her empty mug down on the table. Gathering the loose strands of hair off her forehead, she tucked them behind her ear, then smiled. 'You make good tea,' she said.

'Miss Lucy. Miss Lucy?' Jeevan called, pushing open the door with one hand, the stretched plastic of heavy grocery bags cutting through the palm of the other.

Upstairs, the organ quietened. Jeevan hefted the bags onto a chair and waited. A shuffling of feet, and a short bespectacled figure wearing a long gown appeared at the head of the stairs.

'Jeevan,' said Miss Lucy. 'Is that you?'

'Yes, Miss Lucy, I went to the grocery store so I thought I'd bring a few things.'

Clutching the handrail, Miss Lucy clambered down the stairs. 'Didn't I tell you I can get my own groceries, boy? You didn't have to go and get me anything.'

'No, Miss Lucy,' said Jeevan. 'I was at the store and I saw that there was a special on flour today and I thought maybe Miss Lucy can make me some pancakes.'

'Pancakes! You want Miss Lucy's pancakes?' A large white smile broke across her face and she said: 'That new girl of yours can't make pancakes for you?'

A tingling behind his jaws caught Jeevan by surprise and he realized he was blushing. 'She isn't my girl, Miss Lucy. She is just some poor woman who needs a place to stay. I don't think she even knows what pancakes are.'

'Send her over here,' said the old lady, turning towards her kitchen. 'Miss Lucy will teach her.'

Miss Lucy's fridge, like everything else in her house, was from another time. Jeevan opened it and put the milk, vegetables and fruit in. He removed three eggs from a carton and put them on the counter along with the flour and sugar.

'Pancakes! Just walks on into my house and says he wants pancakes,' Miss Lucy muttered as she brought out a bowl and took a skillet down from its hook.

Jeevan pulled up a chair and sat down.

'Don't just sit there, boy,' said Miss Lucy, handing him the bowl. 'Make yourself useful. Isn't that just like a man. Put the bag of groceries on the counter and sit on down. My Chester was like that too. Cook me this steak, Lucy, make me some meat loaf, Lucy. That man liked to eat.'

Warming the chair of a dead man he had not met, Jeevan felt a twinge of sadness at his absence and at the presence of this woman who would probably not forget him till death or creeping senility claimed what was left of her. When the first of the pancakes began to sizzle, Jeevan stood up. 'Let me see if Henry is around,' he said.

'He can come,' said Miss Lucy. 'But that dog of his has to wait outside. I don't want that beast running around in here, urinating in my house.'

Oscar had not, to Jeevan's knowledge, ever urinated or even threatened to urinate in Miss Lucy's house, but he decided to keep this fact to himself. As he walked out of the kitchen, there was a knock on the front door.

'That Henry already?' called Miss Lucy. 'He can smell these down the street.'

When Jeevan opened the door, he found himself face to face with two women. The taller of these was a black woman in her mid-thirties, dressed in a dark, sharply cut business suit, her cheekbones brushed back with a hint of blush. The shorter woman was older, white, and dressed simply in pants and a light unmarked sweatshirt that effectively concealed the exact structure of her body.

'Mr Chester Murray?' said the younger woman. 'I'm Victoria Washington from the New Baltimore Consortium, and this is my colleague, Mary Symcox.'

'I'm not Mr Murray,' said Jeevan.

'Is Mr Murray home?' said Victoria, stepping into the house.

'Why do you want to meet Mr Murray?' asked Jeevan, stepping back out of habitual politeness, then realizing he perhaps shouldn't have.

'And you are …'

The older woman had come past the threshold too. She had opened a folder she was carrying and was looking at an architectural drawing. She made a mark on it with a pencil and then began looking around the room as if she was searching for something.

'I am Jeevan Sharma.'

'Are you a relative or dependent of Mr Murray's?' Victoria said. 'We need to meet Mr Murray on very important business.'

'Who is it, Jeevan?' came Miss Lucy's voice.

46

'Mrs Murray,' said Victoria, raising her voice. 'I'm Victoria Washington from the New Baltimore Consortium, with my colleague Mary Symcox. We're here to talk to you and Mr Murray about your house.'

'What business do you have with my house?' said Miss Lucy, coming out of the kitchen.

'Mrs Murray, you must have received a letter from the City of Baltimore informing you that your house is in the project area of the Lower Charles Village Revitalization Project. The New Baltimore Consortium has been set up to ensure that all residents and homeowners whose property is being acquired are taken care of in every possible way.'

Victoria paused. Mary Symcox looked up from her folder.

'Jeevan,' said Miss Lucy, her gaze not wavering from Victoria's face, 'what's this girl talking about?'

'Mrs Murray, the City sent you a letter at this address two weeks ago informing you about the project. That letter also stated that representatives from the consortium would be visiting you to discuss your relocation options and to offer you any assistance you might need in this process.'

'Relocation,' said Miss Lucy, her head moving from side to side as she weighed each syllable. 'Who's relocating?'

'Mrs Murray, didn't you read the letter?'

'What letter, girl?' Miss Lucy said. 'What letter are you going on about? Jeevan, do you know anything about any letter?'

'Let me check, Miss Lucy,' said Jeevan. He normally went through her mail every few weeks to make sure she hadn't missed a utility bill, but it had been almost a month since he had last looked. Shuffling through the envelopes, he found the letter Victoria Washington had been talking about.

47

'It's here, Miss Lucy,' he said.

'What does it say?'

It was a long letter with many annexures. The project area stretched from 29th Street in the north to North Avenue in the south, from Howard Street in the west to St Paul Street in the east. The plan was to demolish all residential and commercial buildings except some with historical or architectural significance. The entire area was to be redeveloped: offices, townhouses and condos, a mall, a library, some new labs and a student center for the university. An artist's rendering of the completed project was included. Jeevan unfolded it and there it was: glass and steel, manicured and clean, with small happy figures walking purposefully down its streets.

'What does it say, boy?'

'It says that all buildings between 29th Street and North Avenue, between St Paul and Howard, are to be demolished so that new buildings can be built.'

'Mrs Murray,' Victoria cut in, 'let me explain. The Lower Charles Village Revitalization Project aims to create a vibrant community in your neighborhood. Do you know that the vacancy rate in this neighborhood is almost sixty per cent? In 1996, only four other neighborhoods had more homicides, only three others had more drug-related crimes. The City, the State of Maryland and Johns Hopkins University have come together to give this neighborhood another chance. And the only way is to start afresh. A clean slate.'

'I am not leaving my house,' said Miss Lucy and started to walk towards the staircase. 'I am not leaving this house.'

'The City has exercised its rights, Mrs Murray. This project is good for the city.'

'I am not leaving this house. You heard me.'

'It's for your good as well, Mrs Murray. The city will buy your house at market rate. We will find you a better house, we will give you a soft mortgage to help start again in a much better neighborhood.'

'You can leave now, girl. Leave my house,' said Miss Lucy, trudging, one foot after another, up the stairs.

'Perhaps I can explain this better to Mr Murray. When will he be returning today?'

Miss Lucy turned at the top of the stairs. 'Mr Murray is dead. He won't be returning today or any other day.'

A door slammed and then the organ began to sound.

'Since the title holder is dead, we will have to talk to the inheritor of this property,' Mary Symcox said. 'I need to schedule an inspection.'

'Can you really force Miss Lucy to leave her house?' Jeevan asked.

Victoria Washington turned to face Jeevan. Her face did not show annoyance or frustration. She had earned the confidence she displayed, Jeevan realized, she had probably fought hard for it. She would dress immaculately all her life, her hair would always be perfectly in place.

'Who are you?' asked Victoria, her normal speaking voice clear over the agitated sounds of the organ.

'I live next door, in number 103.'

'Louder, I can't hear you.'

'I live in number 103,' Jeevan said, cupping his palms around his mouth.

She turned towards Mary and gestured at her folder.

'Mr Shabbir Ahmad,' Mary yelled.

'My name is Jeevan Sharma,' he said, softening his voice halfway when the organ came to an abrupt stop.

'Our records don't show any renter at your address, Mr Sharma,' said Mary.

'I am Shabbir Ahmad's cousin, I am living there temporarily,' said Jeevan, immediately regretting his choice of fiction. But if there was an anomaly in his story, the women didn't detect it. The organ started up again, softer this time, sadder.

'We will be meeting Mr Ahmad later this afternoon,' said Victoria.

'Can you really acquire this house?' Jeevan asked again.

'Mr Sharma,' said Victoria, enunciating each word separately, 'eminent domain is the law. The City of Baltimore has the right to acquire a property for use in the public good. This project meets the standards for the use of eminent domain. If you don't understand what I am saying, I suggest you talk to your lawyer.'

Jeevan stood on Miss Lucy's porch, watching the two women leave as Henry came walking up the street.

'Who was that?' Henry asked.

'How did the Orioles do last night?' Jeevan asked.

'Shutout the As. Eleven-zero.'

'Did Cal play?'

Henry snorted. 'Did he ever – three for three with two RBI. Now, who were the fancypants? Church ladies?'

'Why don't you come in, Henry,' Jeevan said. 'Miss Lucy was making some pancakes when these people came. She made a lot of batter and now she's ...'

'Upset,' said Henry, and they both looked up to the first

floor from where the organ was proclaiming its player's state of mind.

'Are you going to tell me what happened, son?' said Henry.

'Yes, Henry,' said Jeevan. 'Come in first. But tie Oscar to the grille before you come in.'

Kay put the groceries in the fridge, dug into her bag for her cigarettes and, walking out of the kitchen into the hall, turned and headed up the stairs to the first floor. She passed the den on her way to the fire escape, then doubled back.

'Matthew?'

'Hey,' said Matthew, not looking up from the computer screen.

'You're home early,' said Kay.

Matthew moved the mouse. On the screen a white bishop moved across green squares.

'Didn't you hear me come in?'

'Yeah,' said Matthew.

'Why didn't you say something?'

A low beep sounded from the computer. The other player had made his move. Matthew gripped the mouse and leaned forward. 'Sorry,' he said.

'I'll be on the fire escape when you feel like talking,' said Kay.

The sky outside was a luminous grey. The drizzle that had accompanied Kay on her way home had stopped. Across the fence, Jeevan's backyard looked washed. Kay's own yard looked sodden and untidy. Perhaps, she thought, she should do something about it. She had wanted to fix up her yard

51

when they lived in Maplewood, New Jersey, but she kept putting it off. It was only when they finally decided to leave that she realized, while packing the garden implements she had bought but never used, that she had always known they would move away from there. This yard too would be hers only for a while. Baltimore was clearly not their last stop. But today, looking at Jeevan's garden and then her own, she felt like it was a mistake, perhaps, to wait for that final move before planting a garden.

'Hey,' said Matthew, climbing out through the window.

'Want one?' said Kay, taking a cigarette out of the pack.

'Umm, yeah.'

They smoked quietly for a while, Matthew looking down at his shoes, Kay looking at him, then looking away at the sky, the yard, the transmission lines, an aeroplane disappearing into the clouds.

'Mom called this morning at work,' Matthew said.

'How's it going up in Brookhaven?'

'Good, good.'

He brought the cigarette to his lips again. Kay waited, as she had waited so many times before.

'Joshua's been invited to testify,' he said finally.

Matthew's elder brother, Joshua, had written a book about the Rwandan conflict. It had come out the year before. One reviewer had said that such depth of analysis and scholarship were rare in a book by a journalist; another had said that the book was suffused with compassion and a novelist's grasp of the fragility and despair inherent in the human condition.

'Testify to what?'

'The Senate Committee on Foreign Relations has a subcommittee on African Affairs. They are holding hearings on democracy in the Congo. Joshua's been asked to testify.'

'Are they close to each other, Rwanda and the Congo?' Kay asked.

'I don't know.'

'It's a great honor for him,' Kay said.

'I know.'

Matthew had studied computer science at Columbia as an undergraduate. His father was a scientist at the big lab in Brookhaven. Growing up, he had felt that there was nothing more exciting than physics. But in his mid-teens he came around to the view that computer science was as fundamental, and, besides, he didn't want people to think he was trying to be like his dad. In Brookhaven, all the kids at school were bright, but Matthew was brighter than most. 'He's the smartest we've seen since Joshua graduated,' one of his teachers had told his mother when he was in high school.

At Columbia, Matthew took all the philosophy classes he could, and all the theoretical computer science classes that were on offer. He was dazzled by the brilliance of the computer scientists who taught there, each one a leader in the field. Sometimes he was disappointed by their attention to details at the expense of the bigger picture, the vast scope of the study of computing. He would go to a professor's office and try to draw him out on the philosophical underpinnings of computability or the possibility of modeling natural phenomena as computational processes. They humored him to some extent but quickly lost patience. When he applied for graduate school, his recommendations

53

were lukewarm: he is intelligent and committed but isn't always good with details.

'I wonder if he's still with that woman with the funny accent,' Kay said. 'Sow-way-toe was such a laa-hk, wasnit. Jo'burg was ap-salue-ly brill-yunt.'

'She's English,' Matthew said. 'That's how they speak.'

'Is that what's troubling you, this testimony?'

In his sophomore year Matthew met Abigail, an art history major. She had read his mother's books on Italian art. Only at Columbia, she would say, can you be dating a guy whose mom's book you have to write a paper on. Her parents loved Matthew and he spent more than one summer with them out on Cape Cod. Matthew's parents liked her too, especially his mother who, despite her worldliness and sophistication, couldn't help feeling validated by the fact that her son had chosen a girl who wanted to be an art historian.

Matthew daydreamed their future sometimes, two college professors at a prominent university, graduate students adoring them, undergraduates having crushes on them, their colleagues jealous of them. Beautiful children, a boat, books with their names on them in the library – it all came to him on mornings when he would wake before Abigail and look at her sleeping in the crumpled bed.

MIT and Stanford didn't want Matthew in their graduate program. Nor did Carnegie Mellon or Berkeley. Brown accepted him and that was good, but Abigail's body language told him that it was not good enough. She had made it to Harvard. The Harvard offer brought her relief rather than happiness. Nothing less would have been acceptable. For

Matthew there was no relief, just a move to Providence. He suggested she commute from Providence, but she said it would be inconvenient. She didn't suggest he commute from Boston. A few months later, they broke up.

'Joshua's doing what he wants to do,' said Matthew. 'And he's good at it.'

'Everyone loved the book,' said Kay.

'It was a good book.'

Matthew's advisor at Brown was Peter Graham, well known in the field of parallel computing for his difficult and interesting theorems. Peter had thrown problem after problem at Matthew and Matthew had struggled. He began to think Peter was giving him problems that were too difficult for him to solve. Peter's other students seemed to get the easier problems. They solved them without much effort and flew off to top conferences to present their results while he sat in Providence, stuck at a crucial step in some proof or the other. He dreaded going into Peter's office, he dreaded seeing the disappointment on his advisor's face; it seemed to be growing with every passing month. A year after he had joined the Ph.D program, Peter said to him, 'Your problem is that you love theorems and hate proofs.' That line went round and round in Matthew's head for weeks. He took it as a challenge. For weeks after that he didn't meet Peter, spending his time combing through the literature. Finally he found a problem that he thought would be significant and formulated a theorem he knew would be path-breaking. And he thought it could be proved. Peter was impressed when he suggested it. Matthew felt like he had turned a corner.

'I didn't like the English woman,' said Kay. 'I got the feeling she was only with him because he was a rising star.'

'He seemed to like her a lot,' said Matthew. 'Mom liked her too. She's very bright, she kept saying.'

Matthew worked hard on the problem. He had just met Kay. She was beautiful and caring, her presence seemed to energize him. When he was with her, he felt like things were okay, he felt like he could take on the challenge Peter had thrown at him. He came up with a construction that Peter thought could work. But he couldn't prove that it worked. He spent nights lying half awake with arrays of computers in his head. Trying to explain it to Kay was useless, she didn't know the math or the computer science that was required, but she was also the only person he could talk to about it. He could see she wanted to help, but she couldn't, and irrationally, that upset him. He fell ill and his delirium was populated with equations and inequalities, series and their sums. Late at night he would brush off Kay's objections and go to the library looking for a clue, but none presented itself. Or he had found a clue, he would think, but it would not lead anywhere. Three months after he had first told Peter about the problem, Peter told him that he had no funding for him for the next semester and perhaps he should consider taking a master's and quitting the program. Kay thought it was a good idea.

Matthew got a job in financial consulting as a programmer. It meant moving to Jersey and wearing pants and collared shirts. Work felt like a halfway house to nowhere, and every passing month Matthew's despair deepened. Kay comforted him, but increasingly she seemed to be short of patience when he went into a funk. Joshua visited them in Jersey and he also seemed to be on Kay's side, telling Matthew to snap out of it, suggesting that he should try to get to the top in his company. When Matthew talked about going back to grad school eventually, Joshua dismissed the idea out of hand.

A couple of weeks after Joshua left, just after Matthew returned from a work trip to Houston, Kay told him she had cheated on him. While he had been away, she had gone to a bar and got drunk and ended up sleeping with some guy she met there. It had happened once before as well, during one of his earlier trips. I'll understand if you want to leave, she said. But he didn't want to leave. If there's something wrong here, he said, let's fix it. It's the right thing to do. They talked about what Kay wanted and he said that she should quit her job if it was making her unhappy and look for a way to go to med school. A few months later, trawling through job postings, Kay found that a lab at Johns Hopkins was advertising for a lab technician.

'What's getting you down, Matt?' said Kay.

'Do you remember when we first met, I told you about this problem I was working on?' Matthew said. 'The one about computing on faulty supercomputers.'

'Peter's problem?'

'No,' said Matthew, dropping his cigarette and rubbing it out with his heel. 'Not Peter's problem. My problem. My theorem. My intuition.'

Kay could see his hand was quivering, like he wanted to strike something. 'Matt,' she said softly. 'What happened, baby?'

'They solved it,' Matthew said. 'Some guys at IBM solved my problem.'

'How do you know?'

'I was on the Internet earlier, just fooling around, looking for this and that, you know, the way I do sometimes. You always tell me, forget about that stuff, it's in the past. Just pretend it doesn't exist. But I can't. I try, but I can't. Sometimes I just surf web pages. I was going through this bibliographic database, DBLP. Fucking DBLP. You know, when I was in grad school, I would often type my name into the author search field in DBLP. I don't know, I guess I hoped that one day, miraculously, my name would appear in it. But it never did, and it still doesn't. And today I was surfing through it and I came across a paper whose title ... I just had to read the title, Kay, and I knew that my problem was solved.'

'Did you look at the paper?'

'One of the authors had it on his home page. I downloaded it. You know the worst thing – it's my construction. It's the same thing I told Peter years ago. I knew it would work, I knew it before the IBM guys even started thinking about the problem. These fuckers proved it works.' Matthew's head had fallen over his chest. Kay touched his back. He was shivering.

'Matt,' she said. 'Oh Matt.'

'It's such a simple proof, Kay, it's so fucking simple,' he said. 'Why couldn't I see it?'

Food Point was full when Jeevan arrived in the evening. Calls of 'Hello Sharma' and 'Salaam aleikum' greeted him as he came through the door.

'You still haven't picked up the copies of your tax form,' he said to the thin African man who sat at one table with two others.

'Just keep it, Sharma man,' he said. 'We don't need those till next year.'

Behind the counter, Sunita was organizing paper napkins. She looked up when he came in, then went back to her task. Rashida sat at the cash register, her order book open in front of her. Jeevan raised his hand to her in greeting and went to the table in the corner. He picked up the Urdu newspaper that lay on the table and laboriously read the headlines. The word 'halaak' – killed – came up several times. On one side, there was a photo of a garlanded man in a kurta-pajama waving from a raised platform.

Sunita put a tray on his table. There were two tandoori rotis in it, a large bowl of chicken curry and a smaller bowl full of beans cooked with potato.

'This is too much,' said Jeevan. 'I can't eat so much.'

'That's why you're so thin,' she mumbled, still looking down at the tray.

'What did you say?'

'Nothing,' she said, turning from the table, then glancing back at him and smiling before hurrying away.

'She made the beans herself,' said Rashida from her spot across the room. 'Especially for you.'

'Especially for you, Sharma man,' said the man who was too lazy to collect copies of his tax return. He turned to his friend sitting next to him and slapped his palm. Some of the people at the other tables snickered. Jeevan lowered his head and began to eat.

Shabbir came out of the kitchen before Jeevan had finished his dinner.

'Enjoying the beans?' he asked, taking the chair across from Jeevan.

'Yes,' said Jeevan.

'Sunita made them especially for you,' Shabbir said.

'I know.'

'Listen,' Shabbir said, turning to Rashida. 'Ask her to give me my dinner. I'll eat with Jeevan tonight.'

Sunita brought out another tray and put it down in front of Jeevan.

'Kheer,' she said.

'Royal treatment for Sharmaji,' said Shabbir.

'Some people from the New Baltimore Consortium had come today,' said Jeevan.

'To your house?'

'No, Miss Lucy's house.'

'What did they say?'

Jeevan looked up at Shabbir. Shabbir returned his gaze.

'They said they were going to meet you later?'

'Yes,' said Shabbir. 'They had come.'

'And?'

'And what? They want to demolish everything between 29th Street and North Avenue.'

'Did you agree?'

'Agree?' asked Shabbir. 'There's no agree-shagree. The City has the power, they are using their power. And we are all going to benefit.'

'Benefit?'

'Jeevan, they're going to buy all the property at market rate,' said Shabbir. 'I had told you long ago this would happen. Remember what I paid for this place? This Food Point? I bought it for one thousand dollars from that woman. And she was happy to get those one thousand dollars. The market rate is now twenty-five thousand dollars. Twenty-five thousand, Jeevan bhai. I told you, sometimes investments take time to mature, but if you make the right investment, it pays. Allah has been kind to us, Jeevan, this is our big opportunity. Do you know the best thing?'

'What?'

'When the new housing is built, every original homeowner of this area will be given the first rights to bid for a property of the same class as the one they used to have. And they will be given a soft mortgage by the City to help pay for it. Think! We will basically get the place at half price. Once these new houses are ready, the rents we can charge here will be eight times what we can charge now. With the malls and the offices, the kind of people who move here will be very different. All these beggars and junkies will be thrown out, no useless people sitting outside their house smoking all day, all these hairdressing and nail-painting shops will go. Third-rate restaurants, like this Food Point of mine, will disappear. There will be doctors and professionals living here, university professors and lawyers. No more mugging, Jeevan, no more bulletproof windows in Seven Elevens, no more shooting and stabbing, no more sirens screaming all night. This hell will become heaven, Jeevan bhai, and we will be landlords in heaven.'

The kheer was creamy, the rice was soft enough, the sweetness not too much. Jeevan took another spoonful. After the pancakes from the morning, more sugar would make him feel light-headed, but the kheer was difficult to resist.

61

'I have won the lottery, Jeevan,' Shabbir said. 'But, you know, even when I was buying my first house, I knew that a neighborhood so close to such a big university wouldn't be allowed to rot for too long.'

'I don't remember you saying that before,' said Jeevan, putting his spoon down.

'You are forgetful, Jeevan bhai,' said Shabbir. 'I always knew something like this would happen.'

'What about the people who are living here?'

'Miss Washington said, We are committed to finding alternate homes for all residents. Plus there is the soft mortgage. They will find much better houses than the holes they are living in now.'

'Maybe they like their holes, maybe they are too old to move,' said Jeevan.

'Come on, yaar,' said Shabbir. 'How old are you – not even forty. You will be fine. You are my ... my ... my ... Rashida, what is Jeevan to me?'

'Trusted friend,' said Rashida, as she returned change to a customer.

'Yes, you are my trusted friend. I will make sure that you get a much better house. Do you want to move to the county? They can find us a place there too, they said, and you can live in it, with Sunita.'

'I am not worried about myself,' said Jeevan.

'You're worried about your friends? That lame Henry and that old black lady? Jeevan, my friend, their time in this world is nearing its end. There are many places in the city where they take care of old people. They shouldn't be living on their own like this, abandoned by their children. What a country! Leaving the old all alone, limping their way to the grocery store.'

'But this is the way they want to live. They love their houses, they love their neighborhood and their friends.'

'You are getting too attached, Jeevan,' said Shabbir. 'Doesn't your Gita say that you must not get attached to this world? These bodies are perishable, Jeevan. And just like our bodies, these houses and this city are perishable. One day they will die, and beyond that death there is another world that awaits us.'

Shabbir's hodge-podge of philosophical utterances brought an unexpected sense of calm to Jeevan. He looked at the face of this man he had known for many years, who had been, for want of a better term, his trusted friend in the city. Behind the puzzlement on Shabbir's face, behind the watchful smugness that was his natural expression, Jeevan saw a version of honesty; a peculiar kind of honesty that leavened this greedy man's ruthless acquisitiveness.

'I'll make a file with all the property papers,' Jeevan said. 'We will need them.'

'Yes,' said Shabbir. 'Also keep the tax papers for all those places and for the restaurant ready and in order. The relocation lady, her name is Mary Symcox, will inspect the houses next week. Make sure that the wiring, the plumbing and the boiler are in proper shape. Also inspect the walls and woodwork carefully and fix them before next week. I'll do it for the restaurant and for my house. You have to do this for all three houses on your block.'

'All three?'

'Do it for Ms Lucy also,' Shabbir said. 'It will help her get a better valuation.'

Sunita came to the table and started clearing the dishes.

'The kheer was good,' said Jeevan, hesitantly. 'Shabbir bhai, will you have some?'

'Of course he will,' said Sunita. 'Do you think I made it only for you?'

Shabbir guffawed.

'This girl is sharp as a knife, Jeevan bhai,' he said. 'Make sure you don't get cut.' Then, when Sunita had stepped away, he lowered his voice, pointed over his shoulder with his thumb, and said: 'So, how are things at home?'

'Fine.'

'Any progress?' Shabbir asked, his eyebrows bouncing suggestively.

'I'll go now, Shabbir bhai,' said Jeevan. 'Let me start getting the papers ready.'

'Get them ready tomorrow, yaar,' said Shabbir. He winked at Jeevan. 'Have a good night's sleep first.'

Jeevan had already pushed his chair back and was walking to the door.

'Thank you, Bhabhi,' he said. 'The curry was very tasty.'

'What about the beans?' Rashida asked, smiling.

'Good, good,' he said, opening the door.

'Arre, Jeevan, listen,' she called after him. 'Kamran had called. He's coming next week.'

Evening on Druid Hill and the light is softening over the reservoir. The basketball court catches its breath after the last game of the day, still quivering from the memory of twists and turns, of balls thrown in looping arcs. A four-by-four drives by, filling the air with a deep throbbing bass line.

Down the hill are train tracks, an abandoned old railway station, a shining new facility for Light Rail wagons, an old stone bridge married – perhaps against its will – into a family of lean concrete on-ramps and off-ramps ruled by a stern and powerful freeway. Hidden from view is a river. It once carved a valley through mountains, a path that men traveled, a passage they laid rail tracks and built roads along. This river's course is now set in stone, its channel narrowed by unmoving embankments.

The white stone Moorish tower stands squat at the top of the hill. Floodlights flick on, making it gleam like a polished, broken tusk. From the foot of the tower is seen a broad vista of the city of Baltimore. Lights have begun to come on: from the modest homes of Hampden in the north to the ambitious buildings of downtown and the Harbor in the south. In another time, smoke must have risen from the dwellings that cover this undulating land, greying the sky above them. Today they are illuminated by an electric glow that catches the dust and stains it orange. Somewhere, the stucco of a rectangular railway station is fading away in the gathering darkness. Not far from it, near North Avenue, seven lit windows on the side of a church tower form a cross. From here no people are seen. But they are there, behind their walls of brick and mortar: talking, eating, breathing, watching TV.

A swathe runs through the city, a narrow strip of houses, bars, body shops, pizza delivery places, convenience stores, churches, offices, pharmacies and Chinese restaurants with five-dollar lunch specials. The plumbing doesn't work. The boilers are defective. The flooring is uneven, the carpeting musty. The walls have bullet holes. No one fixes these buildings, no one comes to their rescue. Those who can, don't care, those who care, can't. And so this land rots and festers and stinks.

What do we do with this place? How do we prevent its poison from seeping into our drinking water? Cleaning it up will cost too much and, besides, we don't know how to do it. Perhaps the best way is to start from scratch. Demolish them, each last one of them. Pulverize them. We need to start afresh. A clean slate. We won't make the same mistakes this time.

3

'CAN'T FIGHT THEM, JEEVAN,' SAID HENRY, SETTLING DOWN ON the steps. 'If they say we have to go, we have to go.'

Oscar came up to Jeevan, his tail wagging slowly.

'Where will you go?' Jeevan asked, running his hand over the dog's head.

'I don't know. Somewhere. Ms Symcox said she will find three places as big as my house. As many rooms, as large as these ones. Maybe she'll find me the right kind of neighbors as well.'

'They're saying you have the right of return.'

'Hmmpf,' grunted Henry. 'Like this is the Promised Land, this neighborhood. The right of return, that's just peachy for everyone concerned, isn't it?'

Oscar sat with his back to the steps, looking out towards the west. Beyond Howard Street, beyond the railway tracks, the sun was beginning to set. Rafts of dark clouds stood anchored in the evening, their edges lapped by a golden surf from the sky's ocean of orange and yellow.

'You know who's behind all this, don't you?' asked Henry.

'Who?'

He leant forward. 'Hopkins.'

'Johns Hopkins?'

'Yeah. Hopkins.'

'Victoria Washington said they were part of it,' said Jeevan.

'Sure she did. They're behind all this.'

When Jeevan first came to stay in Shabbir's house, he had been very taken with the university campus that was a few blocks north of it, spending several hours strolling through its greenery and imposing brick buildings. But he had tired of it quickly. It felt like an enclave. Its porous boundaries seemed to keep out the city around it. Now he went to the campus only when he needed to pick up forms from the government library that was located inside the university library. Sometimes he wandered through the stacks and looked at some of the books. Occasionally he sat on the library's steps, watching Indian students playing cricket on the quad.

'When this neighborhood first turned bad thirty years ago,' said Henry, 'I said to myself, Even if the City doesn't bail us out, Hopkins will. The shootings started, people started dealing drugs; they didn't do anything. Girls got raped in the Dell. Hookers started turning tricks in the alleys. They didn't do anything. People started leaving, people who had lived here for decades, who had been born here, they all left. But all Hopkins did was put up little maps with colored dots on them. Avoid this place after dark, don't walk alone, carry some money at all times. I used to say to myself, Strange that a major university is okay with all the shootings and muggings that go on around it. They've got to do something about it. Otherwise those kids whose big-shot daddies have bought them BMWs will stop coming here. Park outside your dorm and your car gets jacked, take your dog out for a walk and someone shows you a knife. Panhandlers and junkies at every corner. So finally they did something about it, didn't they? They decided to clean up the mess. And we're part of the mess.'

'Hey,' said Matthew, walking up to the stoop. 'Orioles trying to catch up with the Angels tonight, Henry.'

Oscar stood up and turned to Matthew, sniffing his shoes. Matthew patted him on the back.

'Is Cal playing?' asked Jeevan.

'Ummm, doesn't he …?' said Matthew.

'Jeevan's having you on, son,' said Henry, his brow unfurrowing, a chuckle racking his chest. 'Oscar, sit.'

'Cal's oh for two,' said Matthew. 'Eric Davis is hot tonight. Two for two with a homer in the bottom of the first.'

'Since when are you an Orioles fan?' asked Henry.

'Some guy had the radio on in the bus,' said Matthew.

'You take the bus?' asked Jeevan.

'Yeah,' said Matthew. 'I drove enough in Jersey. We'll buy another car soon, I guess.'

'When you move on up to the county,' said Henry. 'Everyone's got to move soon anyway.'

'I heard about that,' said Matthew.

A delivery truck rolled down the street. On its side was an image of a larger-than-life young woman – an inviting smile, small tight clothes, holding a bottle in one hand – beckoning anyone who looked at the truck towards it. Three men and one dog turned and watched the woman roll down the street till the truck carrying her turned into the alley and she disappeared from view.

'You know this boarded up building back here?' said Henry, addressing Matthew. 'This used to be a factory. The McCormick Spice Company. They used to bottle spices right here. They would make the lids of their dispensers by punching holes into little metal discs and dump the punched-out bits in the alley. We used to scramble to find them, pick up as many as we could. It was play money for us kids. We could buy things from each other with that money. I still have a tin full of it somewhere. Sometimes we'd run to Howard Street or Sisson Street and wait on the bridge for the train to come by. We'd bet on the number of cars it had. When my dad found out I was betting, he gave me a hiding with his belt. That's how it was in those days, just unbuckle your belt and whack, whack, whack.'

'You've lived here since you were a kid?' asked Matthew.

'Seventy some years,' said Henry. 'It wasn't like this then. On the weekends my dad and I would walk all the way down to Lexington Market. We'd buy bunches and bunches of bananas and carry them back, start selling them once we crossed North Avenue. He'd give me a nickel if we made some money that way, and I got to eat bananas all the way back. They weren't like these swollen, tasteless ones you get in the store now. I could eat those bananas till I was sick.'

'Seventy years is a long time,' said Matthew.

'Never wanted to live anywhere else,' said Henry. 'A few summers out in Hagerstown playing ball, a few months in Germany during the war. Apart from that, it's been Baltimore for me. Right here. I was born in a house down the hill on 22nd Street, not far from the tracks. Came back from Germany and everyone said, Learn a trade, or go to college, but the book smarts I never had, and the only mechanical skill I learned was how to put bat to ball. So, I just took what job I could get. Started driving a truck, found a girl I liked, and moved to a house on Howard Street near 29th. A couple of years, no babies, then she found a man she liked more than me and off she went. Never found another I liked enough to ask her to marry me. The old folks died in this neighborhood. And yeah, their son was around to help them all the way there. How many people can say that? They didn't need strangers to take them to the hospital, no sir. Now it's just Oscar and me, and these old houses and the people who live in them. Like this Jeevan Sharma, who doesn't talk much but is a good guy, or Miss Lucy, who plays her organ night and day and makes darn good pancakes. And soon they'll be gone too, and so will I.'

Oscar got up and padded his way across to where his master sat. He looked up at him and whined once.

Henry put his hand out, and his dog began to lick it with slow, gentle strokes. 'Good boy,' said Henry. 'Good boy.'

Darkness had fallen, and as Matthew looked at Henry sitting on the stoop, he wondered what it would be like to live an entire life within a square mile of right here, of any place. His own acquaintance with places had been different. Since adolescence he had known that he would leave Brookhaven and never live there again. In New York, as an undergraduate, he had been seduced only partially. Like other New Yorkers he had painstakingly put together a detailed topography of the city – swearing by one pizzeria, condemning another, marking his favorite part of Central Park, enjoying being in one subway station and disliking another, picking one bar in each neighborhood, choosing, always choosing, including and excluding – but unlike many others, he had never felt that this map was his own, he had never felt that it could contain his entire life. Providence was beautiful but marked with the pain of what he had gone through there; it would never be free of that association. Maplewood, New Jersey, with its railway station parking lot and its quiet streets was too much like the place he was expected to live his life in, his life together with the woman he had chosen to be his wife. And perhaps it was under the weight of this expectation that their life there had collapsed. And now, here he was in Baltimore, in this neighborhood that was about to be wiped out. This time, it wasn't he who would leave but the place itself. He felt no regret, just a curiosity as to how a man who had lived all his life here must feel, and a twinge at the thought that he would never know either that man's contentment at having layered decades of living onto one neighborhood, nor his wrenching sadness at having that neighborhood taken from him.

'You have a lot of history here,' said Matthew.

'Yeah, I do,' said Henry, rising from his seat.

'No, I mean, this is an old neighborhood,' said Matthew. 'It probably has some historical buildings, maybe some architectural significance. Aren't those things protected by the law?'

'Are they?' asked Jeevan.

'I think they are,' said Matthew. 'I'll find out about it.'

'It's no use, boy,' said Henry. 'Places like this don't have a history. No Declaration of Independence was signed here, no battle was won or lost here. Just some people working hard and trying to get by.'

Oscar looked up, then turned and began walking. Henry adjusted his grip on the walker. He paused for a moment, looking at a point on the sidewalk somewhere behind Jeevan. Then he felt a tug at the leash. 'I'm coming, boy,' he said to Oscar. 'Let's get home and see if the Os caught up to those Angels after all.'

'So I said to him, dude, wasabi isn't the answer to every question,' said Kamran.

Laughter drove Kay's drink up her windpipe. A spray of saliva and vodka landed on Kamran's arm. 'Sorry,' she said, touching his shoulder, her body still shaking with laughter. 'So sorry.'

'I'll get you a tissue,' said Matthew. 'Would you like another drink?'

'Yes, please,' said Kamran, holding out his empty glass.

'You're hilarious,' said Kay. 'I'm so glad we met you. And your dad has been so nice to us.'

'You guys are way cooler than his other tenants,' said Kamran. 'If I ever came to this house earlier, it was always to attend some Pakistani kid's first birthday party.'

'That's interesting,' said Kay.

'Not really,' said Kamran. 'You guys are probably the first white people to live here in a long long time.'

Early in his senior year at college in Philadelphia, Kamran

had met a girl at a concert. Alex was a junior at Temple. She was funny and she liked the same bands Kamran did. The first time she came over to the house, his roommates – five Pakistani guys who prayed five times a day and played games all night when they weren't studying – seemed to like her. They said she was cool and they laughed at her jokes – although she was very different from their other female friends, some of whom wore headscarves and long sleeves. But soon, Kamran noticed that his roommates began to fidget whenever she came in, going into their own rooms or into the kitchen after sitting silently for a while. They began to avoid him as well, even when she was not over. At the table or on the couch watching TV, he began to feel that there was something they wanted to say, something they were holding back.

'When I was in grad school, we had a lot of Indian guys in the Ph.D program,' said Matthew. 'They were really smart.'

'At Irvine, we had a lot of Asians,' said Kay. 'They were cool.'

'The Chinese at grad school always stuck together,' said Matthew. 'Very few of them made friends with non-Chinese.'

'Tell Kamran about that friend of yours,' said Kay, 'the one who was single.'

'Oh yes,' said Matthew, snorting with laughter. 'Xiao was a funny guy. We were supposed to call him Sean, but I always called him Xiao. He was one of the few who would hang out with the rest of us. One day I said to him, Xiao, there are all these cute Chinese girls in the department and you're a good-looking guy. Why don't you get yourself a girlfriend? So he says, No man, they're all taken. And I was like, Come on dude, you're cool, you're funny, all these other guys are total nerds. Why don't you pull one? His eyes grew big, he sputtered like, no, no, there will be war!'

The excitement Kamran had felt when he first met Alex waned in the face of his housemates' disapproval. Although she spent nights in his room, they didn't have sex. I'm not ready for this, he had said to her the first time they had come to the verge of it. They had argued, but she had felt more perplexed than rejected, and eventually she had pretended to understand. Then, one of Kamran's former roommates – he had been a senior when Kamran was a freshman – came to Philly for a few days. He took Kamran aside and told him that the others in the house were not comfortable with him dating a white woman. What's more important to you, dude? he asked. A few days later, Kamran told Alex he couldn't see her anymore. The following weekend, he moved out of the house.

'So, how long have you lived in New York?' asked Matthew, handing Kamran his second drink.

'Like two years.'

'Matthew was at Columbia,' said Kay.

'That's cool,' said Kamran. 'I don't go up there much, too many Columbia students in their college sweatshirts. It's Manhattan but not really, you know what I mean?'

Kay looked at Matthew, but his face was impassive. 'Where do you live?' she asked.

'In Brooklyn,' said Kamran. 'Do you know Park Slope?'

'No,' said Kay.

'It's really nice,' said Kamran. 'And much cheaper than Manhattan. What's the point of living in a walk-in closet and paying eight hundred dollars for it?'

'Isn't Brooklyn dangerous?'

'Not like it used to be,' said Kamran. 'Not like here. And Park Slope is getting better all the time. Steve Buscemi lives there, and Paul Auster.'

As a child Kamran would often go to Jersey City in the summer. Shabbir had a cousin who lived there. One of those summers on the peninsula across the Hudson from Manhattan, Kamran decided he would live in New York some day. When he graduated from college, he moved back to Baltimore and started working at the *Sun*. But living in Baltimore with his parents felt like a step backwards. So he kept applying for jobs, mainly in New York, till he finally landed one on the copy desk of the *New York Times*.

At work, his very first week in the city, he met Max. In the evenings and on weekends, Max was working on a book about the indie music scene in Oregon. His wife, Anna, was studying to be a chef. Max and Anna decided to tutor Kamran. They showed him the brunch places they liked in Brooklyn and told him what to order, they introduced him to rock musicians in small basement venues on the Lower East Side, they encouraged him to shop for clothes in Soho. His reticence when it came to drinking wine and eating pork amused them at first, then irritated them, but they enjoyed his company and he liked it when they laughed at his jokes. Max, we need to find Kamran a girlfriend, Anna would say every now and then. They would take him to their favorite bars and push him to go and talk to this girl or that.

'I'm stepping out for a cigarette,' Kay said. 'Anyone?'

'I'll come,' said Kamran.

Matthew shook his head no.

'How are you finding Baltimore?' Kamran asked, outside on the porch with their cigarettes lit.

'It's okay,' said Kay.

Her face had taken on an orange glow from the street lights, there was a thoughtful expression on it as she brought her cigarette up to her lips. Kamran noticed her nose, it was chiseled and shapely without being delicate.

'I've always wanted to be a doctor,' she said. 'And this is the best opportunity I'm going to get. So, you know, if it means living here for a bit, that's okay.'

'But you could have moved closer to campus, or to Roland Park or Guilford or something – why here?'

'Matthew,' she said. 'The moment he saw this place he said, We should live here. We saw a lot of places but each neighborhood had some problem – too yuppy, too preppy. Finally, I was like, just choose something.'

'Yeah,' said Kamran. 'It's charming in its own way.'

'You grew up in this neighborhood, right?'

'Yeah, I did,' said Kamran. 'But that feels like a long time ago.'

The first summer after Kamran moved to New York, Max and Anna convinced him to come to Europe with them. Anna wanted to study Mediterranean food, and Max wanted a break. They spent a month traveling through Greece and Italy. In Athens, Kamran drank wine for the first time in his life. In Rome, he ate pork. In Milan, he got drunk and went home with a girl he had met on the dance floor at a club. The next morning, stumbling back to the hotel, he realized that he didn't remember much of the night before, the night he lost his virginity.

Back in New York, Kamran decided he wanted to date a Pakistani girl. It meant that Max and Anna's friends from Portland who visited occasionally, or Anna's classmates at the culinary institute, or most of his co-workers, were ruled out. Max shrugged his shoulders at this decision; Anna argued against it. Kamran was adamant: If she hasn't grown up Pakistani in America, she won't understand where I'm coming from. So they started going to the two or three South Asian parties that happened fairly regularly in Lower Manhattan. Kamran was amused, at first, to find the music his parents listened to being mixed with funk and hip-hop, but slowly he began to enjoy these dark, crowded venues where you could eat kabab and roti while drinking a vodka-tonic, and where the girls looked like they might rock a salwar-kameez or a sari if they wanted but preferred to dress in tight, trendy clothes.

'My parents weren't happy when I said I was moving to New York,' said Kamran. 'Maybe they thought I'd move back to Baltimore for good, get married to a nice Pakistani girl and run Food Point for them. But it doesn't work that way, does it?'

'My mom's like that too,' said Kay. 'She still thinks that eventually I'll move back to California. San Diego, LA, even Riverside, as long as it's California. I used to think that too, you know, that I could never live anywhere but California.'

'You don't now?'

'I can live anywhere but California.'

'Yeah,' said Kamran. There was a story here, he realized as he watched Kay stub her cigarette out and wrap her arms around her chest, her eyes looking out at the parking lot across the street. Kamran felt like asking her something, but he didn't know what the question was.

Kay turned finally, looked at him and smiled. 'So, who do you hang out with in New York?' she asked.

'I have some friends from work,' said Kamran, finding himself unwilling to talk about Max and Anna, and finding himself surprised at this unwillingness.

'You guys party a lot?'

'A little.'

The Pakistani girls he met at South Asian parties found Kamran different from many of the other men there: he wasn't a dentist or a lawyer or an investment banker, but he wasn't an artist or an activist either. He was funny and cute, they thought, and charming in his diffidence. And so phone numbers were readily given and dating began. But all the girls turned out to be imperfect in one way or the other. Some of them were too wild: they drank too much and got sick and had to be taken home too often, or they had slept with too many men and had too many one-night stands, or they ate pork. Some of them were not wild enough: they didn't want to party anymore now that they were dating one person regularly, wanting to stay at home instead, cooking Indian food and watching Indian movies. Some of them were too intellectually engaged: they were into human rights, they were critical of US foreign policy, and they used the phrase 'people of color' too often. Others were unaware of the world around them and didn't have much to talk about except their families and friends. To Kamran each of these faults appeared to originate in their experience of growing up Pakistani in America. New York was full of men in their early twenties who were dissatisfied with the women they dated, but the advice that came from popular culture and from Max and Anna was of little use to him. Kamran was in this alone.

Matthew came out onto the porch. Kamran and Kay turned towards him. He stretched. 'It's late,' he said.

'Yeah,' said Kamran. 'I was just leaving.'

Kay gave Matthew a look.

'Hey,' said Matthew. 'I was just saying. We can hang out a little more.'

'No, really,' Kamran said. 'My mom will wake up when I get in.'

'Parents,' said Kay.

'Yeah.'

'Did your dad say anything about the demolition?' asked Matthew.

'He mentioned it,' said Kamran.

'I met Henry the other day,' said Matthew. 'He seemed pretty bummed out about it.'

'Henry's lived here forever,' said Kamran.

'That's what he said,' Matthew said.

Kay looked at her husband. He had wanted to talk about this all night, she realized, he just hadn't known how to bring it up. 'Where will he go?' she asked.

'I don't know,' said Matthew.

'Henry will be all right,' said Kamran. 'I'm sure he'll find something. My dad was saying, everyone here will get a lot of money.'

'It's sad though, isn't it?' said Kay. 'And for Miss Lucy. They've all lived here a long time.'

80

Kamran felt a shiver of embarrassment at his earlier dismissal of Henry's situation. It was difficult to explain to Matthew and Kay that he didn't love the place he grew up in. He instinctively understood that most people would find such a sentiment reprehensible, most people wouldn't even understand what it meant. But they were both looking at him expectantly, especially Kay. 'We should do something about it,' he said.

'My god,' said Sunita, a smile breaking out on her face. 'This place is so crowded.'

As they walked across Pratt Street to the mouth of the Inner Harbor, Jeevan felt Sunita clutch at his arm. He looked over at her, but she was unmindful, taking in the Sunday afternoon scene on a beautiful summer day.

'Look, look,' she exclaimed, pointing at a small child holding a sticky cloud. 'Candy floss! I want some. Will you get me some candy floss?'

'You want candy floss?' said Jeevan, surprised not so much at the object of the request but at the manner in which it had been made.

'I like candy floss a lot,' she said, tugging at his arm.

'Oooh,' said a white-haired woman, stopping in front of them and looking Sunita's sari up and down. 'That's really gorgeous.'

'Thank you,' said Sunita shyly.

'And you're quite pretty too, hon,' said the lady.

Sunita tittered and blushed.

'Y'all have a nice day now.'

Jeevan felt his heart racing as he saw himself and Sunita the way the old lady had seen them: A not-so-young but not old Indian man of medium height, simply but neatly dressed, walking into the Inner Harbor with a pretty young woman dressed up in her best sari, a matching bindi on her forehead, her hair washed and plaited, her left arm linked with his right one. Jeevan had seen many such tableaus, and for a moment he saw this one too from a distance. Then a rush of panic came, like the feeling of being alone at night in a neighborhood far from home with no cab in sight.

'Let's go this way,' said Sunita, still a little flushed from the encounter.

At least the candy floss seems forgotten, thought Jeevan, following her as she walked towards the water.

A white water-taxi was phut-phutting off towards Fort McHenry, its blue canopy fluttering as it went. Next to it stood a large preserved warship from another era, whatever menace it might have once posed softened by the sounds of excited children cajoling their mothers to take them on board. A live band was playing upbeat tunes in the small amphitheater near the water. A large plastic tip-jar half full of dollar bills sat in front of the bass drum.

'Have you been here before?' Jeevan asked.

'Once,' she said.

Jeevan waited for her to continue, but she said nothing. Her grip on his arm slackened. They walked on for a bit, her gait growing heavy, then Jeevan stopped and turned to her. 'What happened?' he asked. 'Did I say something wrong?'

'No,' she said, her head down as if she were looking at her left foot, 'it's not that.'

'I am sorry, I didn't mean to …' said Jeevan.

'You didn't do anything,' she said, and looked up at him. Her eyes searched his face. She tried to smile. 'Shall we find a place to sit?' she asked.

They walked past the cruise ships and the Science Center and found an empty bench on the southern side of the Harbor. Across this last incursion of the Chesapeake Bay, on the water near the aquarium, the paddle boats were fussing around like a flush of ducks. Sunita seemed to be looking at them from the bench. She sighed, clucked her tongue, then sighed again.

'For the first few months, I knew nothing,' she said finally. 'I was away from Meerut for the first time, different country, couldn't understand what anyone said. Every second night he would go out: one day there was a party at the restaurant, one day some catering job. Sometimes he would come home late, smelling of alcohol and cigarettes. Other times he didn't come home. Then the next morning he would say, I fell asleep in the restaurant. I used to get angry, sometimes I would cry. I don't know anyone here, I miss home, why do you leave me at night? He would say, I need to earn money to feed us. And when we have a child, then what? he would say. We have to save money for him as well. I believed him, why wouldn't I? And I wanted to have a baby also, but, but, he never wanted to … you know …'

'What?' asked Jeevan, then blushed when he realized what she was saying.

'My bhabhi and my friends had told me that men always want it, especially in the beginning,' said Sunita, smiling despite herself, probably at the memory of those conversations.

'But he never wanted it. And I felt a little relieved. It was scary, it also hurt a little. I liked it, but I also felt ashamed about how it felt. Now look at me, shamelessly telling you all this.' She glanced up at Jeevan. There was a mixture of pain and embarrassment and shyness in her face. Before he could say anything, before he could figure out what he could say, she continued: 'But it's okay. You are a good man. I don't know why, but I feel like you are a good man.'

Jeevan shifted in his seat. He smiled at her, but didn't say anything.

'Why aren't you married?' asked Sunita.

'Me?' asked Jeevan. 'I don't know.'

'How can you not know?'

'I mean, no reason, it just never happened.'

'You never found the right girl,' said Sunita, making a statement, not asking a question.

Jeevan stifled a laugh.

'Why are you laughing?' she asked, mock annoyance on her face.

'Just like that,' said Jeevan, throwing up his hands in an exaggerated gesture of innocence.

She laughed too.

'Then?' said Jeevan.

'I think it was at least eight months before I found out that all those late nights were not spent at the restaurant. They were spent with her. And do you know how I found out? The doorbell rings in my house, I open the door, and there's a woman, a tall woman with dirty yellow hair. She starts shouting and screaming at me. Half the things she is saying, I don't even understand. But I do understand she is saying that my husband is actually her husband and that she doesn't want to share him. I didn't know what to say to her. I just shut the door and locked it from inside. She shouted and shouted for a while, then she left. Now I knew why, when I met the wives of his Indian and Pakistani friends, they would sometimes look sad when they talked to me or call me poor girl when they thought I wasn't listening. He had been lying to me all this time. Everyone had known. I was the only donkey who didn't know anything, and didn't suspect anything.'

The Orioles game had finished and groups of people in baseball caps and black and orange T-shirts with the bird logo on them strolled by. Two white men in shorts wearing slightly drunk expressions came walking by, one with his hands on the other's shoulders.

'I've seen fire and I've seen rain,' the one in front was singing, somewhat tunelessly.

'I've seen sunny days that I thought would never end,' his friend responded.

'I've seen lonely times when I could not find a friend,' said the first, his hands flailing forward at the end of the line.

'But I always thought that I'd see you, baby, one more time again,' they sang together, as they stumbled along up the paved promenade.

'He didn't come home that night,' said Sunita when the singing duo had passed. 'Or the next night. When he finally came, he said he was sorry but he wanted to stay with her. She was no longer happy with meeting him two or three times a week. She was pregnant, and she wanted him to live with her. I refused. I'm your wife, I said. This is my house. I

85

won't leave. Where will I go, in this country, no relatives or friends? Where will I go?'

'What did he say?' Jeevan asked.

'What could he say?' said Sunita. 'He just started staying out more and more. Even when he was home, he wouldn't talk to me. He stopped touching me. For months and months I lived alone while my husband lived with me. And the worst part was, I couldn't tell my mother. I couldn't go home. My mother kept saying, I miss you, I want to see your face, come at least once. I lied to her: We don't have any money, he has taken a loan to start his own business, we can't afford a trip to India. But I knew that he would never come with me, and even if I made an excuse for him and went alone, the minute my mother saw my face she would know something was wrong. I stopped calling her. I said, I'll write letters, phone calls are expensive. I knew one day she would say, Let me talk to my son-in-law. What would I say then? I had to sit down and write long letters, making up things about where my husband took me and what he bought for me, what he liked to eat and how he loved me so much. I lied and lied and every time I wrote one of those letters, I cried. How many months this went on for, I don't know.'

She paused to run her hands down her face like she was wiping tears, although Jeevan didn't see any wetness in her eyes.

'Then, one day, he started saying that I have to leave the house. He would come home and shout at me, call me names, threaten me. I won't move, I won't move, I kept repeating. Till the day he hit me. One slap across the face was enough. I wasn't scared. Not at all scared of him. The truth is that one slap woke me up, I realized that I had to leave this man, for my own sake. So I went to Rukhsana baji, she had always been very nice to me, and I told her, Baji, I need your help.'

A brown-skinned man playing a tune on a small wooden Andean pan-flute walked by the bench. His notes resonated and layered on each other, creating a mystical effect that was incongruous in the sunny American afternoon. He stopped near the bench and opened out a small folding table on which he laid out the other flutes he had been carrying, and a bowl.

'That instrument has a beautiful voice,' said Sunita, her face still, her eyes distant.

'Would you like some candy floss?' asked Jeevan.

'Mama, it's no use fighting the City. You can't win,' said Rhonda, setting her Starbucks cup down on the table. 'Jeevan, why don't you tell her?'

Jeevan looked at Miss Lucy's daughter. Her high cheekbones caught the light in a way that made him think what a beautiful woman Miss Lucy must have been when she was younger.

'It's a difficult situation,' he said, nodding.

'Now don't you go over to her side,' said Miss Lucy. 'And get the cup off my table before it stains it.'

Jeevan stood up and reached for the offending piece of drinkware, but Rhonda got to it before him.

'There's a little left,' she said, and raised the cup to her lips.

Miss Lucy mumbled something and turned her face away from her daughter.

'What's that?' asked Rhonda.

'Nothing you want to be caring about,' said Miss Lucy.

Jeevan, still on his feet after the aborted attempt at clearing the Starbucks cup, cleared his throat. 'I have to go,' he said.

'You sit down,' said both women in one voice.

Jeevan sat down.

'I've told her so many times, Jeevan,' said Rhonda. 'Come to Charlotte and live with us. What's left here for you? We've got a nice house. There's a bedroom just for you.'

'What about my organ?'

'That organ again! Mama, I've told you a hundred times, we'll buy another one, a smaller one that can fit into a normal-sized room. Besides, how are we ever going to get that thing out of your tiny parlor?'

'I'll stay where my organ can stay,' said Miss Lucy.

'We worry about you, Mama. Richard and I want to look after you.'

'I can look after myself,' said Miss Lucy.

'It was different when Daddy was alive,' said Rhonda, turning to face Jeevan as she spoke. 'He would have wanted her to be with us after him. I know it.'

'You don't know anything,' said Miss Lucy.

'Rhonda wants to help,' Jeevan volunteered.

'I don't need help from the likes of her,' snapped Miss Lucy.

'It's always been like this, Jeevan,' said Rhonda. 'When he was still here, it was always, We don't need your money, Rondie, your daddy's alive, isn't he. And Dad was like that too. What kind of man takes money from his little girl, Rondie? You never met my daddy, did you Jeevan?'

'No,' said Jeevan.

'Chester was a proud man,' said Miss Lucy.

'And stubborn,' said Rhonda. 'Just like Mama here. Maybe that's why they went so well together, Mama and Daddy, both of them too proud for their own good.'

Jeevan looked at the photo of Miss Lucy and Chester that sat on a side table, taken at the Famous Ballroom decades ago. It showed a woman in her late thirties and a man just a few years older, dancing, looking into each other's eyes. It was not a wedding picture, Jeevan thought, nor was it of them when they were so young that the living person bore no resemblance to the person in the photo. It was a photo of a man and a woman in a phase of their lives that they knew even then was the best time they would ever have. This was the time when they had assumed their place in the world, when they had already become who they would be. These were the faces that their children would remember, that the world, if it cared to, would associate with them.

'It's a beautiful photo,' said Rhonda, her eyes following Jeevan's gaze. And for a few moments there was silence.

'You know, Jeevan,' said Rhonda, her voice calmer but still determined, 'even when Daddy fell ill, he didn't take money from Richard. Instead, he borrowed money from that ...'

Her voice trailed off.

'From whom?' asked Jeevan.

'From Shabbir,' she said reluctantly.

'Shabbir?'

'Yes,' said Rhonda. 'It was before you came.'

'I didn't know about this,' said Jeevan.

'You handle all of Shabbir's finances, don't you, Jeevan?' asked Rhonda.

'Yes,' said Jeevan. 'But I don't know anything about this.'

Rhonda looked at Jeevan. He could see she was evaluating his denial, weighing it against what she knew of him.

'Shabbir gave Chester the money,' said Miss Lucy. 'Before Chester died, he said he squared it up with Shabbir.'

Try as he might, Jeevan could not recall anything he had seen in Shabbir's papers that had to do with a loan to Chester. Over the years, Shabbir had trusted him with more and more of his finances, even giving him access to documents from earlier years. Jeevan had organized them and filed them, not just in Shabbir's office – a small room near the kitchen at Food Point – but also in his own head. If there were papers for this loan, he thought, Shabbir had hidden them from him.

'Anyway,' said Rhonda, looking away from Jeevan finally. 'It doesn't matter. The point is, the City is going to acquire your house and you will all have to move. It's better – really, Mama – move out of this place, this dirty neighborhood, all the gun play and drugs, pimps and whores on the street. This city is no place for decent folk to live in.'

'The girl thinks she's too good for the place she grew up in,' said Miss Lucy. 'She's got no love for her house or her neighborhood. Now that she's got her light-skinned husband with his hair all straight and funny, she thinks she knows something about what folk are decent and what aren't. What are decent folk, Jeevan? Those friends of her man's, talking like they're the Queen of England and sending their children to Jack and Jill? Those folk are decent and we folk are pimps and whores. That's what this girl thinks. She just wants to go on climbing up that hill with that fancy man of hers.'

'Don't drag Richard into this,' said Rhonda. 'He's a good man. He treats me right, and he works hard for his money. Richard wants to help you. It's a shame, he keeps saying, your mother living there all alone. She should live with us.'

'And his fancy mother,' continued Miss Lucy. 'I saw the way she looked at me. She didn't say a word to me at the wedding. And don't think she was falling over herself to welcome the daughter of these parents into her family either.'

'It's been fifteen years, Mama,' said Rhonda. 'I'm not going to keep apologizing for Sheila's behavior for fifteen years.'

'I didn't raise my child to be brown-nosing a black woman who thinks she's white. The Lord knows I didn't.'

'What did you expect me to do, Mama?' said Rhonda, her voice rising. 'Marry some nappy-headed Negro and be a janitor's wife for the rest of my life?'

'Your father was a nappy-headed Negro,' said Miss Lucy. She paused for a moment and said: 'So was your brother.'

Rhonda's face contorted. She looked like her mother had slapped her.

There were photos around the house and once, when fixing some tiling, Jeevan had found a closet full of clothes that must have belonged to Myron; they were for a man much slighter than Chester had been. Shabbir had told him about Myron, and how he had died in a shootout on the corner of 25th and Maryland, just a few hundred yards from the house he had been born in. But not once, till now, had

Miss Lucy ever talked to Jeevan about Myron, or even uttered his name.

'I hate this place,' said Rhonda. 'I've hated it from that day. You know which day I'm talking about Mama, you know what I'm saying. I was the one who answered the door that evening, I ran down to the corner. By the time you came, Myron was dead already, but I saw him alive, lying on the sidewalk, bleeding from his stomach. He knew he was going to die, every kid here knew what it meant to be shot, but he didn't believe it. Rondie, he said, Rondie, he shot me. He just kept saying that till his eyes stopped seeing.' Her face collapsed into her hands and she wept. Miss Lucy got up and hobbled around the table. She put her arms around her daughter. 'My child,' she said. 'My honey child. Your brother is with the good Lord in heaven. Sometimes at night, in my dreams, I see him and my Chester, standing with the angels, smiling at me. He is at peace now.'

Jeevan rose from his chair and quietly let himself out.

On a light stucco wall at the end of the block, large spray-painted black letters say WE LOVE YOU JJ. In front of the LOVE a blue D has been sprayed, making it LOVED, then obscured again, partially, by black paint. In front of that wall stand some young people, their faces somber, lighting candles with a cigarette lighter someone is passing around. Across the street, around the corner from the store whose front bears the legend 'Miracle on 33rd Street' are more black letters: RIP JJ.

The road dips down to the Jones River and its various bridges towards the west. Across the expressway, behind the hill, the sun is low on the horizon. Cars roll up the street: people exiting the highway, going home. Some of them honk as they pass the crowd that is beginning to gather at the corner. These are short bursts of sound, and somehow they are able to transcend the registers of frustration and exhilaration that car horns are designed to produce.

A woman carrying a leather-bound Bible in one hand walks down the street, a candle in her other hand. Behind her, a woman leaning her head against a man's chest walks slowly, taking solace in the arm her companion has thrown around her. Two women, dressed neatly in black, their veils curled over their hats, support a woman by her limp hands. Her head nods from side to side as she walks.

The remaining candles are lit. A few stragglers join the party. The woman with the Bible opens it and begins to read. A few of the young men shift from side to side, their loose clothes swaying as they move. The candles shine off the large round hoops that some of the young women wear. The Bible reader looks up and continues to speak. One of the older women closes her eyes and raises a hand.

Traffic slows as it passes the scene. A few cars speed up. The street lights come on, orange and soft. The candles glow yellower in their light. The Bible is shut now and the crowd parts to allow the woman who was reading from it to lead them as they walk down the street. She talks as she walks, words of prayer, some of which are answered by sobs, some with gestures and some with words. Wax rolls down the candles, singeing some hands, congealing on fingers.

A squad car turns onto the street at the next corner. It moves slowly along with the procession for a while. The driver looks straight ahead. His partner's face is impassive and stony. His eyes scan the crowd. Then the car accelerates and drives away, its red and blue lights unlit, the large painted letters on its back receding into the falling dusk.

4

THE FIRST TIME MATTHEW HAD READ THE PAPER WRITTEN BY the IBM researchers, he had skimmed it quickly on his computer screen, going straight to the part he knew was crucial. The construction fundamental to the proof was there, more or less the way he had drawn it for Peter on the whiteboard in his office the day he had gone in and told him about the problem for the first time, the only time in his stay at grad school when he had impressed his Ph.D advisor with something he had said. What he hadn't drawn, and what these people had added, were a few arrows explaining how it was supposed to work. He followed the arrows – the arrows that made the drawing into a proof, that would have made his drawing into a proof if he had known where to place them – then looked at the equations and glanced through the arguments. His stomach clenched repeatedly as he read, his head grew heavy. Finally he stopped reading. They had solved his problem. They had beaten him to it. He closed the file, slammed his laptop shut, and walked out of the building to smoke a cigarette that his body did not crave. Standing outside in the late afternoon – the sun beginning its downward slope, glinting off the edges of bus-stop roofs – he had wondered why he felt like his research career had just ended. How could something that was already over end again?

For a few days after that, he had found it physically difficult to speak to anyone. TV excruciated him. Food tasted flat. In the evenings at home, he sat at his laptop for hours, playing chess on the Internet, losing steadily but playing on. Kay noticed. He could tell because her manner with him softened. But she didn't say anything. Then, after a particularly miserable weekend, on a Monday morning sitting on the pot, his mind wandering over his work plans for the week and some bills that needed paying, he had suddenly found himself thinking: Maybe there's a way to improve their theorem. It took him by surprise, and for a few seconds his mind went blank and he became aware of his heart beating in his chest. He thought: It's possible. There's always a better theorem, a neater proof. The more he thought about it, the more convinced he became. There was bound to be a way forward. He would have to read the paper carefully and understand the proofs in detail. He could do that. He would print out the paper, it was easier to focus that way. Yes, yes, he thought, I need to take a printout.

He logged in as soon as he got to work and pulled up the paper on his desktop. Just as he was about to click on the print icon, he saw his boss standing near the printer. How would he explain this? It wasn't a particularly formal office, many of the people here had computer science or math degrees. It wouldn't be considered unusual if someone printed out a research paper. But Matthew hesitated. He knew that if someone asked him about it, he would be in trouble. No one would think of his yearning for a researcher's life as an expression of contempt for the kind of work that was done here. But if someone accosted him right now, Matthew was afraid he wouldn't be able to hide either his yearning or his contempt.

At lunchtime most people left the office. He evaded his lunch group, saying he had a sandwich in his bag and wanted to get some things done. He opened the paper again on his computer. What would Kay say if she found out? She wouldn't find out. He didn't have to tell her. But what if she did? She was right, wasn't she, in saying, Let it go. She had seen him in Providence, she had seen what he had gone through, she had been there through all of it. It wasn't fair to her. But he just wanted to see if there was some way to improve the result, that's all. Most probably there wasn't, and that would be the end of that. But what if there was?

His fingers trembled over the enter key. It's just a printout. Come on, it's just one fucking printout. How would Peter react if he came to know about this? Peter, with his disappointed face and his one-line dismissals of Matthew's many attempts, would probably roll his eyes and sigh. Maybe Peter's right, maybe I'm not good enough. Why am I trying to do something I'm not smart enough to do?

On that question, his finger dropped and a little printer icon appeared in the corner of the screen. Matthew sat frozen, staring at the laptop but not seeing a thing. Across the room, there was a rumble as the wheels began to turn.

Matthew jerked to his feet and ran to the printer. Looking over his shoulder, greeting a passing janitor unusually cheerfully, he silently urged the machine to work faster. When it stopped churning, he reached for the pages lying face down on the tray and picked them up. The recycle bin sat, blue and inviting, near the shredder, and for a moment Matthew wavered. Then he slid the pages into the maw of the large office stapler that sat on the table and, just like that, he pressed down on it and quickly returned to his cubicle.

The rest of the day, his mind kept returning to the paper. In a meeting with his boss, listening to his colleagues banter over coffee, he kept thinking about the printout in his bag: a corner folded from being stuffed in hastily, sitting next to his discman and earphones, a book on Probability, some discarded cling wrap from sandwiches that had been carried in the past and an old issue of the *New Yorker* Matthew hadn't got around to recycling. That evening, when the bus had, to the best of his knowledge, crossed the city line into Baltimore, Matthew reached into his bag and pulled out the paper.

The abstract went quickly. He didn't need to be told what the question was and how they had answered it; he knew it as well as anyone else did or ever would. It was the abstract he had wanted to write. The introduction slowed him down. He found the same grandiose claims about the relevance of the question that he had thought he would make. Bullshit, he thought, it's just theory and you guys know it. Your model has too many simplifications, the mathematics is too neat. The only reason you care about this is because you know that the research community cares about it, and the only reason they care about it is because they have to care about things to be taken seriously as scientists. Okay, so you guys are smart, we get it.

He folded the paper into his bag and sat back.

Around him people chattered on or sat silent, waiting for their stops. This is real, he thought, this going to work every day. There's no glory in it, just the satisfaction of working to earn a living. He had that, and he didn't need anything else. But as the bus rolled through the evening, the urge to retrieve the paper from the bag grew, and with it came a feeling of being alone. He wanted to talk to someone about the paper, thrash out the thoughts he had, write his equations on a whiteboard and throw questions at someone. Even if that person just stopped him where he made a mistake and helped him with a few calculations, that would be enough, even if that person didn't answer, even if they just listened and understood. He was good enough to do this, but he couldn't do it alone. Kay didn't know any of this, she had struggled through calculus in college. Besides, she had said very clearly that she wanted him to forget his grad school experience and move on. Some of the people at work might have understood, but none of them was interested. They just cared about stock prices and the market, TV shows and buying new cars, holidaying in Hawaii. Outside the circumscribed world of grad school and research labs, no one cared about these things. But Matthew cared, even if it meant he would have to care on his own.

That night, after Kay had fallen asleep, Matthew got out of bed and went to his table. Loading up the chess program, he played a few games, then went out and smoked a cigarette. It was almost one in the morning before he picked up the paper and began reading the proofs. He verified each argument, sometimes getting stuck over one sentence for ten or fifteen minutes till it became clear, sometimes moving on, knowing that he didn't fully understand the reasoning but accepting it anyway. A few of the arguments were vague, and a couple of times he got excited at the thought that he might have found an error. But when he worked it through, he found that the reasoning was solid, it had just been written loosely. He solved each equation himself and went over every step as carefully as he could. The proof was sound, there didn't seem to be any error. Nor could he think of improving the result in any way. He went back to the chess server, there were still people there looking for games, some insomniacs, some people from other time zones sneaking in a game while at work. He began playing, but kept nodding off. At one point, he woke with a start to find he had lost a game because he had fallen asleep and his clock had run out. By the time he went to bed, it was past four.

One long sleepy day later, he went back to the paper, going over the description of the previous work on the problem. He had read almost all of the papers that were mentioned but there were a couple that he hadn't seen before. Perhaps, he thought, he needed to look at those papers. Maybe there was something in them that would open out a new possibility. It would mean he would have to go to the Hopkins university library. He had avoided the campus the few weeks they had been in Baltimore. But there was no easier way to get those papers.

He left work a little after lunch, claiming he had a dental appointment. Forty-five minutes later, he was deep in the basement of the library, scanning the stacks for the conference proceedings and journals he needed. Making copies of the papers, he took them to an empty table and sat down to read. Two hours later – struggling through equations and explanations, fighting the urge to go out and smoke, and once even looking around to see if there was a computer on which he could perhaps log in and play a game of chess to clear his mind – he was no closer to finding a way to improve the result. There was still an hour before he could return home, so he put away the papers and walked up the stairs to the coffee machine. Stepping out onto the quad with his coffee and a cigarette, he saw there were some Indian students playing cricket. He sat on the steps and watched as one of them ran in and threw what looked like a tennis ball at another who was holding a flat bat. The bat swung vertically to meet the ball and missed it. The ball went through to another player, who was standing behind the batter. As the ball was being relayed back to the man whose job it appeared to be to throw it, a thought stirred in Matthew's mind.

He recalled a lecture from a class Peter had given early in Matthew's time at Brown. Perhaps there was a way of using the proof Peter had talked about, maybe it could be adapted to this setting. He reached into his bag and brought out one of the papers he had read. With this new idea in his mind, it read completely differently. There is a chance, Matthew thought, a slim chance. He would have to look at the text Peter had used. His copy of it was at home, but he wanted to look at it right away and he couldn't go home for at least an hour. Draining his coffee in a gulp and stubbing his cigarette in the mud, Matthew stood and turned to go back into the library. He ran down the stairs to where the security guard sat. A woman's bag was being inspected, so Matthew had to wait his turn. His leg shook with impatience, but the guard continued to sift through the bag at his own relaxed pace. He turned in annoyance and his eye fell on a noticeboard that stood to one side of the library's entrance. In one corner was a printed A4 sheet that said

SEMINAR

Sorting and Re-sorting in Parallel
Professor Peter Graham
Dept of Computer Science, Brown University
Shaffer 101
12 p.m., Thursday, 15 May 1997

Sunita came walking down the street, a plastic bag in one hand, her sari's pallu trailing behind her in the breeze. She climbed up the stairs and stopped, startled, when she saw Jeevan sitting on the porch in the dark.

'Why don't you turn the light on,' she said, reaching back with her free hand and drawing the pallu around her shoulder.

'It's okay,' said Jeevan.

'You didn't come tonight.'

Jeevan nodded.

'Have you eaten?' she asked. 'I thought so,' she continued, without waiting for his answer. 'I brought some sabji and daal. There's some rice from the afternoon. I can make some chapatis if you want. Come.'

She breezed into the house. Then, realizing that Jeevan hadn't moved, she opened the door again and said: 'Come.'

All Jeevan could see was a dark female form standing over him, sari wrapped around it, framed in an open doorway, outstretched arm holding the door open for him.

'I'm coming,' he said.

Sunita put a plate in front of him and shoveled some rice into it. 'Do you want some chapatis?' she asked.

'No.'

'I can make them,' she said. 'It won't take time.'

'This is okay.'

She took a pan off the stove and spooned cauliflower and potatoes into his plate.

'Not so much,' he said, raising his hand.

'Okay,' she said and lifted everything except a single floret of cauliflower off his plate. Jeevan looked up. 'You complain too much,' she said, smiling, then dumped it all back into his plate.

When he had finished eating, Sunita cleared the dishes and said: 'That cassette player in the closet upstairs, does it work?'

'I don't know,' said Jeevan.

'Shabbir bhai gave it to you, right?'

'Yes, but I've never used it.'

'I'll get it.'

She brought the old machine down, took it to the living room, dusted it off with a cloth and plugged it in.

'I don't have any cassettes,' Jeevan said.

'Rashida baji lent me one,' she said. 'Come, sit here, let's listen to it.'

Clicking the cassette into place, she pressed a button. A low hum, and the whirring of the roller was replaced by the sound of strings, and then a woman began to sing. Jeevan sat up at the sound. Lata Mangeshkar's voice settled on his ears like salt on a hungry man's tongue. His eyes closed involuntarily. His muscles relaxed and his head dropped over his chest.

'*Baahon mein chale aao*,' sang the voice, '*humse sanam kya purdah …*'

'This is my favorite song,' said Sunita. 'Do you know it?'

'Yes,' said Jeevan, raising his head, his eyes blinking open.

'My mother would say, She's shameless, running after him, telling him to come into her arms,' said Sunita, sitting down at the other end of the couch from Jeevan. 'I would fight with her. No, she isn't, I would say. She loves him, she knows he loves her. What's wrong with it then?'

'Nothing,' said Jeevan.

'Jaya Bhaduri looks beautiful in this song, doesn't she?' said Sunita. 'I loved her long hair, tied loosely halfway down, and then a long plait. I always wanted to keep my hair that way, but my mother would tie my plait really high.'

'Your hair looks good like this,' said Jeevan.

Sunita looked at Jeevan. Her lips curled into a smile. 'So you like the way my hair looks?' she said, flipping her plait forward.

Jeevan looked away.

'You know,' said Sunita, edging towards him on the sofa, 'I know why you are so quiet all the time.'

The song finished. After a hiss-filled pause, the next one started. Sunita got up and went over to the cassette player.

'Once more,' she said. 'Is that okay?' She turned to face him while the tape spooled back. 'It's a girl,' she declared. 'You are a failed lover. That's why you mope around like Devdas.'

The cassette finished rewinding with a click. Sunita pressed play and came back to the sofa. She sat on her side facing Jeevan, one leg curled up on the sofa. 'Am I right?'

'Devdas used to drink,' said Jeevan, turning towards her. 'I don't drink.' Once again the song started playing, a woman singing to a man, Jaya Bhaduri to Sanjeev Kumar on the screen: '*Baahon mein chale aao, humse sanam kya purdah …*'

'What was her name?'

'Whose name?'

'The girl who broke your heart.'

Jeevan laughed, and Sunita laughed with him. 'No girl broke my heart,' he said.

'So you've never fallen in love with anyone,' said Sunita. 'I don't believe it.'

'Umm …'

'See, see, I knew it,' said Sunita. 'What was her name?'

'Harpreet.'

'A Sikhni! Was she beautiful? These Sikh women are very fair, that's why all you men think they are beautiful.'

Jeevan smiled and shook his head. 'You are mad,' he said.

'So what happened with Harpreet?' asked Sunita.

'Nothing happened.'

'I'll tell you what happened,' said Sunita, rising from the sofa.

'You used to wait for her on the roof every evening,' she said, her right hand shielding her eyes as they searched an imaginary horizon, her neck moving from side to side. 'And she would come, blushing and shy.'

Jeevan waved his hand in denial.

'She said she would love you for ever,' she said, her two hands clasping each other in front of her chest, her head tilted to the right.

A smile broke on Jeevan's lips.

'But one day her father saw the two of you together.' Her eyes opened wide in mock anger, her back straightened.

Jeevan couldn't help but laugh.

'You pleaded with him,' she said, her eyes taking on a plaintive look, her hands folded. 'I love her, I will make her very happy, please let me marry her.'

'Stop,' said Jeevan, his stomach beginning to knot with laughter. 'Please stop.'

'But he was firm,' she said, resuming the angry-eyed father pose. 'My daughter will never marry a Hindu. So he found a Sikh boy and arranged her marriage.

'You said to her, Let us run away, but she said, I cannot break my father's heart.' Turning away from Jeevan, Sunita covered her mouth with the back of her hand like she had just broken into tears.

'When her wedding procession came by your house, you sang sad film songs and drank all night,' she said, tilting an imaginary glass into her mouth and swaying on her feet. 'Next morning, you decided to leave India forever!'

Jeevan held his side with one hand and motioned with the other. 'Stop, please stop,' he said.

'So,' said Sunita. 'Is that what happened?'

'No, no,' said Jeevan, breathing deeply through his mouth

as he tried to recover. 'We never talked. I used to see her on my way to work. I don't think she even noticed me.'

'Poor you,' said Sunita, sitting back down and leaning towards him, her chin poised on her palm. 'The fire was only on one side.'

Jeevan shrugged his shoulders.

'You men are all the same,' said Sunita. 'You don't understand anything. When I was in Meerut, in the evenings when I went out for a walk with my friends, all the boys in the neighborhood would come out. Some of them would pass remarks loudly, talking about how they would bring stars down from the sky for us, or how I was as beautiful as a fairy from heaven, or some stupid filmy dialogue like that. Others would sing songs, some were soft romantic songs, some not so soft. And then there were other boys, like yourself, who would just stand and stare and stare. All donkeys! We never paid any attention to them and they never realized that if they'd just had the courage to look one of us in the eye and talk like friends, we would have talked to them and made them our friends.'

'Maybe they wanted to be more than friends,' said Jeevan.

'If they did, they first had to be friends,' said Sunita. 'We girls talked a lot about the kind of man we would marry. Some said, He should be handsome like Salman Khan, some said, No, no, Salman Khan is very short, I want a tall man like Amitabh Bachchan. Others would say, I like Anil Kapoor's hairstyle. But when all that kind of talk was finished, when we got serious, we all agreed that we wanted to marry a good person, someone who would look after us, who would care for us and our children.'

'Even if he was ugly?' asked Jeevan.

'Such a person would never be ugly in my eyes,' said Sunita, and Jeevan saw that the eyes that would never see a caring person as ugly were fixed on him, their brown irises resplendent around the small black pupils through which she saw him. Catching his lingering gaze, her eyes blinked, her head bowed. Then she glanced up, her cheeks flushed, and looked down again.

'Do you like Urdu poetry?' he said, getting up and walking to the cassette player.

'Yes,' she said, also standing up, holding her body as if she expected to be led somewhere. 'It's very romantic. But I don't understand all the difficult words.'

'Don't worry,' said Jeevan, pressing the stop button. 'I'll explain them to you.'

She sat back down and looked up at him. He thought of sitting down, then decided to stay on his feet.

'This is by Jaun Elia,' said Jeevan. With the music switched off, his voice was resonant in the silence recently vacated by Lata Mangeshkar's song.

'When you come, you will find me lost
My solitude has nothing in it but dreams
You want to decorate my room
My room has nothing but books
These books have done me great injustice
There's an enigma in them, and my mind, afflicted by it,
Can never know the pleasure of good news
Can never find peace in this life.'

'It's pretty,' said Sunita, rising to her feet. 'But it's not very romantic. Anyway, there are hardly any books in your room.'

What do we do with all this?' asked Kamran, stepping out from under the arched entrance of the library. 'This guy built this, that guy built that. These houses sold for this much, those people loaned the money. The streetcars took them to work, the neighborhoods came up around the streetcar lines. That's great, but how does that help us?'

Kay adjusted her bookbag on her shoulder and looked up at him. He isn't really into this, she thought. Should I even be here with him? 'Let's get some coffee,' she said.

We've got to do something about this, Kay had said. Kamran wondered what they could actually do. How could they prevent the demolition? The argument that people wouldn't want to leave places they had lived in for years didn't stand. The neighborhoods they could move to were safer, cleaner and better. It didn't make sense to say that the compensation package was inadequate; it was clearly more generous than most previous packages had been. And many of these people, especially the ones who still had some significant portions of their lives to live, would probably want to move to a place that didn't feel like a prison, so community action, even if they knew how to go about organizing it, would probably not take off. It had been Kay's idea to go to the library. There's history here, she had said. Maybe that's the way to go. And so Kamran had returned to Baltimore for the weekend. Kay had asked him to.

'Matthew didn't want to come?' Kamran said, as they walked past the cathedral, down Mulberry Street towards Charles.

'No,' she said. 'It was his idea, the history thing. But when

I asked him to come, he said, It's not going to work. He can be very negative sometimes.'

Kamran felt stung by the statement. He hadn't been all that positive himself. She had noticed, he was sure she had noticed. 'Yeah,' he said, 'sometimes you've got to just put your doubts aside and go for it.'

Kay favored him with a smile. He's trying, she thought.

'You see this grey stone?' he said, pointing at the cathedral.

'It's beautiful,' she said. 'It's a grand building.'

'It's gneiss. Quarried right here in Maryland, near Ellicott City. It's a metamorphic rock. Probably started forming hundreds of millions of years ago, right here in Maryland.'

'In the Maryland of a hundred million years ago,' said Kay, smiling.

'Yeah, back when Baltimore was just a little village with a harbor.'

'Nice work, Encyclopedia Brown.'

'You're the one who forced me to spend four hours in the library on a Saturday afternoon,' said Kamran. 'Not that I didn't enjoy it.'

'You didn't have to come.'

There was an amused light in her eyes that shone on Kamran and felt like illumination. She's married, he thought to himself. Sucks that she's married.

At Louie's Bookstore Cafe, the late afternoon was in full swing. In the bookstore section, a woman stood reading at a mike in front of a neat square arrangement of nine chairs on which three people sat listening to her intently over the chatter of the diners who sat in the cafe section. Kamran and Kay were taken past the small tables crowded with large plates and shown a spot in a corner. Above their table, on plain canvas, a frantic, stylized collection of lines in spray-can black spelt a single word: ADUMBRATE.

'I can barely read what it says,' Kay said. 'Ad-umb-rate. What does that mean?'

'Like, to hint at, or outline,' said Kamran, making a face. 'Very clever.'

'Why clever?' asked Kay, looking back at the indistinct word with its fat angular serifs. 'Oh, I get it.'

'Besides, graffiti shouldn't be framed,' Kamran said. 'I mean, the whole point is that it's art that lives outside the gallery, outside private collections, outside temperature-controlled rooms. Where's the danger in this? Where's the impermanence? Put graffiti into a frame and it's no longer graffiti.'

'Impermanence isn't always cool,' Kay said quietly.

Kamran's tirade against the appropriation of artistic dissent faltered. Annoyance gathered within him. But when he looked across the table, the sight of her face – contemplating the menu, a restful expression on it – disarmed him. He wished she would look up and smile, to indicate that she was over it, whatever it was, but also to apologize to him for cutting him off like that, for misunderstanding him. But she kept studying the menu, and he kept waiting.

'Hey! How are you guys doing today?' said a bright-eyed woman holding a little notebook and a pen.

'We're great,' said Kay, and Kamran relaxed at the genuine cheer in her voice.

'Can I get you guys something to drink?'

Over coffee, the conversation rolled serene and

comfortable. Kay talked of the time in high school when she was a reluctant cheerleader, of how her mother had been proud of her and people at school had admired her. 'But I didn't date the jocks, which struck people as odd.'

'I can't believe you were a cheerleader,' said Kamran, when, in fact, what he couldn't believe was that he, Kamran Ahmad, was having coffee with a former cheerleader.

Kay talked about her first boyfriend and his sweet grandmother, who always addressed her as 'mi niña bonita', and carried on whole conversations in Spanish with Kay who struggled to follow along.

'When I was in college,' said Kamran in response, 'I dated this one white girl and my housemates, all Muslims, mainly from Pakistan, were dead against it.'

'Really?' asked Kay, not sure why college roommates would be 'against' something like that, or why it would matter.

'Yeah,' said Kamran. 'It was crazy.'

'So you moved out?' Kay asked.

'Yeah,' said Kamran.

He didn't, thought Kay.

'You've dated white girls since?' she asked.

'Oh yeah,' said Kamran. 'Sure I have.'

He hasn't, thought Kay.

The waitress returned just as Kay was trying to think of an excuse to get up and go home.

'What are you getting?' Kamran asked, and Kay looked down again at the menu she had been holding all this time.

The coffee came. Kamran told his funny New York stories of the outrageous but not dangerous behavior of Max's incipient rock star friends on the Lower East Side, of nerds at work who checked out new Union Square lunch places by working through the menu one sandwich at a time, of precocious Park Slope seven-year-olds preferring sushi over peanut butter and jelly sandwiches for lunch. Kay settled into the afternoon, following each narration with an anticipatory smile, responding with 'Oh my god' or 'That's too funny' or 'No way he said that', and laughing freely at the punchlines. She eagerly took in the litany of bagel shops and performance spaces, upscale restaurants visited during Restaurant Week and tenth-floor art galleries, outdoor summer concerts and organic food stores, noting, sometimes with bemusement, the detailed description Kamran gave of each place, the involved instructions on how to get there by subway or on foot.

Coffee dried in their mugs, which were then cleared. But not before they had ordered appetizers. The late afternoon's patrons had left and their tables were taken by early diners. After the appetizers, they decided they might as well order drinks and a light dinner. So they called the waitress back and ordered again. By the time they finished their food and moved to dessert, some of the tables were being readied for their second seating.

'You guys look like you want to spend the night here,' said the waitress, smiling at Kamran as she removed the dessert plates. 'There's a futon in the back, just in case.'

'Oh we're not, I mean, we're not like ...' said Kamran, blushing furiously, then realizing he had misunderstood: 'oh, you meant ... umm ...'

The waitress was looking intently at Kamran, her head

cocked to one side, her eyes glittering with amusement. This was clearly a funny story she was going to hoard for later.

'We'll just get the check, please,' said Kay.

On Charles Street, night was casting its yellow and grey shadows on the sidewalk's stucco. Taxis were rolling up the street, heading north, but Kay didn't wave down any of them, and so neither did Kamran. Instead, they walked downtown. Through large picture windows they could see that the restaurants were full of diners – their forks or chopsticks or glasses of wine raised, their faces animated in conversation – and waiters carrying trays high near their chests, focusing on navigating the maze of tables. People dressed for the evening walked in twos and threes into darkened bar rooms, disappearing from the street's view. An ATM vestibule waited, empty and neon white, for the business that would come its way as the night wore on.

Kamran and Kay walked through the Saturday night energy of downtown. Skirting the Inner Harbor, they climbed up a long, steep flight of steps to Federal Hill Park.

'Let's sit there,' said Kay, pointing to a bench that faced north.

They sat and looked down at the Harbor and to the buildings beyond it. Over to the west, the baseball stadium's lights were on.

'Looks like a game's on today,' said Kamran. 'I wonder if Cal is playing.'

'That's Jeevan's joke,' said Kay. 'Henry never tires of it.'

Kamran chuckled. 'Henry and Jeevan are quite a pair.'

'You've known both of them a while, haven't you?'

'Since I can remember.'

'Isn't it strange to see people you knew as a kid grow old?' said Kay. 'I see it and think, I'll grow old too someday. But I can't imagine it, not really.'

'Yeah?'

'I don't know if I am ready to grow old,' said Kay. 'It's like I feel there's stuff I need to do before that. You know, like go to med school, become a doctor, maybe have kids, a house. It's not like I feel there's a clock ticking and I need to get these things done before it ticks down. It's more like I feel that till I get these things done, I won't grow old. Does that make sense?'

North of the Harbor, the large tent of the Pier 6 concert pavilion shone like a lantern. The sound of guitars playing emerged from it and crossed the black waters of the bay to where Kay and Kamran sat. A flute sounded over the guitars and the drums took off.

'Is that Jethro Tull?' asked Kay.

'Could be,' said Kamran. 'Can't believe they're still doing shows. I mean, who goes to a Jethro Tull concert?'

'My dad proposed to my mom at a Jethro Tull concert,' said Kay.

'Oops.'

'That was a long time ago,' said Kay, taking Kamran's hand.

Kamran looked down at the two hands embracing on the bench. His right hand, the one Kay held, felt clammy and warm. The rest of his body shivered. He looked up at Kay, but she was looking across the Harbor at the concert pavilion.

'Then there are other times when I feel that I'm being stupid,' she said.

'Stupid about what?'

'You know, about time. About doing the things I want to do.'

Seen in profile from where Kamran sat, Kay's face had taken on a thoughtful look. Her skin looked smooth, touchable.

'My mom always said, Medicine is difficult, it takes years,' Kay said. 'And I thought, Whatever. I'll get to college, do my pre-med courses. I'll show her I'm good enough. But college didn't work out the way I'd thought it would. It could have, if I hadn't met this guy I ended up dating for years. I should have seen it. I should have seen it right in the beginning, that he wanted a certain kind of girlfriend, someone a little more like his West LA friends' girlfriends. I should have made it clear, I guess, that I needed him to back me up, to tell me I was good enough. But I didn't, and so I kept needing him to be a certain way for me and he kept needing me to be a certain way for him, and by the end of college I was a pharmacist.'

'There's nothing wrong with being a pharmacist,' said Kamran.

'No, there isn't,' said Kay. 'It's a steady job. No matter what happens, people always need medicine, right? But that's not what I wanted. What I wanted was a guy who would be there for me while I tried to become what I wanted.'

She drew her hand back from Kamran's. The cool evening air dried his palm.

'Maybe that's the mistake I made,' Kay continued. 'Thinking that I needed a guy, thinking that I couldn't go it alone. Imagine that, it's the end of the twentieth century and I'm still thinking that a woman needs a man ...'

'Like a fish needs a bicycle,' said Kamran.

Kay's gaze, when it turned on him, was not so much reproachful as distant.

'Sorry,' said Kamran.

'It's okay,' said Kay, hurt spreading across her face. 'That was funny.'

Kamran's head sank onto his chest. With the thumb and forefinger of his left hand, he massaged his temples. Then he looked up, reached out with his right hand and took her hand in it.

'I'm sorry,' he said. 'Really.'

Kay withdrew her hand from his. 'And then there's Matthew,' she said, absently flexing the fingers of the hand that had been in Kamran's a moment ago.

'What about Matthew?' asked Kamran, looking at her hand as it opened and closed.

'He has these silly dreams of being a computer scientist. He thinks I don't know that he's trying again to solve some problem. Getting out of bed in the middle of the night and going to his computer – like I can't tell when he gets up and when he comes back.'

'What's the problem?'

'I don't know,' said Kay. 'Some paper he was working on when he was in grad school. He couldn't do it then, and now some other people have written that paper. He's taken it hard. He just found out some time ago. Now he's trying to do something, I don't know what. He doesn't tell me because he thinks I wouldn't like it. And you know what? He's right.'

'Why?'

'It's always about him, his ambition, his failure, his

117

aspirations,' said Kay. 'In his family, you need to be an intellectual to be a success. You need to have written a book about conflict in Africa or something. That's great, I mean, but he doesn't see what it's doing to him. Sometimes he gets carried away by all that. And I'm like, In this whole picture, where do I fit in?'

'But I thought he changed jobs to come to Baltimore so that you could take classes while working at Hopkins?'

Kamran's innocent question drained the fight from Kay's body. She crumpled into the bench. Her neck fell back and her eyes closed. Her arms tingled with the need to be touched. She wished for a moment that Kamran would take her hand – she almost reached out for it, then stopped because she realized that it wasn't Kamran's touch she needed, it was Matthew's.

'You okay?' Kamran asked, suddenly anxious at the nighttime emptiness of the park.

They sat without speaking for what seemed like a very long time. The concert ended on the other side of the Harbor and the lights went out in the pavilion. The food court went dark, the paddle boats were parked. East of where they sat, from somewhere near Fells Point, four criss-crossing searchlights carved patterns on low-lying clouds. The curved lettering of the Dominos Sugar sign looked like a hot iron ready to brand the night sky. There were people awake everywhere, in the clubs, in the bars, in their homes, on porches and decks – talking, flirting, laughing, dancing, partying – but from up on Federal Hill, not a single one could be seen.

It was almost midnight when they flagged down a cab on Light Street.

'Hey Kamran!' said the cab driver, as they bundled into the backseat. 'What's up, brother? When did you come in from New York?'

'Asad bhai?' said Kamran, his eye falling on the tag that proclaimed the cab driver's name, Asadullah Rehman. 'You're driving a cab now?'

'Yes, brother,' said Asad. 'Not as smart as you. Should have studied harder in high school.'

'We were in high school together,' said Kamran, turning to Kay. 'Asad bhai was a year ahead of me. Asad bhai, this is my friend Kay. She's Abba's tenant.'

In the rearview mirror, Asad's eyes met Kay's. The look he gave her, before nodding, then looking back at the road, went straight to her stomach and made it tighten.

'This boy, in high school, always with the books,' said Asad, addressing Kay. 'Not like me, always chasing the girls.'

Asad paused, waiting for Kay's response. But no polite laughter or witty repartee came. Kamran didn't try to fill the gap either, his thoughts going back to the time in school when Asad used to tease and taunt him, taking his bullying as far as he reasonably could with a skinny kid whose father knew his own father.

'How is Shabbir chacha?' asked Asad.

'He's fine.'

'And Jeevan uncle? I heard your dad got him a girl.'

Kay shifted over and put some space between herself and Kamran.

'Jeevan uncle is fine.'

'Shabbir chacha really loves that Hindu,' continued Asad. 'Tell him to find me someone too.'

'I'll tell him.'

Kay yawned deliberately and shut her eyes. Asad caught Kamran's eye in the mirror and said in Urdu: 'She's sleepy, take her home and put her to bed.' Then he winked, and Kamran felt like reaching through the partition and taking hold of his fat hairy neck and pressing down till his eyes rolled back into his head.

'Excellent,' said Shabbir, his footfalls echoing as he came down the stairs. 'This house is excellent, Miss Lucy.'

Mary Symcox looked up from a file she had open in front of her. Behind her, in one empty corner, lay a paper bag shaped around a bottle. Next to it were a few shards of glass and a small oblong object with a bowl at one end. Miss Lucy was standing over these, her head bent.

'Have you seen how big the room upstairs is?' asked Shabbir. 'You can put two organs in it and it would still not be full.'

'It is larger than your organ room by one foot in each dimension,' said Mary Symcox.

Miss Lucy walked to the window facing the street.

'Did you see the front lawn, Miss Lucy?' asked Shabbir. 'We can put some chairs there for you. This Waverly is much greener than our neighborhood. Look at the trees. So much better. In our place, it is all tar and concrete.'

Beyond the patch of grass pockmarked with dandelions that Shabbir was calling a lawn, a woman pushed a grocery cart filled with cartons of a grape-flavored drink down the street.

'Much better,' said Shabbir. 'And the shops are so close.

The Waverly farmers' market is just two minutes away, every Saturday. And on Sundays, in the winter, people are tailgating and barbecuing in the parking lot, Miss Lucy, before the football game. It's like a party, every home game.'

Miss Lucy did not turn. The day's light shone through the window, around her small body, and entered the room. Looking at Miss Lucy's narrow shoulders, Shabbir remembered the robust woman he had first met, so many years ago, when he was new and friendless in Baltimore. For a moment, he felt like taking her back to 26th Street, depositing her in her own house and asking Mary Symcox to leave. But this is better, he thought, fighting back the feeling. What is there for this old lady? And who can stop what has to be? Allah is the guardian of the weak. He is merciful.

'Mrs Symcox,' Shabbir said, 'isn't Johns Hopkins buying Eastern High School?'

'They already have.'

'Once they renovate it and move their offices into that building, the property prices here will go straight up, won't they?'

'I guess they will,' said Mary Symcox, glancing over at Miss Lucy.

'This is a good location,' said Shabbir. 'A good location to own a house.'

From Mary Symcox's expression, Shabbir could make out that she didn't agree with his peremptory assessment of the quality of this location. 'And you will see,' he said, louder than necessary, 'after Hopkins moves in here, they'll clean up this neighborhood. All these shootings on Greenmount will stop, their campus police will patrol the streets.'

Mary Symcox continued to look skeptical. This woman is not an ally, thought Shabbir. But at least she keeps quiet.

'Mrs Murray,' said Mary Symcox, turning away from Shabbir to the window, 'I have to inform you that according to our rules, the compensatory property must have the same number of rooms as the property being acquired. We are also required to ensure that the rooms are of roughly the same size as the corresponding rooms in the property being acquired. This property, 713 East 33rd Street, has one living room, one parlor, a kitchen on this floor and two bedrooms and two bathrooms on the first floor. Each of these rooms has dimensions that match or exceed the dimensions of the corresponding room at your current address, 109 West 26th Street, according to the measurements we have on file.'

'Hmmpf,' said Miss Lucy.

'Of course they are bigger rooms, Mrs Symcox,' said Shabbir. 'We trust your judgement.'

There was a mumbling sound from Miss Lucy, her shoulders moved as she spoke.

'What did you say, Miss Lucy?' asked Shabbir.

'I said, can we go home now,' said Miss Lucy, in a clear, hoarse voice that bounced off the windowpane, back to the two people who stood in that empty, dimly lit room.

'Perhaps this will be your new home, Miss Lucy,' said Shabbir, the salesman's disingenuousness in his voice replaced with the soft tones of an old friend.

'I didn't birth two children here,' said Miss Lucy, her back as straight as she could hold it. 'My husband didn't fall down dead here.'

Mary Symcox looked up from the file she had been

holding open. Shabbir sighed and walked towards the old woman who stood by the window.

'Miss Lucy,' he said, touching her on the shoulder, 'you must be strong. You must have faith in your god. That house on 26th Street is not your final home, Miss Lucy. Your final home is in the sky with your god. Till then, if living here is your destiny, you must accept it.'

Miss Lucy turned to face him. 'Shabbir,' said Miss Lucy. 'Shabbir. You remember when you first came to Baltimore? You remember? Chester brought you home one night, saying, Look what I found down the street, Lucy. Feed this man, Lucy, this man needs to be fed.'

'I can't forget that, Miss Lucy.'

'You weren't like the others who came from elsewhere, not even wanting to talk to folks, just sticking to their own. You weren't like that.'

'Your Chester was like an older brother to me, Miss Lucy.'

Mary Symcox closed her file and wandered away to the kitchen. Miss Lucy turned and watched her walk away, then looked again at Shabbir's face. She took a step back and sat down on the window-sill. 'He was like that,' she said, her hand stroking her breastbone, her brow furrowing and relaxing, over and over. 'Always like that.'

'Yes,' said Shabbir. 'He was like that.'

'Always bringing people home,' she said, her head beginning to bob. 'Feed this boy, Lucy. Make some pancakes, Lucy.'

'He loved his pancakes,' said Shabbir. 'I like them too, Miss Lucy. But you don't make them for me, only for Jeevan.'

123

'I'll make them for you too, boy,' said Miss Lucy, her voice strained and hoarse, her hand reaching for her head. 'Just come on over to Miss Lucy's.' Holding her head with both hands, Miss Lucy slumped forward.

'Miss Lucy!' said Shabbir, reaching forward and arresting her fall. 'Mrs Symcox! Mrs Symcox! Come quickly.'

There is a 'bing' and the STOP REQUESTED sign lights up. In the back, a gangly man in a denim jacket rises. A large woman in a floral printed dress and sunglasses tries to stand up, then sits back down. Denim Jacket stops in front of her long enough for her to hold onto his arm and hoist herself to her feet, then walks on, his headphones swaying in front of him like a stethoscope.

'These kids nowadays, they watch a little TV and think they know something,' a large black woman dressed in a nurse's scrubs is saying. Across from her, two women are nodding in agreement.

A radio is on somewhere near the middle of the bus. It sits on a man's lap, softly projecting the static-like sound of a stadium audience. 'That one's out of here,' a booming voice proclaims, its staged enthusiasm undampened by the radio's low volume setting. 'See … you … later!' The radio's owner seems unaffected by the excitement at the stadium, he continues to look out the window. Behind him a young man in a cap, more interested in the radio than its owner, turns to his friend: 'That's what I'm talking about, man.'

'So, I told the boy,' the nurse continues, 'Aunt Ginny'll make you pancakes from the box and then Aunt Ginny'll make you her own pancakes.'

Next to Aunt Ginny sits a man in a brown uniform, white curly hair at his temples, a condescending smile on his tired face. Women.

The driver pulls tickets out of the dispenser and hands them to two teenage boys whose eyes are barely visible under pulled-down baseball caps. Then she shuts the door and, having steered the bus back on its way, cocks her head to one side and adds herself to Aunt Ginny's audience.

'Nothing like home-made pancakes,' one of Aunt Ginny's interlocutors says.

Outside the bus, the neighborhoods of Harford Road slip by, trim and well kept. There is rust on some of the chairs in the lawns and a few of the garden ornaments are of the cheaper variety. There are cars parked along the road that came out of dealerships in the eighties. Through the broad windscreen, the driver spots two women standing at a bus stop. She turns the steering wheel towards the right but one of the women waves her on. The other continues looking up the empty road.

'Some gravy on those pancakes,' the bus driver says, turning the wheel back to the left. 'Butter.' The engine hums louder as she steps on the gas.

The uniformed man's condescension wavers. He moves his jaw in a discreet gulping motion. A girl sitting near the middle of the bus looks at her mother and smiles. Her mother keeps looking ahead.

'He eats those pancakes and he says, Aunt Ginny, you're right. He says, Aunt Ginny, can I have more of your pancakes? And I say, First throw that box in the trash, boy.'

The bus driver slaps her hands on her thighs in appreciation of Aunt Ginny's story, and for a moment the bus drives itself.

5

OSCAR SAT ON HIS HAUNCHES, GOLDEN FUR LAMBENT IN THE diminishing evening light, looking up at Miss Lucy's house. His tongue was hanging out of his mouth but his eyes were patient. Seeing Jeevan climb down the steps, his tail wagged slowly. A friendly high-pitched sound came from his throat and he looked over towards Jeevan's stoop where his owner sat.

'Henry?' said Jeevan, running his hand over Oscar's head.

'Hmmpf,' said Henry, not rising to meet him.

Jeevan walked over to Henry. Oscar followed him, immediately resuming his patient pose in a spot from where Henry's face was directly visible. Jeevan moved the walker to one side and sat down a step below Henry.

'It's late,' said Jeevan.

'Hmmm,' said Henry.

'How long have you been sitting here?'

'Not long.'

No cars were passing by on Howard Street. No pedestrians

walked by. The train tracks stood quiet. Under the silence was a gentle electric hum, constant as ever, suddenly audible.

'How is she?' Henry asked.

'The doctor said it was minor,' Jeevan said. 'Shabbir bhai got her to the ER in time.'

'A stroke,' said Henry.

'Yes,' said Jeevan. 'But a minor one.'

'Should she be home?'

'They said we could take her home.'

'Yeah,' said Henry. 'Isn't cheap to spend a night in the hospital.'

'Shabbir paid for the ER.'

'Yeah,' said Henry, a grunt of laughter escaping him. 'Shabbir's a good guy. Doesn't always look that way, but he is.'

'They had gone to look at a house. Mary Symcox, that lady from the New Baltimore Consortium, came to take Miss Lucy. She's supposed to show each homeowner three different houses.'

'Miss Lucy went?'

'She didn't want to go. Shabbir bhai convinced her.'

'He could talk the stripes off a zebra, that Shabbir.'

'He went with her,' Jeevan said.

'He would, wouldn't he?' said Henry. 'He wants to see the house himself.'

'He cares for her,' said Jeevan.

'Yeah,' said Henry. 'And for himself.'

Jeevan balked.

'You know what I mean,' said Henry. 'Don't act like you don't know what I am talking about.'

Jeevan rose to his feet and turned to face Henry. 'I don't know what you are talking about,' he said, and for once, his accent grated on Henry's ears.

'So you don't know about the loan Chester Murray took from Shabbir?' Henry said, rising to his feet and reaching for his walker.

'Rhonda said something about it when she was here,' said Jeevan, lifting the walker and placing it within Henry's reach.

'Don't take me for a fool, Sharma,' said Henry, taking a grip on the walker and stepping onto the sidewalk. 'You handle Shabbir's things. You know everything about him.'

'That's what Rhonda thinks too,' said Jeevan, sitting down on the lowest step.

Henry looked down the street. Oscar stood up and started padding in the direction of home. He had taken a few steps when Henry called from behind: 'Wait, boy.' Henry turned back to Jeevan. 'You really don't know about this?' he said. 'The loan Chester took from Shabbir.'

'No.'

'Chester wrote a note saying that if he couldn't repay the loan, the house would go to Shabbir.'

'But Miss Lucy said he paid the money before he died,' said Jeevan.

'Hmmmpf,' said Henry. 'He would have, if he had any to pay.'

'But where does the house come into this?' asked Jeevan.

'It's surety,' said Henry. 'You think Shabbir would give a loan without collateral?'

'How do you know?'

'I was one of the witnesses,' said Henry. 'I signed that piece of paper. Miss Lucy was there when I signed it.'

'But then …'

'Why didn't he claim the house when Chester died? He has the property deed now, Chester handed it over to him. Why didn't he turn that old widow out onto the street? I don't know. I kept thinking he would, but he didn't.'

'I've never seen this piece of paper,' said Jeevan.

'I guess you don't know everything there is to know about Shabbir then, do you?' said Henry, putting his hand on Jeevan's shoulder.

'So it isn't Miss Lucy's house,' said Jeevan. 'It isn't even her own house.'

'No,' said Henry. 'It isn't.'

A tiredness came over Jeevan, a wave that passed down his body, curling it inwards. His eyelids scrunched shut and his head hung down, heavy and immovable.

'Jeevan?'

Jeevan's head hung down over his chest, moving slowly from side to side.

'Jeevan,' said Henry. 'Come on now, Jeevan.'

But Jeevan could not speak. Not because he had nothing to say, but because his mouth refused to let him form words. He sat there with his head down and his eyes shut, feeling like he would never rise from where he sat, never open his eyes again, never speak another word.

Perhaps a minute passed, perhaps more, and Jeevan felt a wetness on his cheek. A long loving tongue was laving his face. 'Good boy,' he said, raising his hand to stroke the dog's head. 'Good boy, Oscar.'

'Will she be okay tonight?' asked Henry.

'The doctor said someone should be with her for the first few days,' said Jeevan. 'Sunita will stay.'

'Sunita?'

'Yes,' said Jeevan. 'I said I'll stay, but she didn't listen.'

'I guess it's better if a woman ...'

'Yes.'

'Did you call Rhonda?'

'Miss Lucy said no.'

'She's a good girl,' said Henry. 'That Sunita of yours.'

'Yes.'

'Hold on to her.'

Jeevan smiled weakly and nodded his head.

'It's late,' said Henry.

'Yes.'

'Try and get some sleep.'

'Yes.'

'Oscar, come on, boy,' said Henry, click-clacking his walker down the street. He had barely gone a few steps when he turned again and walked slowly back to where Jeevan sat.

'Orioles playing on the West Coast today,' he said. 'Oakland. When I came out, it was the bottom of the third. It'll go on past midnight.'

Jeevan looked up at him.

Henry hesitated, waiting for Jeevan to say something, then said: 'Cal's playing.'

Jeevan was overcome by a feeling that threatened to burst out of his chest into the silent night. He took the handle of the walker in his right hand and squeezed it tight. Then he took a deep breath and released it. 'Good night, Henry,' he said.

Kamran was sitting on the stoop, headphones in his ears, his head bobbing, when Kay returned home.

'Hello there,' she mouthed, waving her hand in front of his face.

'Hey,' said Kamran, removing the headphones.

'What's up?' asked Kay, sitting down next to him.

'I've been working hard,' said Kamran.

'At what?'

'At your project?'

'My project?'

'Yes,' said Kamran, waving his right hand above his head at the buildings that stood behind him. 'This project.'

'I thought that was our project,' said Kay, smiling.

'Right,' said Kamran. 'Our project.'

His face had a quizzical expression on it. His hair curled over his brow, one lock falling separate from the rest. Men, thought Kay, they can be such boys sometimes. 'So, what have you been working hard at?' she asked.

'I spent most of the day downtown,' said Kamran. 'I just got back.'

'What were you doing downtown?'

'I went to the City record office.'

'What's in the City record office?'

'A lot of stuff,' said Kamran, standing up and glancing over at the front door of her house.

'Oh sorry,' said Kay, jumping up. 'Why don't you come in? I'll make some coffee.'

Later, when the coffee had percolated, they sat in the living room. With the blinds drawn, it was dark and cool. Kamran stretched out on the couch. Kay sat down next to him.

'So I found out that these three houses were built by Rankin Realty in 1928,' said Kamran. 'They had actually bought this tract almost twenty years earlier and constructed on Howard Street and on 29th Street within a few years. But this street didn't have any houses till 1928. In fact, they leased part of the land out to the McCormick Spice Company in 1915.'

'They probably didn't think anyone would want to live near the tracks,' said Kay.

'I guess,' said Kamran.

'But then they changed their minds.'

'Yes,' said Kamran. 'Hard to say why.'

Kay looked at her watch. It was almost five-thirty. Matthew would be home in half an hour. Matthew, she thought, my husband Matthew. She rose from the couch and picked up her mug. 'More coffee?' she asked.

When she returned to the living room, Kay sat on a chair across from the sofa. 'So what do we do now?' she asked.

'I also found this,' said Kamran, digging a booklet out of his bag.

'How to apply the National Register criteria for evaluation,' said Kay, taking the booklet from him. 'What is this?'

'It's a National Park Service bulletin. It tells you how to determine if a building or a site is eligible for inclusion in the National Register of Historic Places.'

'Do you think ...'

'Maybe,' said Kamran. 'Maybe.'

'How will we know?' asked Kay.

'We'll have to read it,' said Kamran. 'There are criteria. Then, if we think this place satisfies some of those criteria, we have to nominate it for inclusion in the National Register.'

'Let's read it then,' said Kay.

'You'll have to come over here,' said Kamran, patting the sofa. 'I brought only one copy.'

'How convenient,' said Kay, getting up and walking across to the sofa.

Kamran read impatiently, skimming whole paragraphs, skipping ahead to later sections. Kay struggled to keep up, getting increasingly irritated. Finally she snatched the bulletin from his hands.

'What?' said Kamran.

'I can't read like this,' said Kay.

'So just tell me where to stop.'

'I would if I could finish reading one complete sentence,' said Kay.

'Whatever.'

Kay didn't say anything. She opened the bulletin and started reading it. Kamran stood up and walked away to the other side of the room. He was mumbling something, but Kay decided to ignore him. Kamran paced up and down the room, waiting for her to look up or say something, but she kept reading.

'Listen to this,' she said finally. 'The quality of significance in American history is present in buildings that possess integrity of location, design, setting, materials, workmanship, feeling and association ...'

'What does that mean, "association"?'

'And,' continued Kay, 'criterion B, that are associated with the lives of persons significant in our past. Isn't that funny?'

'Not ha ha funny, no,' said Kamran.

'I mean, we could say that Miss Lucy is a person significant in our past, couldn't we?'

'You just moved here, dude,' said Kamran. 'You've known her like a month tops.'

'Ouch,' said Kay.

'No, no, what I meant was … I mean, I don't think that their "our" means us,' Kamran said. 'It's like, you know, a bigger "our".'

'Yeah,' said Kay. 'That's what's funny. It's an "our" that includes us, but it's so big that it doesn't mean us.'

'Right, right, right,' said Kamran. 'That is funny.'

'Come here,' said Kay. 'Let's read this.'

Kamran went over to the sofa, feeling chastened, and sat down next to her. She didn't give him the bulletin. He had to look over her shoulder to read. They were still reading half an hour later when Matthew came home.

'What're you guys looking at?' he asked, putting his bag down on the side table.

'Hey baby,' said Kay, getting up and going over to him. She kissed him lightly on the lips. Kamran also stood up, and watched as she put her arms around her husband.

'Hey Matthew,' he said. 'It's a bulletin that explains the criteria for nomination to the National Register of Historic Places.'

'Cool,' said Matthew. 'I downloaded it a few days ago at work. I think there may be something there.'

'Like what?' asked Kamran.

'Here,' said Matthew, holding his hand out. 'Show me that.'

'You want some coffee, baby?' asked Kay.

'Do I ever,' said Matthew, leafing through the bulletin that Kamran had reluctantly handed him. 'Here,' he said finally. 'This might be it.'

'What is it?' said Kay, handing Matthew his coffee.

'It's criterion A, events,' said Matthew. 'It says properties may have significance under this criterion if they are associated with events significant to the cultural traditions of a community.'

'Not getting it,' said Kamran.

Kay took the bulletin from him and looked down at the page he had been holding open.

'The trains, man,' said Matthew. 'The rails are an important part of this city's cultural tradition.'

'What's that got to do with us,' said Kamran. 'We can't ask for this block to be designated historic just because it's near the tracks.'

'No, dude, I'm talking about the train motifs.'

'What train motifs?' asked Kamran.

'The ones outside,' said Kay.

'Which ones?' said Kamran.

Matthew led them out onto the porch. There, on the stucco window lintel, there was a detail of a steam locomotive with steam issuing from its nozzle. On the mantel, there was a horse at full gallop.

'It's like they're racing,' said Kay.

'There are similar details on Jeevan's house and Miss Lucy's house,' said Matthew. 'I checked.'

'And look at this,' he continued, pointing at the large emblem at the center of the grille door.

'What is it?' asked Kay.

'It looks just like the emblem of the B&O railroad company,' said Matthew. 'But the letters B&O aren't there.'

'It looks generic,' said Kamran.

'Could be,' said Matthew, walking down the steps to the sidewalk. 'Come down here.'

Out on the street, he turned back towards the block and pointed upward. A procession of steam engines ran across the long trim that skirted the top of the three houses. They seemed to evolve in design from modified horse carriages – the ones over Matthew and Kay's house – to full-blown steam locomotives from the early twentieth century – the ones over Miss Lucy's house.

'Wow,' said Kamran.

'You mean you never noticed this in all these years?' asked Kay.

'I must have,' said Kamran. 'I guess I never registered it.'

'Pun intended?' asked Matthew.

'What's that?'

'You never registered it,' said Matthew, putting his hands up to air-quote 'registered'.

'That's funny,' said Kamran.

They stood looking up at the three houses.

'Do you think this is enough, baby?' asked Kay.

'No,' said Matthew. 'I mean, I haven't seen anything like this anywhere else in Baltimore. But then, I haven't been around much.'

'Yeah,' said Kamran. 'I don't know if this is enough.'

'Let's find out,' said Kay.

'Yes, we should,' said Matthew, turning to her and then realizing that she had been addressing Kamran.

⋖⋗

It was past 2 a.m. when Jeevan finally got out of bed and went down to the kitchen. He put a saucepan full of water on the stove and looked around for the tea leaves. They weren't on the counter where he kept them. He opened the cupboard above the sink and found that there were only spices and rice, flour and puffed rice where he had earlier stored his plates. In the cupboard next to it, the one that had stood empty for the many years he had lived here, he finally found the tea, neatly stored in an airtight container.

Standing over the stove, he realized that he was boiling enough water for two people. Lifting the saucepan, he tipped half its contents into the sink. Returning the vessel to the fire, he waited for the water to come to a boil.

Shabbir had hidden the contract from him. It didn't make sense. There were aspects of Shabbir's dealings that were much worse, some of them illegal. All those Jeevan knew intimately. Shabbir even discussed their modalities with him. For some of those things, if Shabbir was caught, Jeevan too would be liable. Then why hide this one thing, this contract that didn't even sound illegal? It was just a straightforward loan against collateral.

The water had started rolling by the time Jeevan noticed it was boiling. He put a spoonful of tea leaves in, turned the flame down and covered it. Turning to the fridge to get the milk, he noticed that taped onto it was a slip of paper on which a grocery list had been written in a small rounded Hindi hand. Potatoes, onions, tomatoes, milk, Fantastik, flour. He wondered why he hadn't noticed it earlier, then realizing it had been left for him, peeled it off and put it in his pocket.

Shabbir owned Miss Lucy's house, and he had kept this from Jeevan. He had known Jeevan wouldn't like it. How had he known? How had he known what Jeevan himself hadn't known? He hadn't thrown her out of her house, Shabbir wasn't like that. Besides, the house hadn't been worth anything to him or anyone else all this time. He wasn't losing anything by letting her live in it. He was probably earning merit with the angels. But now the house was worth something. It was bound to, eventually. Shabbir had known this all along. They say that in a hundred years even the fate of garbage changes. A sleeping investment had suddenly woken up. This hell was going to become heaven, Shabbir had said. And Shabbir was going to give up the angels' merit. Shabbir was going to be a landlord in heaven. But what about hell's tenants?

Jeevan added milk to the pan and put the flame up again. He let the tea come to a boil, then simmered it for a few minutes till it took on a dark color. Sitting back at the table with a warm mug in his hand, he took a sip. It's good tea, he thought. I make good tea.

A line from a poem came running through Jeevan's head: When you come, you will find me lost. He had said this line aloud recently, he thought. Where? To whom? It came to him again and he felt that this internal voice that was reciting the line – just this line, not the rest of the poem – was stressing the 'when you come'. The 'you will find me lost' was getting lost, standing away from the 'when you come'.

He spoke the line out loud, but in this audible iteration the emphasis had shifted back to 'you will find me lost'. It didn't sound right. No, it sounded right, as it should sound.

It just didn't sound right at this moment. Should I recite the next line? he thought. But there was no urge to do so, so he didn't. Who had he recited the poem to recently? And why?

He finished the tea, washed the cup and, realizing he wasn't sure anymore where he should put it, left it next to the sink. There was no reason to believe sleep would come now, but he didn't feel like sitting in the kitchen either, so he walked back up the stairs. When he reached the topmost step, he paused.

In front of him was the door to Sunita's room: this room that had been a store for Shabbir's boxes; that had occasionally been a dormitory for the children of Shabbir's visiting relatives; that shared a wall with Miss Lucy's organ room – Jeevan had sometimes sat with his back touching the wall when the organ was playing. Now it was Sunita's room. For the first time since it had taken on this new role, Jeevan opened the door to Sunita's room.

A narrow bed with a brightly colored bedspread was the only piece of furniture in the room now, but it managed, on its own, to make it feel like a warm, welcoming place. There was no dust anywhere, the cobwebs had disappeared. On one wall there was a small cork board with a few photographs tacked onto it: A young man and his new wife on their wedding day, an older Indian man sitting stiffly next to his wife, a girl in pigtails holding her father's hand. Jeevan looked closely at the little girl – that same smile, mischievous, on her face. Growing up doesn't change everything.

He turned from the board and looked around the room. His eyes rested on the closet. For a moment he hesitated, then he walked up to it and opened it. The first thing he saw was a postcard of Ram and Sita, he with his bow slung on his shoulder. Sita looked out of the postcard, benevolent, content. In front of the postcard was a small oil lamp with a burnt wick standing in it and an incense stick-stand with the narrow purple stubs of three consumed incense sticks poking out of it. Jeevan shut his eyes and bowed his head.

When his eyes opened, he noticed there were saris folded carefully and stacked on the shelf below. He picked up the one on top. It was white with a mustard border, a line of gold-colored thread along the edge of it. He ran his finger over the gold thread. Suddenly he remembered who he had recited the poem to. Sunita. He had recited it to Sunita. It ran through his head again: 'When you come, you will find me lost.' He quickly put the sari back, shut the closet and left the room, slamming the door as he went.

The graduate students entered in bunches: the Indians with their shirts tucked in, the Chinese looking a little lost, the East Europeans talking loudly, the Americans serious and bespectacled. Watching them come in from his chair at the back of the room, Matthew found himself oscillating between yearning to be one of them and relief at not being trapped in that life. He scanned their faces for signs of stress, uncertainty, for a lack of self-confidence. But if any such feelings lurked within – and surely they did, he thought – they weren't discernible on the surface.

At the head of the room, fiddling with his laptop, stood Peter. He looks just the same, thought Matthew, not a hair different from what he had been then. In fact, even the shirt he was wearing seemed vaguely familiar. It felt like nothing had changed for Peter, not a thing. It was as if Matthew had drifted far out to sea while Peter had remained at anchor, steady and unmoving.

'Right then,' said a mousy looking man, once Peter's laptop had been successfully connected to the overhead projector. 'We're happy to have with us today Professor Peter Graham from Brown University. Thanks for making the long journey all the way from Providence, Peter.'

When the polite titters had subsided and the introduction had been made, Peter took the floor. Matthew shifted in his seat. Had Peter seen him? Had he recognized him? If he had, he gave no indication of it.

'It's good to be back at Hopkins,' said Peter. 'Hopefully someone will take me to a crab house before I take the flight back to Providence.'

His introducer gave him a thumbs up amidst another round of forced laughter.

Peter spoke of the new work he was doing. Matthew followed along for the most part. There was real difficulty in what Peter was doing, Matthew saw that in his objective moments. At the same time, he couldn't shake the feeling that a lot of what was being discussed was a little contrived. The research did deserve an audience, but Matthew couldn't help feeling irritated at the eagerness with which the audience was receiving what Peter said. The frequent, admiring questions and comments annoyed him. Peter held the podium with ease, Matthew admitted to himself, irritated at his former advisor's smug self-assurance.

The talk ended with a seemingly sincere round of applause for the speaker, and the room emptied quite quickly except for Peter and his host and a couple of students who stood around waiting to talk to the speaker, perhaps to be introduced to him by their own advisors, and begin a process of networking that they would then carry forward to conferences and seminars as their careers proceeded. Matthew rose from his chair and walked out of the room.

Outside, on the quad, a Frisbee was being thrown back and forth. Matthew stood and watched. I have to talk to him, he thought, his eyes following the rapidly rotating disc as it cut a lazy arc through the air. That's why I came, isn't it? I have to talk to him, I have to.

But his legs didn't move. He could hear his heart beat loudly. The hands that hung by his sides seemed to belong to someone else.

'Heads up, dude!' came a voice breaking through the haze.

Matthew looked up and saw that the Frisbee was swirling through the air in his direction. It seemed to be moving slowly, inexorably, towards him. He felt his torso move backwards but he didn't duck, or try to move. At the last moment a gust caught the Frisbee from below and it bounced upward, missing his head by a few centimeters and crashing into the column behind him.

'That was close,' said a familiar voice from behind Matthew. He turned to face it.

'I know you,' said Peter.

'Matthew. Matthew Fleischer.'

'Matthew Fleischer,' said Peter, rolling his tongue over the name. 'What are you doing here?'

'This way, Peter,' said Peter's host, catching up with him.

'I live in Baltimore now,' said Matthew.

'That's good,' said Peter, turning to acknowledge his colleague, who had already begun leading him through the quad to the parking lot.

'I saw a notice for your talk,' said Matthew.

'You a student here now?' asked Peter, walking down the steps behind his host.

'No,' said Matthew. 'I work in Towson.'

'Where's Towson?'

'Just north of Baltimore. But I live close by. I come to campus sometimes, to the library. That's where I saw the notice.'

'Good, good,' said Peter, quickening his step to catch up with his host, who was rapidly making his way across the quad.

'I had an idea about the problem we had been working on,' said Matthew.

'Remind me,' said Peter. 'What problem was that?'

'Emulation of faulty meshes with constant slowdown.'

'Oh, that one,' said Peter, shifting his laptop bag from his left shoulder to his right. 'Bernard Levinson and his summer intern solved it a year ago.'

'But their analysis is amortized,' said Matthew, stepping sideways to avoid the laptop bag as it flailed towards him. 'I think I can get rid of the pipelining delay.'

Peter stopped and turned to face him.

'And I can improve the constants,' said Matthew, his stomach quivering as he spoke.

'There's nothing left in that problem,' said Peter. 'No one is interested anymore.'

'You remember, in the parallel computing class you talked

143

about isoperimetric inequalities,' said Matthew. 'If we can prove an isoperimetric condition about the faulty situation, we can do something.'

'Still talking in generalities, Matthew,' said Peter, turning to look for his colleague, who was now walking back to where the two of them stood.

'I have a proof,' said Matthew, although he didn't.

'Someone you know?' asked the mousy professor, stepping up to them.

'A former student,' said Peter.

'That's nice.'

'Look, Matthew,' said Peter, 'I'm kind of in a hurry right now. There's a two-day workshop next week at Rutgers. Bernie Levinson will be there as well. He'll be presenting the emulation work. If you want to come up there, maybe we can talk more about this.'

'Right,' said Matthew.

'You can find a link on my homepage,' said Peter.

'I'll be there,' said Matthew.

The two professors turned and walked away towards the parking lot. As they went, Matthew heard Peter's host ask Peter: 'Should we ask him to lunch?' Peter shook his head and continued walking.

'Hey there!' said Kay, tapping Sunita on her shoulder. 'That's a lot of chickpeas.'

Sunita turned with a start. Two of the four cans she had been holding slipped and fell, rolling down the aisle.

'I'll get them,' said Kay.

Sunita pushed Kay's grocery cart to one side and waited.

'Matthew and I love chana masala,' said Kay, back from successfully rounding up the itinerant cans.

'You like Indian food?' asked Sunita.

'Love it. We used to live in New Jersey,' said Kay, like she was delivering a punchline.

Sunita laughed with Kay, although she didn't quite get the joke.

'Particularly chana masala,' said Kay. 'It's our favorite Indian dish.'

'He likes it a lot as well,' said Sunita.

'He? Jeevan? Great. Do you make it often?'

'Yes, at least once a week,' said Sunita. 'I will make it for you.'

'That would be great,' said Kay. 'I used to make it sometimes when we were in Jersey. It doesn't turn out the same, though. I used to just get the powder. There were, like, these Indian grocery stores not far from us.'

'There is one in Baltimore also,' said Sunita. 'Bombay Bazaar. On Pratt Street. It's a little far from here.'

'But you probably don't use those powders, right?' said Kay. 'You probably make it from scratch.'

Sunita grinned, her neck dipping forward. She looked over her shoulder, then lowering her voice, she said: 'I also just use the powder. But my mother thinks I grind my own masalas. Every second letter, she asks me if I am making sure the masala is properly ground and if I have all the ingredients. I just say, Yes Ma, it's all okay. Sometimes I tell her that this or that is not available, just so that she believes me.'

Kay laughed out loud. Sunita was shaking with quiet laughter.

'Moms,' said Kay. 'They're the same everywhere.'

They pushed their carts through the aisles together, chatting as they went, quietly noting what the other was buying. Sunita's 'This watermelon is very nice, I bought some yesterday' was repaid with 'Their potato salad is delicious, do you eat potato salad?' 'Why do you need so much wheat flour?' Kay said, soon after Sunita asked her: 'Why do people eat black-colored bread here?'. 'Just hang some yogurt overnight, it's very light and very tasty' was Sunita's response to Kay's 'I really should switch to low-fat cream cheese'.

Later, after checking out – Kay chose paper, Sunita plastic – they emerged onto St Paul Street.

'Would you like some coffee?' asked Kay. 'We could stop at Donna's.'

'Okay,' said Sunita, who had passed by Donna's several times without ever entering.

They sat at a table overlooking the street. Sunita ordered tea, then had to ask for milk again separately.

'Miss Lucy has been quite ill,' Sunita said.

'Oh,' said Kay. 'I didn't know. What happened?'

'She had a stroke.'

'Oh my god, I had no idea,' said Kay. 'How is she now?'

'She is better,' said Sunita. 'She is recovering.'

'Which hospital is she in?'

'She is at home.'

'Who's looking after her?' asked Kay. 'Does she have a nurse?'

'I have been staying there at night.'

'Really? That's very nice of you.'

'He said he would stay. So I said, No, this is a woman's job.'

Kay brought her coffee to her lips. In another time, at another place, if this was someone else, she would have said something about this 'woman's job', she thought. But Sunita spoke with such ease that it seemed rude to contest what she said.

'I mean,' said Sunita, her eyes searching Kay's face, 'I mean, Miss Lucy is a woman, no, so she needs a woman to stay with her. To take her to the bathroom and everything.'

Kay put the mug down on the table. 'Yes, of course,' she said. 'You know, I can stay over too if you need a break.'

'Thanks,' said Sunita. 'It's okay. Maybe just one or two more days. Already she is complaining, I am not a child, stop treating me like a baby.'

'It must be difficult,' said Kay.

'No, no,' said Sunita. 'I have never had to look after a mother-in-law. This is a small thing.'

'She's almost like a mother-in-law to you,' said Kay.

'Yes,' said Sunita. 'I am almost married to a man who is like her son.' She laughed out loud.

Kay's rib cage shook with a spasm of silent laughter. 'Had you met Jeevan before you moved in with him?' she asked.

'No, never,' said Sunita. 'Rashida baji said he was a good man, and I trusted her.'

'Wow,' said Kay. 'You must really have a lot of faith in her.'

Sunita shrugged. 'She is very caring,' she said. 'But then, my mother is also very caring. And the man she chose for me

147

was not a good man.' Pouring more tea into her mug, Sunita stirred it slowly.

'I'm sorry about that,' said Kay.

'It's okay,' said Sunita. 'Sometimes these things happen.'

'Yes,' said Kay. 'They definitely do.'

Sunita looked at the woman who sat across the table from her. Kay's eyes had a soft, sad light to them. This girl has also suffered, she thought. 'But you know,' she said, 'when Rashida baji first suggested I should live with him, I was not sure. Not that, How can I live with a man I am not married to? I had already accepted that what they say about marriage – that it ends only when you die – is not always true. There was this feeling, this fear that this time too I would meet the wrong man, not the man I am destined to spend seven births with, not that true husband who I would recognize immediately.'

As Sunita spoke, Kay felt something build in her chest, starting in her stomach and spreading through her entire upper body. Sunita's words fell on her like heavy rain, washing over her and relaxing her muscles. She felt like saying something when Sunita paused, but she didn't know what it was she wanted to say.

'Are you okay?' asked Sunita.

Kay realized that Sunita had reached across the table and was stroking her forearm. 'Yes, thanks,' she said, putting her hand on Sunita's and squeezing it.

Later, as they walked home from Donna's, hefting their groceries, Kay said: 'So, do you think Jeevan is the one?'

'Maybe, I don't know,' said Sunita. 'Sometimes when I see him, I have this feeling that I know him from before.

There is something about him that makes me feel so … so, I don't know, so comfortable.'

'Sounds like you're in love, girl,' Kay said, making an effort to lighten her voice.

Sunita blushed. 'I don't know about love-shove,' she said. Then, her eyes darting up to Kay's face: 'Maybe.'

They waited for the pedestrian signal to turn green at the corner of 29th and Charles. The evening that surrounded them appeared to change hue from grey to light to grey again. Kay put her hand on her companion's shoulder. 'I'm really happy for you,' she said.

'Chester,' Miss Lucy slurred. 'Chester Murray! You get those dirty shoes out of my living room.'

'Miss Lucy,' said Jeevan, getting up from his chair and coming across to the bed. 'Miss Lucy.'

Miss Lucy's lips pursed. She swallowed and her mouth opened.

'Would you like some water?' said Jeevan, picking up the glass that sat on the table next to her.

'Jeevan?'

'I'm here, Miss Lucy. Would you like some water?'

Jeevan held the glass to Miss Lucy's lips.

'How are you feeling now, Miss Lucy?'

'Where's that girl of yours?' asked Miss Lucy.

'She's gone to the grocery store,' said Jeevan. 'I told her to take a nap before coming back here in the evening.'

'She's a good one, boy,' said Miss Lucy. 'You better hold on to her.'

Jeevan smiled. 'I will, Miss Lucy.'

'What an obedient child,' said Miss Lucy. 'Yes, Miss Lucy. No, Miss Lucy. Anything you say, Miss Lucy.'

A feeling of immense relief surged through Jeevan. He tried to laugh, but could only smile. 'Is your right arm feeling better?' he asked.

'Don't worry your head, son,' said Miss Lucy. 'Miss Lucy isn't paralyzed or anything like that.'

'No, that's not …'

'And you can tell that girl of yours to stop ordering me around,' she said, removing the covers from her body. 'I'm just fine.'

'Miss Lucy, don't get up.'

'And why can't I get up on my own two feet in my own house, boy?'

'The doctor said …'

'You and your girl,' said Miss Lucy. 'The doctor said this and the doctor said that. Now get this into your head: I'm fine. I had a bad headache, it's gone now.'

She brought her legs down and pushed her body up onto them. Jeevan stood up. Her long gown swayed a little as she tried to find her feet. Jeevan put his hand out and supported her. She didn't brush him off. Taking a few slow steps towards the bathroom door, she stopped and turned to Jeevan, who was following her with his hand on her back. 'You coming into the bathroom with me, boy?'

'No, Miss Lucy.'

'I didn't think so.'

Later, down in the kitchen, Miss Lucy sat at the table and ate the soup Sunita had left for her on the stove. 'You got something you want to talk about, Jeevan?' she said, setting her spoon down finally.

'No, Miss Lucy.'

'Sure you do,' said Miss Lucy. 'I raised children, son. I can see it in your face.'

'Yes, Miss Lucy.'

'What is it?'

'It's about the house, Miss Lucy.'

'What about it?'

'Henry told me that Mr Murray had taken a loan from Shabbir,' said Jeevan, 'that this house was collateral for that loan.'

'Henry should mind his own business.' Miss Lucy put her spoon in the soup bowl and stood up.

'So you know about this, Miss Lucy?' Jeevan asked.

'Yes.'

'But that day when Rhonda was here …'

Placing the dishes in the kitchen sink, Miss Lucy turned on the faucet.

'Leave it, Miss Lucy,' said Jeevan. 'I'll do it.'

'Hmmpf,' said Miss Lucy, continuing to rinse the bowl.

Jeevan stood behind her and watched. 'Did Mr Murray repay the loan?'

'He would have,' said Miss Lucy, 'if he hadn't died on me first.'

'How much money had he borrowed?'

'What does it matter now?'

She walked out of the kitchen, leaving Jeevan standing there on his own. 'Forget it, Jeevan,' she called from the other room. 'Don't worry yourself about it.'

'I think Shabbir wants to take the house from you, Miss

151

Lucy,' said Jeevan, walking into the living room where Miss Lucy sat on her chair, her head back, her eyes closed. 'It's worth money now.'

'Oh child,' said Miss Lucy, 'Shabbir wouldn't do that to this old woman. He isn't like that.'

'But …'

'Come,' said Miss Lucy, opening her eyes. 'Come sit next to me, boy.'

Jeevan walked over and sat on the couch near her. She looked at him and smiled. 'Wipe that worried look off your face, Jeevan,' she said, reaching forward and holding his hand. 'I know what Shabbir is capable of, son. The Lord knows that Shabbir is not the most righteous of men. But he will not take the roof from an old woman's head. That he will not do.'

'But Miss Lucy …'

'The Bible says, We all have sinned, we all fall short of the glory of God.'

Jeevan squeezed her thin bony hand. 'But Miss Lucy,' he said, 'there's still the City …'

'This is my house, Jeevan. My children grew up here. I cooked for my husband in this kitchen. No one can take this house from me. Even if they bring it down brick by brick, it will still be my house. Even if they carry me from here – and I swear to you, boy, that I will never leave on my own feet – it will still be my house. You understand that?'

'Yes, Miss Lucy.'

'Come upstairs,' said Miss Lucy, rising to her feet. 'I dreamt that Chester came home and said, Lucy, play *Amazing Grace* for me this evening. He didn't like dressing up for church, he didn't, but he was strong with the Lord, that man.'

Jeevan stood up and gave Miss Lucy his hand.

'You like it too, don't you? *Amazing Grace.*'

'Yes, Miss Lucy.'

They walked together to the stairwell.

'Miss Lucy,' said Jeevan, as he helped her on to the first step, 'how much did Mr Murray borrow?'

'You don't give up easy, do you?'

'No, Miss Lucy.'

'It was eight thousand dollars.'

The lit end of a cigarette rose and fell rhythmically in the yard across the fence. Jeevan watched from his side as Kay stood, her back to her house, staring over the fence at the transmission lines – long narrow streaks of reflected streetlight orange. In the distance a train sounded a weary horn, a tired injunction to anything that might wander into its way as it hauled its load down the tracks.

Finally the cigarette burned down to its butt and Kay turned.

'Hello,' said Jeevan.

'Jeevan. How long have you been standing there?'

'I just came out.'

Kay walked up to the fence that separated their yards. Her face, Jeevan saw as she came closer, was somber. Her eyes looked tired. She smiled at him.

'I met Sunita at Eddie's today,' she said. 'She's really nice.'

Jeevan nodded.

'Is she at Miss Lucy's tonight?' asked Kay.

'Yes,' said Jeevan.

'I told her I'd be happy to stay over a couple of nights if she wants a break.'

'Thanks,' said Jeevan.

'How is Miss Lucy now?'

'She's getting better.'

Kay rested her chin on the fence and smiled again, a broader, more mischievous smile. 'Sunita really likes you,' she said.

The train that had sounded its approach earlier was upon them now. Its rolling wagons trundled into the tunnel, making a racket that allowed Jeevan to say nothing without being rude.

'You like her too, don't you?' asked Kay when the train had passed.

Jeevan made to shrug his shoulders, then stopped. He scratched his head and looked away from Kay. 'She is a nice person,' he said.

'You do like her,' declared Kay.

Jeevan turned back to face her. He tried to put on a serious face, but the edge of his mouth kept quivering into a smile.

'You can say it,' said Kay. 'Go on, say it.'

'There is nothing to say,' said Jeevan.

He does, thought Kay, he totally totally does. She felt like jumping over the fence and hugging, or at least touching, Jeevan. Maybe there's something there that will rub off, she thought.

'It's late,' said Jeevan.

'Hey, before you go, there's something I wanted to tell you,' said Kay. 'Kamran and I have been trying to figure out if we can save this block somehow.'

'Save this block?'

'Yes, like, have it declared a historic place or something,' said Kay. 'They can't demolish a historic place. You won't have to move from here, nor will Miss Lucy.'

'This block is historic?'

'Kamran got this document,' said Kay. 'It says that if a place is associated with significant cultural traditions, it can be declared historic.'

'This place is significant?'

'We don't know for sure. Kamran found out that the builders had left this particular block vacant for a long time, then built on it in 1928. It may have something to do with the railroad, because they put these railway-themed decorations on the houses. You've seen those, right?'

'Yes,' said Jeevan.

'We're going to find out about them,' said Kay.

'We?'

'Kamran and I.' Kay's face had a question on it, an expectation of a joyous response, that turned into a worried furrow on her brow as she waited for Jeevan to speak.

'What about Henry?' said Jeevan finally.

'What about him?'

'Even if this block stays, Henry's house will go.'

'Oh,' said Kay. 'Right.' She tip-tapped the fence with her hand for a bit, then said: 'He can move in here.'

'Here?'

'Our house,' said Kay, her right hand splaying backwards. 'I mean, we're just renters, right? We can move. We can go to the other side of Charles Village or to Hampden or something. There are tons of apartments on University

Parkway. We'll find something. We could even go to Towson. I can commute. Matthew would hate that though.'

'You are very generous,' said Jeevan.

'No, no, come on. I'll come back and visit you guys. We'll sit on the steps and chat.'

Jeevan laughed.

'Why are you laughing?'

'You'll miss us,' said Jeevan.

'Yes, I will,' said Kay, smiling.

'Once you find out why this block is historic, you will save it from being demolished. Then Henry's house will be demolished and you will shift to Towson so that he can live here. Then you will miss us and come back to visit.'

'Yes,' said Kay, laughing out loud now. 'That's exactly what I'm saying.'

'I'll give Miss Lucy the good news,' said Jeevan.

'No,' said Kay. 'Don't say anything to her now. If it doesn't work out, she'll be even more disappointed. Let Kamran and me work on this some more first.'

Jeevan nodded.

'Okay,' said Kay. 'Good night then, Jeevan.'

'One minute, Kay,' said Jeevan.

'Yes?'

Jeevan pursed his lips, as if he were thinking of something, then said: 'You know, I have known him since he was a child.'

'Who?'

'Kamran,' said Jeevan. 'When I came here, he must have been ten-twelve.'

Kay felt an uneasiness in her stomach as Jeevan spoke.

'I played with him,' said Jeevan. 'I took him to the dentist. I made paper boats with him when it rained. I watched him grow up. And when he went to college, I felt like any father feels when his son leaves home.'

'You guys are very close,' said Kay. Although, she now realized, Kamran had hardly ever mentioned Jeevan in all the time they had spent together.

'I don't know,' said Jeevan. 'Helping raise him was my duty. Sometimes duty and love get mixed with each other. But that is not what I wanted to say. What I wanted to say was that I have seen this boy grow up into a man. I know him. People who meet him in adulthood may never come to know him that way.'

'Jeevan,' said Kay, 'why are you telling me all this?'

Jeevan nodded in response. Then he nodded again. His head tilted to one side, his hand opening as if he were talking to himself. 'There is no reason,' he said. 'No reason. Sorry.'

'You don't have anything to be sorry for,' said Kay.

Jeevan smiled at her. 'You are a very generous person,' he said.

The intersection of Charles and 29th lies lazy in the morning sun. Traffic lights slung on a cable sway gently in the breeze, their metronomic changes marking the slow passage of luminous time. The branches of a cherry tree, blossoms incipient, sway, then fall still, waiting for the next gust.

On the south-eastern corner, a white marble Jesus stands in the middle of a manicured green churchyard, hands spread wide to gather the sunshine, the gentle benediction falling from the sky. On the steps of the cathedral, a group of men wearing black and women in lavender huddle around two people who have just been married. There is a clicking sound and the silence is pierced by laughter. The photographer looks down at his camera. The bride adjusts her grip on the bouquet.

To the south, Charles Street is a tunnel of visibility. In the middle of this shimmering vista stands the Washington Monument, its crowning statue not much higher than this point. There is a moment of confusion – how can something always seen from below be level with the eyes?

Up the hill comes a Lexus – silver-tan, shining smooth, windows darkened – rolling on gleaming chrome rims. Its sunroof is open to the sky, and from this portal emerges a sound that is loud, sharp and melodious. The notes bend upward and down, a joyous laid-back keening sequence that flows out of the car's body and fills the morning in deep yellow tones. The bass drum thumps to the end of the bar, building a need for a voice, which comes sliding in at just the right time. 'One two three and to the four,' it says, 'Snoopy Doggy Dogg and Dr Dre is at the door.'

6

THE FIRST THING JEEVAN SAW WHEN HE ENTERED THE HOUSE was Sunita sitting on a chair with her face in her hands. Opposite her on the couch sat a man, thin to the point of being skinny, his hair combed down. His face might have been called handsome once. He stood up when Jeevan walked in. 'So, this is the fellow,' he said.

Jeevan put down the grocery bags. 'Who are you?' he asked.

'Who am I?' said the man. 'What I want to know is, who are you? Who are you to take a married woman and keep her in your house?'

Jeevan bent down and picked up the grocery bags from the floor. He walked to the kitchen and started emptying them onto the counter. The man came after him. 'Answer me,' he said. 'Where are you running off to?'

Sunita let out a loud sob.

Jeevan opened the fridge and put the milk in. The vegetables and fruit went in next.

'Hey mister,' said the man, tapping him on the shoulder. 'Stand up and face me.'

'One minute,' said Jeevan, getting up, folding the plastic bags and putting them into a drawer near the sink. 'Now tell me,' he said, turning to face the man.

'Tell you? I have nothing to tell you. I'm here to take my wife back with me.'

'Your wife?'

'Yes,' he said, gesturing over his shoulder. 'Her. She's my wife. Don't pretend you don't know anything.'

Jeevan walked past the man, back into the living room. 'Is this man your husband?' he said.

Sunita raised her head slowly. When her hands parted, Jeevan saw that her eyes were red. She nodded.

'Do you want to go with him?'

Sunita shook her head.

'She doesn't want to go with you,' said Jeevan, turning to Sunita's husband.

'What do you mean, doesn't want to go? How can she want or not want? She's my wife. She has sworn in front of the fire that she's my wife. She has to come with me.' He stepped forward and caught hold of Sunita's arm. 'Come,' he said. 'Get up.'

Jeevan felt his temples begin to throb. Something like a metal ring expanded in his head. His right hand trembled, but he didn't let it leave his side. He stood where he was standing and waited for his muscles to go slack.

'No,' said Sunita, tearing the man's hand off her shoulder.

'What do you mean no?' said her husband. 'You have to come.'

Sunita stood up. She looked at Jeevan, then back at her husband. 'I don't have to do anything,' she said.

'You slut,' said the man, raising his hand.

'Don't hit her,' said Jeevan. 'Don't dare hit her.'

'No,' said Sunita. 'Let him hit me. Let him hit me as hard as he can.'

The man's hand fell.

'No,' she said, grabbing his hand. 'Hit me. Hit me. Come on, hit me.'

Sunita's husband pulled his hand back. He looked at it, then at Jeevan, and finally at Sunita. 'Neetu,' he said in a hoarse voice, 'I'm sorry, Neetu. I have been very bad to you, Neetu. Please come back, Neetu.' He started to hit his forehead with his fist and weep.

Jeevan went up to him and put his hand on the man's shoulder. 'Go home now,' he said.

Sunita's husband allowed himself to be led to the door. Jeevan opened the door and gently pushed him out of it.

'Neetu,' he said once more, but didn't look back as he said it. Jeevan stepped out with him.

On the sidewalk, Sunita's husband turned to Jeevan and said: 'Okay, Bhai. You win. You can have her.'

Jeevan gestured slowly with his hand: go.

'Enjoy her,' said the man, his lips curling. 'But then, you must have done that already.'

'Go now,' said Jeevan.

'She's round and full,' said the man, his hands tracing an imaginary woman's contours. His hips bucked forward, as if he were holding onto someone. 'Just right for some hard fucking, haan? Uhhn Uhhn Uhhn.'

Jeevan stepped back.

'But she's nothing compared to the women I have fucked, Bhai,' said the man. 'These Indian women, they don't even take their clothes off in bed. Find a white woman, Bhai. They'll take you in their mouth and suck you. You can even cum in there if you want. Just hold the head when you do. They'll eat it all up. You want to fuck the ass, just ask. It goes in smoothly, like a banana.'

'Go away now,' said Jeevan.

'Why should I go?' said the man, taking a step towards Jeevan. 'Does your father own this place that you will tell me to go away?' He put his hands on Jeevan's chest and pushed. 'You dirty bastard,' he said. 'You worthless low-caste worm. Happy to live with someone else's wife. No shame. I'll send you what's left of my dinner once I've eaten.'

Jeevan put his hand up. 'All this is useless,' he said. 'Just go away now.'

'Arre sisterfucker,' said the man, 'even Lord Rama threw his wife out of the house because she had been in another man's house. And you, you want to live with another man's wife. Thooo.' His spit landed at Jeevan's feet.

'What's going on here?' said a voice from behind Jeevan.

Henry was coming up the sidewalk towards them.

'Now who is this lame guy?' said Sunita's husband. 'Is he also fucking Sunita?'

'What did he say?' asked Henry.

'He asked, in Hindi, if you were also fucking Sunita,' said Jeevan.

'Hmmpf,' said Henry, pushing his walker a little faster. 'I'll answer him myself. In English.'

Sunita's husband and Jeevan waited for Henry to reach them. Oscar came up to Jeevan and licked his hand.

'What's your name, boy?' said Henry, resting the walker right in front of Sunita's husband.

'Mohan Kumar,' said the man.

'And who are you?'

'That slut Sunita's husband.'

'Well, Mr Mow Hand Coo Mar,' said Henry, gripping the front bar of the walker tightly with his left hand and freeing his right hand, 'here's my answer to your question.'

Henry's right fist struck Mohan Kumar below his left eyebrow. His neck jerked back. He staggered, then lost his balance and fell over. Jeevan stepped up, inserting himself between the fallen man and Henry. He helped Mohan Kumar to his feet and said: 'Now go.'

Mohan Kumar put his hand to his left eyebrow – the skin under it was beginning to darken – then looked at his hand. There was blood on it. He looked at the two men, took a deep breath, then turned and walked to the corner, got into his car and drove away, honking loudly as he went.

'Orioles and Tigers tonight at Camden Yards, Jeevan,' said Henry, jerking his right hand repeatedly once Sunita's husband's car was out of view.

'Is Cal playing?'

'Sure is,' said Henry, who was now examining the knuckles of his right hand closely, trying to pat back into place little scraps of skin that had torn off.

'Matthew didn't come?' asked Kamran, lifting his beer mug off the bar.

'No,' said Kay, settling onto the stool next to his. 'Said he didn't feel like going out.'

'What can I get you?' said the bartender, coming over to where they sat.

'I'll have a Stella, please,' said Kay.

'These guys have like hundreds of different brews from all over the world. You've got to try this one,' said Kamran, holding his glass out to her. 'Blanche de Chambly. It's a white beer from Quebec.'

'It's nice,' said Kay, taking a sip.

'I love the citrus flavor,' said Kamran. 'Should I ask him to get you one?'

The bartender looked at Kay expectantly.

'I'll stick to Stella. Thanks.'

The Brewer's Art was beginning to fill up. A weekday population of women located somewhere between casually sexy and outright dressed up handled their beers delicately or aggressively – if they were trying to make another kind of point – and laughed at the one-liners offered up to them by men whose hair had taken a lot of careful adjustment to achieve the requisite disarray. Perhaps all these people would be deciding between brands of toilet paper at the store or cleaning their kitchen counters or accompanying a nephew to the neighborhood sandbox tomorrow, thought Kay, but tonight they were here, being what they needed to be.

'Let's get a booth,' said Kamran when the Stella arrived.

He led them to one of the many recessed seating areas, the smallest one, and settled in on one end of the single couch placed there. Kay sat next to him. A waiter came by and lit the tea light on the table with a cigarette lighter. Kay reached into her bag for her cigarettes.

'I've done it,' said Kamran, watching her light her cigarette.

'What?' she said, blowing out the first round of smoke, then looking at the tip of the cigarette to see if it was properly lit.

'Criterion A,' said Kamran, his face gleaming with repressed excitement. 'I've nailed Criterion A.'

'No way,' said Kay, sitting up. 'No fucking way.'

'Way,' said Kamran. 'Can I bum a smoke?'

'Sure,' said Kay, handing him the packet and the lighter.

Kay waited while he lit his cigarette. 'So,' she said when he was done, 'tell me.'

'I went to Rankin Realty's office yesterday,' said Kamran.

'Rankin Realty, the guys who built the houses,' said Kay. 'They still exist?'

'Sure they do,' said Kamran. 'They have a big office downtown.'

'And?'

Kamran took a hard drag on his cigarette and drained his beer. Leaning over, he caught the bartender's eye and gestured to his empty glass. The bartender nodded. 'I told them I'm writing a piece for the *New York Times* about rowhouses in Baltimore. Showed them my ID. They totally bought it. I got a meeting with Edward Rankin IV. Fourth generation of the family in the business, get it? Edward Rankin the fourth. Like Louis the fourteenth and shit.' Picking up the fresh beer that a waiter had put down on the table, Kamran downed a third of it in one gulp. 'So this guy, Rankin the

165

fourth, was really excited to hear I wanted to write about his company for the *Times*. He said he had old papers, letters and stuff, and that I could look at them. It took me four hours yesterday and all of today, but I found it.'

'What did you find?' said Kay, her impatience beginning to turn to irritation.

'It's like this,' said Kamran, stubbing out the cigarette although there was at least a quarter of it left. 'By 1927 the Rankin company had built tons of houses all over the city. Seven of the tracts of land they had built on were near the tracks, and they had built them up, almost completely. But they had left the strips of land right on the tracks vacant, thinking that nobody would want to buy a house that faced the railtracks.'

'But our block is …'

'Exactly,' said Kamran, taking another large sip of his beer. 'Damn, this is tasty.'

'Why did they build our block then?'

'The Fair of the Iron Horse,' said Kamran, setting his glass down and wiping his mouth with the back of his hand.

'The fair of what?'

'The Fair of the Iron Horse,' said Kamran. 'In the fall of 1927 the B&O Railroad celebrated its centenary by holding a large railroad fair in Halethorpe. They displayed a bunch of locomotive engines. There were engines from all the hundred years of the B&O.'

'The engines on the trim at the top of the houses,' said Kay.

'Exactly,' said Kamran. He signaled to a waiter. 'I'll have another one of these. Blanche de Chambly. Do you want something?'

'I'm good.'

'Almost one and a half million people came to the fair,' said Kamran. 'Can you imagine, in those days, one point four million people? Rankin the second was there too, he mentioned that in his note.'

'What note?' said Kay, picking up her Stella, still half full, as Kamran's beer arrived.

'Rankin two had an idea,' said Kamran. 'The fair showed that there was massive interest in railroads. He wanted to take advantage of this. There were seven trackside plots on which his company had building rights. He planned to build a total of twenty-five moderately priced houses there.'

'And give them a railroad theme,' said Kay.

'Damn straight,' said Kamran, putting his beer down and running his hands through his hair. 'I've got to pee. Do you want another beer?'

'Sure,' said Kay, putting the Stella to her lips and tilting the bottle up.

Kamran rose to his feet, stumbling a little, almost knocking the table over, then righting himself.

'You okay?' asked Kay.

'Cool, cool, I'm cool.'

Kay suddenly needed that second beer more urgently. She looked towards the bar and waited for the bartender to glance up from his work. At the bar sat a man – blonde, his smartly cut shirt open down to his chest. He saw her looking in his direction and raised his beer towards her. Kay felt the blood rush to her cheeks. Before she could stop herself, she smiled at him. The man swung himself off the bar stool and walked across the room, looking directly at her, half-smiling, half-smirking.

'Hey,' he said when he got to her.

'Hey.'

'This seat taken?' he asked, pointing his beer to the spot next to her on the couch.

It is, thought Kay. 'No,' she said.

'Jason,' he said, holding his hand out once he had settled in, his thigh rubbing against hers.

'Kay.'

'So, Kay,' said Jason, 'you from around here?'

'Isn't that like the oldest line in the world?' asked Kay, feeling energized and alert.

'Hey,' said Jason, a grin spreading across his face, 'sometimes it's best to go with the tried and tested.'

'Right,' said Kay, intensely – uncomfortably – aware of Jason's closeness. 'Better safe than sorry, I guess.'

'What the fuck is going on here, dude?' Kamran's voice seemed to come from far away.

'Nothing,' she said.

Jason looked up at Kamran, his eyes narrowing. Then he looked at Kay. 'I'm out of here,' he said.

Kamran put the two beers he was carrying down on the table and sat at the end of the sofa farthest from Kay. He finished the rest of his earlier beer in one swig, then took a sip from the fresh one. Kay didn't touch hers.

'I wanted to tell you about the horse,' said Kamran, not looking at her, his voice slurring.

'What horse?'

'The horse on the windows,' said Kamran, picking up his beer again. His hand brought the glass up to his nose, then readjusted it so that it was at his lips.

'Stop drinking,' said Kay.

'Whatever,' said Kamran. 'Do you want to hear about the horse or not?'

'Let's go home, Kamran,' Kay said, standing up.

'There was a race,' said Kamran. 'Like, you know, like between an engine and a horse.'

'I'm going to pay,' said Kay, taking the beer from his hand and putting it out of his reach on the table. 'Then we're going home.'

'It was, like, a race,' said Kamran.

When she returned to the table, Kamran was sitting with his head leaning back against the wall, his eyes open wide. The beer sat where she had left it. 'Let's go,' she said.

Outside, Kay helped Kamran up the steps to the street.

'I did all this work,' he said, one hand on the rail, one around her waist. 'I spent all this time.'

'You have,' she said. 'This is good stuff.'

'Did I tell you about the horse and the race?' he said, turning his face towards hers.

'Yes, you did.'

When they reached the street, there was no cab in sight. Kamran swayed slightly but she didn't move to catch him. He tapped her on the shoulder.

'What?' she said, her face turned towards downtown, from where the cabs would come.

'Look at me,' he said.

She turned to him. 'What is it?' she said.

He took her face in his hands. His face started coming towards her. The stale smell of beer, with a hint of orange peel on it, hit her nose. She caught his hands and wrenched

169

them off her face, stepping back as she did. Kamran stumbled forward, almost falling.

'Don't you want me?' he said, his head moving from side to side as he tried to stand up straight. 'I thought you wanted me.'

When Sunita opened the door for him, Jeevan saw she had been crying. Her hair was open and bedraggled. She noticed him looking at it and tried halfheartedly to push it back off her face.

'Are you feeling all right?' asked Jeevan.

'Yes,' she said, looking down.

'Can I come in?'

Sunita's head jerked up. 'Yes,' she said, then moved back a step.

Jeevan walked into the room. The sound of Sunita shutting the door behind him startled him. An irrational feeling – is it right to be alone with a girl in a closed room? – came to him, almost making him turn and leave. But it passed, and he sat down on the bed, facing Sunita. 'This room looks nice,' he said.

'Thank you,' she said, standing with her back to the door.

'It used to be a storeroom,' said Jeevan. 'It looked very different.'

He's trying to make conversation, thought Sunita. It would have brought a smile to her lips on any other day, and this thought saddened her further, and made her feel like she had somehow been separated from herself. 'I'm sorry about what happened today,' she said.

'No, no,' said Jeevan. 'Why sorry?'

'If you had not come back, he would have got tired and gone away.'

'I'm sorry.'

'No, no, no,' said Sunita, clutching the doorknob with her right hand, her head resting against the door. 'I'm sorry. You were so good. You are so good.'

Jeevan stood up and took a step towards her. Then he stopped.

'It was not a good idea,' said Sunita. 'My coming here was not a good idea. I should have said no to Rashida baji. I don't know why I thought ... I thought ... I don't know what I thought.'

Jeevan's hand rose in a question, then fell back to his side. He kept looking at her face.

'He says to me,' Sunita continued, 'even Lord Rama refused to take his wife back after she had lived in Ravana's house, but I am willing to take you back. Who is Rama here and who is Ravana! I forgive you, he says. He! Forgives me! Hmmmpf.'

Jeevan sat down on the bed. And even as he sat, he realized that his action had incensed Sunita.

'And you,' said Sunita, her voice rising, 'why didn't you say something to him? Why didn't you hit him? Any other man in your place would have slapped him hard across the face.'

'Henry punched him,' said Jeevan.

'He did?' said Sunita, disbelief punctuating her teariness.

'Hard,' said Jeevan. 'On his face.'

Sunita giggled. 'Maybe I should marry Henry,' she said.

Jeevan took advantage of this lull to quickly rise to his feet. He walked towards Sunita, then turned around and walked past the bed to the window. Outside, the street stood quiet and dark. On 27th Street, a taxi drove by, briefly visible as it passed the connecting alley.

'If you want me to go away,' said Sunita, 'I will go.'

Jeevan turned from the window and strode up to where she stood. He put his hands on her shoulders. She looked up, streaky-eyed and surprised. Jeevan bent his head forward and touched her lips with his. Sunita's mouth opened slightly, her hands slowly curled around his back.

When they separated, Sunita was smiling. Tears were rolling down her face. Jeevan took her hand and turned towards the bed. Sunita pulled back.

'I'm not that kind of girl,' she said.

Jeevan dropped her hand. 'I'm sorry,' he said.

Sunita stepped forward and took his hand. 'I'm joking,' she said. 'I am that kind of girl.'

They stood by the bed, facing each other. Sunita reached up with her right hand and touched Jeevan on the cheek. She moved her hand over his jaw, down to his neck. Jeevan's eyes closed on their own. He tilted his neck forward so that his face went deeper into her hand, so that her touch went deeper into his skin. A long silent breath escaped him.

I am here, thought Sunita, addressing him without speaking. I am here for you.

When Jeevan opened his eyes, they were glistening. He smiled at Sunita in a way that she knew instantly she would not forget for a long time. Jeevan touched her midriff like he was feeling for a baby's kick, gently caressing her, then poking a finger into her belly button.

'Ooh,' said Sunita. 'What are you doing?'

'Nothing, nothing,' said Jeevan, not withdrawing his finger. 'Just, you know . . .'

'You are very naughty,' said Sunita, and this declaration sent a thrill through Jeevan.

Her lower lip caught between her teeth, Sunita wriggled her abdomen around Jeevan's finger, sending a current of arousal to his groin. His legs shifted in his pants, making space for the stirring between them. He withdrew his finger from her belly button and moved his hand up. Sunita bent forward to meet it. Jeevan palmed her breast, running his fingers over the nipple that stuck out through her blouse. Sunita's back arched at his touch. He pushed his body against hers, his mouth seeking her mouth again, this time more urgently. She ran her hand up his trousers, looking for, then finding, his penis under the layers of clothing.

'Wait,' said Jeevan, stepping away. He walked to the light switch and flicked it off.

Sunita giggled. 'Do you want to hide something from me?'

Jeevan came back to her, his face now lit by the streetlights filtering through the window.

'No,' he said, his hands falling slack at his sides, his chest pushing outwards.

Sunita unbuttoned his shirt. She ran her hand over his chest, bent forward to kiss his nipples. 'My lord,' she said, rubbing her face over his stomach. 'You are my lord.'

Jeevan's body stiffened at these words. His penis began to lose its hardness.

'What happened?' asked Sunita. Her right hand groped his telltale softness, then withdrew to her side.

'I'm sorry,' said Jeevan, stepping back.

'What happened?' she asked again.

Jeevan made to button his shirt, then dropped his hands. He sat on the bed. 'I'm sorry,' he said.

'Is it because I am another man's wife?' she asked, standing over him. 'Do you think I am dirty?'

'No, no, no,' said Jeevan, his head shaking from side to side. 'It's not that. Please don't say that.'

'Then what is it?' said Sunita.

'I, I ...'

Sunita put her hand on his right cheek. Tilting his head up towards her, she said gently, 'Say what you want to say.'

'I cannot be your lord, how can a man like me be your lord?' said Jeevan in a voice so small and strangled that Sunita's whole body filled with the need to take hold of him and never let him go.

'You don't understand,' she said, going down on her haunches and looking up at his face, still cradled in her hand. 'You are already my lord. You have been my lord for many many births.'

They made love enveloped in a halo of tenderness. The physical shocks that ran through Jeevan's body came through his mind in a mellow stream. Sunita's name ran round and round in his head till he could no longer tell when he was saying it out loud and when he wasn't.

Every muscle of Sunita's body was aware of Jeevan's penis moving in and pulling out. The sensation spread radially, a pleasure that built slowly, steadily – a progression towards a distant desired destination. Sunita floated towards this point on a choppy sea, the eddies taking her forward and back. For a moment, just before her orgasm came rolling through her senses, she felt like she was standing at the side of the bed, watching the two of them. Her mind emptied of all thought, and for that one moment, Jeevan became a feeling to her, an awareness, a pinprick of perception.

In the morning, when Jeevan woke – Sunita's back full against his chest – it felt like there had never been a morning in his life when he had woken alone in an empty bed.

By the time Kay returned home, it was past twelve. Matthew was sprawled on the couch, one leg up on the table, an empty bag of chips on his chest. On TV a woman with a tight body was working out on a sleek machine while a large muscular man looked on approvingly. At the bottom of the screen, a phone number flashed repeatedly under the words 'Order Now!'

'What're you watching?' asked Kay.

'Nothing,' said Matthew, pointing the remote at the TV and pressing a button. The TV didn't go off. 'We need new batteries for this.'

'There are some in the dresser drawer upstairs,' said Kay.

Matthew swung his legs off the couch and walked up to the TV. He pressed a button below the screen and the picture disappeared.

'You said you wanted to sleep early,' said Kay.

'Yeah,' said Matthew, returning to the couch and slouching down on it.

'I'm going up,' said Kay, turning towards the stairwell.

'How's Kamran doing?' said Matthew.

Kay looked back at him over her shoulder. Why can't he just say he wants to talk, she thought. Just come out and say it. 'He's fine,' she said, walking to the chair across the sofa and sitting down. 'In fact, he's found out some stuff.'

'What kind of stuff?'

'About the block,' she said. 'It was built to commemorate this rail fair in 1927.'

'The Fair of the Iron Horse,' said Matthew, sitting up.

'You've heard of it?'

'I read about it a bit,' said Matthew. 'It was for the B&O centenary.'

'That's what he said, there was something about it in some old documents he found at Rankin Realty's office.'

'He went to Rankin?' asked Matthew. 'Shit. Of course. That's the obvious place to go.' He was sitting on the edge of the couch now, nodding his head rapidly. His eyes were squinting at the coffee table, his lips pursed.

'You've been investigating?' said Kay.

'It makes sense,' he said. 'The engines on the trim are all the major ones displayed at the fair. From the Tom Thumb to the King George V. And that explains the B&O logo style decoration on the front door grille.'

'You didn't tell me you were snooping around on this,' said Kay, her initial annoyance mellowing into something sadder.

Matthew looked up from the table at her. 'Sorry, baby, I didn't want to get you excited till I actually turned up something.'

'But …'

'And, besides, it never even struck me to go to Rankin Realty. Kamran's a journalist. He knows these kinds of things, I guess. That's cool, he's found out this stuff. Now you guys just have to build the case and contact the state.'

'Yeah,' said Kay. 'That's what we guys have to do.'

'The horse thing, baby,' said Matthew. 'It's Tom Thumb racing the horse. That was a big deal back then, the new steam locomotive trying to show it was faster than a horse drawing a wagon full of people. And you know what?'

Kay didn't take the cue.

'The horse actually won,' said Matthew, amused. 'But the engine had drawn ahead before something malfunctioned and it came to a grinding halt. Isn't that funny?'

'That's funny.'

'That's why the windows have the horse and the engine drawn on them,' said Matthew. 'It's totally commemorative. We are so Criterion A, baby.'

'Are you sure?'

'Except,' said Matthew, the excitement draining out of his voice, 'except maybe if there are other such blocks and if they are better preserved or something, we might not have a claim, or it might be weaker.'

'Kamran said they had planned seven such blocks at various places along the railtracks.'

'Seven,' said Matthew. 'Where are the other six?'

'He didn't say,' said Kay.

'He didn't find out?'

'No, he must have, I guess. I don't know. We kind of couldn't finish having the conversation.'

'What does that mean?' Matthew asked. 'You couldn't finish the conversation.'

'Kamran got drunk,' said Kay, her eyes meeting Matthew's. She paused for a moment, holding his gaze. 'It's not what you're thinking.'

He licked his lips, then nodded and looked away. They sat in silence for a minute. 'I have to go to Jersey tomorrow,' he said finally.

'Jersey? Tomorrow? For what?'

'Work,' said Matthew.

'Work? On the weekend?'

'There's a workshop, like a seminar, at Rutgers,' he said. 'I want to go for that.'

'What kind of workshop?'

'Peter was here last week,' said Matthew, taking a deep breath, rising from the sofa. 'He gave a talk at Hopkins. I told him about the stuff I've been working on.'

'What you've been doing at night?' asked Kay.

Matthew paused. She knows. His body eased at the thought. How long has she known? 'Yes,' he said. 'It's that problem I told you about, the one I had been working on in grad school. The one that these other guys recently wrote a paper on.'

'Right,' said Kay, her eyes fixed on his feet as he paced from the couch to the TV and back.

'I had some ideas about it,' said Matthew. 'Then I found out that Peter was visiting. So I went to his talk. He told me about this workshop. One of the authors of that paper is going to be there. I thought I should go.'

'How long has this been going on?' said Kay. There was

a hardness in her voice that made Matthew stop and turn to her.

'Not that long,' he said. 'Just a couple of weeks or so.'

'Why didn't you tell me?'

'But you've known,' said Matthew. 'Right? You knew I was working at night, right?'

'But you didn't tell me,' said Kay, standing up and facing him. 'I knew, but you didn't fucking tell me.'

'Baby,' said Matthew, coming up to her. 'I'm sorry. I should've told you.'

Kay turned away. 'You've been skipping work and going to seminars. What else have you been up to? Going to the library behind my back?'

Matthew's arms hung by his side and, for a moment, they felt like deadweights. He wanted to raise them, do something with them, but he didn't know what they could do. 'Yes,' he said. 'I have.'

'Why, Matt?' asked Kay. 'Why didn't you tell me?'

'I didn't know if anything would come of it,' he said. 'I was just fooling around a little. I thought if something developed, I'd tell you then.'

Kay rubbed her chest with her hand. Her shoulders heaved. She turned to him. 'Matt, why are you doing this to yourself?'

'I think it can work, baby,' he said. 'Really.'

'You thought that earlier as well.'

'I know, I know,' said Matthew. 'And that was wrong. Then. It's different now.'

'What's different now?'

'I don't know,' said Matthew. 'I'm older. I feel like, you know, better about myself.'

'You feel better about yourself?' said Kay. 'Really?'

Matthew flinched. He took a step back, then turned. 'I need to do this, baby,' he said, sitting down on the couch. 'I need to take another shot at this. I think I can do it this time.'

'There's a lot of I in that, not so much we,' said Kay, her back to him.

'Look, I said I'm sorry,' said Matthew, a tide rising in his head. 'I should have told you. Don't crucify me for that.'

'I'm not talking about that anymore,' said Kay, turning and walking up to the couch where he sat. 'I'm not talking about what you've already done, I'm talking about what happens now. You want us to move again, go back to Providence, or Jersey? You want me to wait tables again while you play games in your lab?'

'I didn't say that,' said Matthew, his head down.

'Then what are you saying, Matthew?' said Kay, going down on her haunches. 'Look at me. Tell me, what are you saying?'

Matthew stood up and stepped away from the couch. 'I don't know,' he said. 'But I want you to do your thing as well. If med school is what you want, and this job is a way to get there, I want you to do it. But I also want, I mean, I think I also want, to try again.'

Kay rose to her feet. 'Do you want it or do you think you want it?'

'I don't know.'

'What are you trying to live up to, Matt?' said Kay. 'Being an academic success isn't everything, it isn't the only thing. So Joshua writes books and you don't, how does that matter? You have a great job that pays well and you have your own life. Isn't that worth anything?'

'It is,' said Matthew, turning his back to her, his voice cracking. 'Of course it is.'

'Matt, baby,' she said, behind him now, stroking his back. 'Have you forgotten how miserable you were there? I was there, baby, I saw what you went through. It broke my heart to see you like that. Why put yourself through that again?'

Matthew's back shuddered, then shuddered again, and Kay realized he was half-sobbing. 'I need to,' he said finally. 'I can't live with myself if I don't.'

Kay's hand fell away from his back. 'Fine,' she said. 'Live with yourself then. You're pathetic. You're so fucking selfish, it's pathetic.'

'Selfish?' said Matthew, spinning around. 'I'm selfish? That's fucking rich coming from someone who has cheated on her husband, not once but twice.'

'You bastard,' said Kay, stepping back from him. 'You fucking bastard.'

'Hey Jeevan,' said Xing, getting off his bicycle. 'Long time no see. Coming in?'

Jeevan smiled at the delivery boy, folded the copy of *Citypaper* he had been glancing through and carefully put it back in the yellow dispenser that stood anchored to a street lamp. 'I'm waiting for Shabbir,' he said.

'There he is,' said Xing, pointing over Jeevan's shoulder. 'See you inside.'

Every now and then Shabbir, who ate at least one rich curry with meat or some kababs at every other meal, would declare: 'All this dal roti everyday gets tiring.' This was understood to be a precursor to his deciding that he wanted to eat at Oriental Lotus, the Chinese takeaway that was a few blocks from Food Point. Rashida never came, always saying: 'One thing my stomach can't digest is noodles.' So, Jeevan was taken along.

'Hello, Mrs Liu,' said Shabbir, striding up to the counter.

'Hey Shabbir,' said the lady, whose hair seemed to have turned whiter since the last time Jeevan had been here. 'Veg Lo Mein, large?'

'Yes, yes,' said Shabbir, pleased, as he always was, at having his regular order remembered.

'And House Lo Mein for Jeevan,' said Mrs Liu. 'Regular size.'

'Yes, Mrs Liu,' said Shabbir. 'Our friend Jeevan can eat all the animals you put in your House Lo Mein.'

'I'll make it for you without pork, Shabbir,' said Mrs Liu, smiling as she clipped the order slip onto the rail above the window to the kitchen.

'You should come to Food Point some time,' said Shabbir.

'Your food is too spicy for me,' said Mrs Liu, raising her hands in mock horror.

'I'll make it for you without spice, Mrs Liu,' said Shabbir. They both laughed.

At the table, as they waited for their food, Shabbir said: 'Sunita's husband had come.'

'Yes,' said Jeevan, tapping the table with his fingers and looking over Shabbir's shoulder at the TV that was mounted just above Oriental Lotus's shopfront.

'What did he want?'

'He wanted her to go back to him,' said Jeevan. On the television, Rafael Palmeiro, the Orioles' first baseman, was promoting Baltimore Gas and Electric in a uninflected monotone that somehow made both him and the company he was endorsing more loveable.

'What happened?'

'Nothing,' said Jeevan.

'He went away?'

'Yes.'

'Do you think he will come back?'

'No.'

Shabbir considered this reply, then his face broke into a wide grin. 'She's yours, Jeevan bhai,' he said. 'Congratulations.'

'Shabbir bhai,' said Jeevan, turning his gaze on Shabbir, 'did Miss Lucy's husband take a loan from you?'

Shabbir's grin slowly reformed into a set expression. 'What are you talking about?' he asked.

'Did you lend Mr Murray eight thousand dollars?'

Shabbir rose slowly. He walked around the table and went to the counter. He picked up one of the plastic glasses set there and poured himself some water. 'Yes, I did,' he said, returning to the table and setting the glass down.

'And you took the deed as surety?' asked Jeevan.

'Who told you all this?'

'Henry.'

'That old fool should mind his own business,' said Shabbir.

'Miss Lucy confirmed it,' said Jeevan.

The innings break was over now and the Orioles were up to bat. A man in a black helmet was standing bent over in a funny fashion at the plate, his bat slung over his right shoulder. When the camera angle changed, Jeevan saw that on his back was a large number 8 and the word 'Ripken'.

'Jeevan,' said Shabbir. 'Jeevan, are you listening?'

'Sorry,' said Jeevan.

'I said, why are you asking me about the loan.'

Jeevan hesitated. Shabbir has been good to me, he thought. Shabbir has always taken care of me.

'Large Veg Lo Mein,' said Xing, putting a steaming box down in front of Shabbir. 'And regular House Lo Mein.'

'Thank you, Xing,' said Shabbir, taking the Styrofoam plate and plastic spoon that Xing offered him.

'And two of these,' said Xing, putting down two individually wrapped orange fortune cookies.

Jeevan reached for the cookies, thought about picking up one of them, then chose the other. He tore the wrapping and broke open the cookie.

'Arre, that is for after your food,' said Shabbir.

The slip of paper read: Your blessing is no more than being safe and sound for the whole lifetime. Jeevan read it, then read it again. A wave of anger rose up within him. 'Are you going to take Miss Lucy's house from her?' he asked, in a voice that Shabbir had never heard him use before.

'Jeevan,' said Shabbir, an edge appearing in his voice, 'that is none of your business.'

A muffled roar came from the TV's speakers. Jeevan looked up to see that Cal Ripken was running, his hands fisted, his facial muscles tensed. He rounded first base and charged towards second. The camera cut to a fielder releasing the ball, then back to second base where Cal was sliding now.

The second baseman collected the ball and swung his glove downward. The umpire, crouched a few feet from the base, dramatically threw both hands outwards. Safe. The crowd roared again. Ripken stood up. The camera focused on his face. He looked satisfied.

Jeevan shoveled lo mein onto the Styrofoam plate. He made as if to pick some up with his fork, then put the fork down. 'Shabbir bhai,' he said, 'are you going to take the house?'

Shabbir took a forkful of lo mein and put it in his mouth, looking at Jeevan as he did. He chewed it slowly, then took a sip of water and said: 'Yes, I am.'

'Why?'

'They're giving block compensation to people who own entire blocks. It's meant for commercial strips, but it applies to residential blocks as well. It will be double the price of the three houses put together.'

'Victoria Washington didn't say anything about this,' said Jeevan.

'I asked her,' said Shabbir.

The shortstop Mike Bordick came to bat with two men on base. Cal was at third base – the catcher Chris Hoiles, at first base now, had moved him along – where he stood talking to the third base coach. Matt Williams, the Indians' third baseman, said something to him that made him smile. The third base coach took his position as the pitcher got into his windup.

'What will happen to Miss Lucy?' asked Jeevan.

The pitch, when it came, was a little to the outside of the plate. Bordick, swinging easily, hit it between first base and second. Hoiles ran, leaping over the ball as he went. Cal had already reached home plate and was bumping fists with Brady Anderson by the time the right fielder collected the ball.

'Cal scores,' said the TV's tinny voice.

Shabbir turned to look.

'They're doing well,' said Jeevan.

'Hmmm,' said Shabbir. Then, turning back to Jeevan, he said: 'Don't worry about Miss Lucy. I will take care of her.'

'How?'

Shabbir mopped up the last of his noodles and stuffed them into his mouth. 'Jeevan bhai,' he said, chewing as he spoke, 'you think you are the only one who cares for other people? You think Shabbir is a selfish, greedy bastard? Maybe you should open your eyes wider and see the world as it really is.'

Jeevan nodded.

'I called you here today, Jeevan, to tell you my plans. Because I thought I could trust you. But how can I trust you if you don't trust me? Tell me, can I trust you if you don't trust me?'

'No, Bhai,' said Jeevan.

'Now listen to me,' said Shabbir. 'I have seen two houses in the county, in Pikesville. They are right next to each other. And they are much bigger and nicer than the house you live in now. They both have backyards and front lawns. And they are in a nice neighborhood.'

Xing walked up to their table carrying three large plastic bags full of food.

'You don't like the House Lo Mein today,' he asked Jeevan, pointing at the full carton sitting on the table.

186

'No, no,' said Jeevan, picking up the carton and beginning to empty its contents onto his plate.

'I have a delivery,' said Xing. 'See you guys later.'

'Rashida and I will live in one,' said Shabbir. 'You and Sunita can live in the other.'

'And Miss Lucy?' asked Jeevan.

'Why so impatient, Jeevan bhai? Let me talk for one second. One of the houses is a little bigger. It has a large bedroom on the ground floor. I measured it. Both the organ and the old lady can stay there. You and Sunita can stay there with her.'

Two men and a woman with a tattoo on her arm and a piercing above her right eye came in. The dark lipstick and heavy eyeliner she wore couldn't hide the essential freshness of her young face.

'And I was, like, are you smoking crack, dude?' she said. The men burst into laughter. One of them offered his hand for a high five.

Jeevan regarded them for a moment, then looked back at Shabbir. 'I'm sorry I doubted you, Shabbir bhai,' he said.

Kamran poured milk onto his granola and crunched the first spoonful of his breakfast. Outside the window, the sun was shining off the rooftops. The street was quiet, parked cars lay silent along the sidewalk, their steering wheels locked in place by red clubs. Over the horizon an armada of clouds was making its slow way across the sky.

'Assalaam aleikum, Beta,' said Shabbir, coming out of his room.

'Waleikum assalaam,' mumbled Kamran.

'When did you sleep last night?' asked Shabbir, sitting down across the table from him.

'Late.'

'You should sleep on time, Beta,' said Shabbir. 'And wake up early.'

'Hmmm.'

'Even two nights ago you came in very late,' said Shabbir.

Kamran poured more milk into his bowl.

'Did you go out with your friends that day?'

'Yes,' said Kamran, bringing the spoon to his mouth.

'Your mother will be making parathas for breakfast,' said Shabbir. 'Stuffed parathas. Aloo and gobhi.'

'Hmmmm.'

'What is this crunchy nonsense you eat for breakfast?' asked Shabbir. 'This is not real food. Keep some space for the parathas.'

'Granola's good for you,' said Kamran. 'Parathas are too oily.'

'You used to love parathas when you were a boy,' said Shabbir, sighing. 'Ammi, make parathas. Ammi, when are you going to make parathas? Allah knows what happened to you.'

'I grew up,' said Kamran.

Shabbir looked at his son – unruly hair falling onto his forehead, strong nose bent over his bowl of granola. He looks so much like Imran chacha, he thought, remembering his father's younger brother. And he has the same stubbornness and temper. 'Who had you gone out with that night, Beta?' he asked, the memory softening his voice.

'Kay,' said Kamran. 'Your tenant.'

'You are spending a lot of time with that girl,' said Shabbir, the tenderness draining out of him.

'Hmmm,' said Kamran.

'What hmmm?' said Shabbir. 'Why are you spending so much time with her? Don't you have other friends in Baltimore? The other day, Asad had come. He said he met you at night near Federal Hill. But you didn't phone him or meet him after that.'

'Asad is a loser,' said Kamran.

'And you are a big winner, haan? How did you become so arrogant? Asad's father is one of my oldest friends in Baltimore. He is like a brother to me, like your chacha.'

'That doesn't make that sleazy cab driver my cousin,' said Kamran.

'What is wrong with cab drivers?' asked Shabbir. 'Don't forget that cab driving paid for your education.'

'I'm not forgetting anything, okay,' said Kamran. 'I just don't want to hang out with Asad and the other Pakistani losers he hangs out with, that's all.'

'Yes, yes, why will you hang out with Pakistanis,' said Shabbir, his voice rising. 'After all, you are not Pakistani. Shall I bring you a mirror? You can check the color of your skin in it.'

'Abba, don't get into a twist over this. I just don't want to hang out with Asad, that's all. He wasn't a friend of mine in school. You thought he was, but he wasn't.'

Shabbir rose from the table. He turned as if to leave the room, then turned back and said: 'Asad said you were with her that night.'

189

'Yeah, I was,' said Kamran. 'Not that it's any of his, or your, business.'

'How dare you?' roared Shabbir, coming up to the table and shaking Kamran by the shoulder. 'How dare you talk to your father like that.'

Kamran pulled away from him and stood up. His chair fell over, clattering on the floor.

Shabbir raised his hand. 'Say sorry,' he said.

'Or what?' said Kamran, battling a fear that reminded him of his childhood. 'You'll hit me?'

Shabbir's hand dropped. His eyes bulged, his breath came short and hard. Kamran stood looking at him, his left hand tensed, ready to block a blow. It had never come before, never from his father anyway, and it would probably not come today either, but his body disregarded this information and waited.

'Beta,' said Shabbir finally, his shoulders sagging perceptibly, his torso racked by a series of deliberate sobs. 'Ranu beta, you are my only son, you are my most precious possession, my life. Why do you treat your old father like this?'

'Dad,' said Kamran, rolling his eyes. 'Dad, calm down. I'm sorry, okay? I'm sorry I said that.'

'Your mother and I have worked so hard all our lives,' said Shabbir, whose sobs did not seem to be producing any tears. 'For what? All these things we have collected are all for you. All my money will be yours. And what do I ask in return? Nothing. Just that you talk to me like a son should talk to a father. But no, you say that your life is none of my business. Why? I am your father, why is your life not my

190

business? If I see you walking around with a married woman, why is it not my business? Do you expect me to sit around and do nothing while my son's life is ruined?'

'Abba,' said Kamran, 'listen to me. It's nothing like what you're thinking. Kay and I are working together. In fact, we have been working on something that's going to benefit you.'

Wiping his dry eyes with the back of his hand, Shabbir said: 'What benefit?'

'Abba,' said Kamran, suddenly excited at being able to tell his father about something he had done, 'the houses you own are historic. And Miss Lucy's house too. The whole block. They were built to commemorate a railroad fair, a hundred years of the B&O railroad. And you know what, this is the only such commemorative block. The company had planned six others, but they never built them because the Depression started and the housing market plummeted. Your property is historic and unique.'

Shabbir sat down at the table. His eyes narrowed. 'How did you find this out?'

'I looked through the City's records,' said Kamran. 'And I went through Rankin Realty's papers. They are the ones who originally built these houses.'

'But the property is not historic right now,' said Shabbir.

'No, not yet,' said Kamran. 'But I think we have a strong claim. We will have to fill a form and submit it to the State of Maryland's Historic Preservation Officer. It'll take some work to fill the form, but I think we can do it. Then they will inspect the property and if they think it meets the criteria, they will designate it. And once it is designated as a historic place, no one can demolish the block.'

'What are the chances of your claim being accepted?' asked Shabbir, getting up and walking to the window.

'I think they're good,' said Kamran. 'All the commemorative detailing, you know, the steams engines on top, the B&O logo on the grille doors. We can also say that we are barely a block away from the Old Goucher campus – that is historic – but the detailing is the kicker, it will all turn on that.'

'The steam engines and horses on the windows,' said Shabbir.

'Exactly,' said Kamran. 'They're all in good shape. So that works in our favor. And there's clear documentation – I have copies – that Rankin Realty planned this as a commemoration. That can't be contested.'

'It needs to be in good shape for them to accept the claim,' said Shabbir, looking out the window.

'I guess so,' said Kamran. 'That's what it says in the bulletins.'

Shabbir turned away from the window, and walked up to Kamran. 'Beta,' he said, 'what is the point of getting into all this? The City has decided that all these buildings are to be demolished. They must have thought of something before deciding. And if these buildings were historic, wouldn't they have themselves decided not to demolish them?'

'Abba, sometimes things get forgotten. Sometimes you have to bring it to the City's attention. This is clearly one of those cases.'

'Hmmm,' said Shabbir, frowning. 'You remember Shahzaib bhai, your mother's cousin from her mother's side? The one who lives in Washington?'

'No.'

'They had visited us once,' said Shabbir. 'You were maybe five or six years old. Anyway, Shahzaib bhai had bought a house in Washington. A few years later, some interfering people had that house and many houses on that street declared historic. Something about some black people living there at some time. In the end, Shahzaib bhai was stuck with that house. He couldn't build any extensions, he couldn't demolish any part of it. Even one window frame couldn't be changed. He was getting such a good offer from someone who wanted to buy his house and the next house. They wanted to build a parking lot there. The moment they found out his house was historic, the offer disappeared. Instead, they built the parking lot on the next street.'

'But, Abba ...'

'But nothing, Beta,' said Shabbir. 'Why should we get into all this historic-shistoric? They are giving us good money for the place. Let us take it and buy even better houses somewhere else. What history is there in this two-hundred-year-old country anyway? In Lahore, every mohalla has a six-hundred-year-old building just sitting there with birds shitting all over it.'

'You're the one who is full of shit,' Kamran mumbled.

'What did you say?'

'Nothing, Abba,' said Kamran. 'I don't think you get it. This is history. It may not be as old as your precious Lahore, but it is old enough for me. And I think it's worth preserving.'

'Allah,' said Shabbir, sighing. 'This boy is as stubborn as his father. Okay, do what you want. Just don't hang around with that married woman. I'm a man, I understand what it means to be young. In my time, I have also done a lot of things. But Allah help you if your mother finds out.'

'What will his mother find out?' said Rashida, coming up the stairs.

'Nothing,' said Shabbir, raising a finger to his lips and looking out of the corner of his eye towards his son.

A cloudy day over the bridge on Sisson Street, and down below, the railway tracks lie waiting. Over to the south, the lines of new cars parked in the dealership lot shine idly. Above them, strings of red, white and blue streamers, their colors bleached out by long days in the sun, flutter gently. Large white lettering on a blue background can be seen, proclaiming the dealer's name. The name is seen at an angle, pointing towards a road that cannot be seen from here.

Green is sprouting out of the cracks in the sidewalk along the bridge. The taller of the weeds sway ever so slightly in the breeze, their tiny yellow flowers moving like the face of a child being rocked to sleep. The concrete panels that line the bridge are adorned with the squat, pointy lettering of graffiti writers who have since moved on to other, more trafficked public walls. Above the panels, the iron railing is a narrow cylindrical canvas for textures of rust.

Beyond the railing, the eye dips to the tube of space that is given over to the railways. The tracks lie confident and easy. The right-of-way, the domain of the train, is manicured with neatly arranged piles of gravel on both sides of the tracks. There is rust down there as well; the rust of once useful pieces of metal. They wait for the slow consumption from within to eat its way through them.

And then the owner of this space, its sole legitimate user, approaches, announced from afar by its lonely whistle, felt in a vibration that precedes it. The bridge braces for its arrival. The tunnel tingles with anticipation. The gravel takes a step back. Sidewalk cracks begin their jostling, the weeds readying to be squeezed. Even the breeze seems to pick up, its eddies running helter-skelter into each other.

Only the dealership is unconcerned. It continues to face the road that runs over the tracks and onward to downtown.

7

MATTHEW SAT IN AN EMPTY ROW NEAR THE BACK OF THE auditorium and watched Ankush talk. Ankush had just entered the graduate program at Brown when Matthew was leaving. He had been a timid guy socially – wispy moustache, synthetic checked shirts tucked into his jeans – who would come alive aggressively in the classroom. Ankush's accent was shifting, Matthew noted. The 'con' in his 'consequence' was moving from the Indian 'cawn' to the American 'caan'. But it hadn't quite got there. His shirt wasn't tucked in anymore, and his hair was cut to a length that wouldn't stand out on a university campus, the oil in it replaced by a more acceptable product. But the biggest difference was the confidence with which he spoke, the ease with which he walked from his laptop to the screen and back. It wasn't hard to see where the self-assurance came from. The work he was presenting had won a best paper award at a leading conference. The expression on Peter's face – Peter was Ankush's advisor, and a co-author on the paper Ankush was presenting – was of pride and satisfaction. His academic heir was going to do him proud.

'This guy is smart,' whispered a voice on Matthew's right.

He turned with a start and found himself looking at a girl leaning across an empty seat towards him, her green eyes shining with a conspiratorial look behind her round metal-rimmed glasses. 'Yeah, he used to be in my lab,' Matthew said, and instantly regretted having involuntarily tried to bask in reflected glory.

'Cool,' said the girl. 'Where's he now?'

'He's still there,' said Matthew. 'I'm not there anymore.'

At the coffee break, Matthew tried to sidle up to Peter. Bagel in one hand and coffee in another, Peter was chatting with a dark man. His braided hair made him look black, but when he spoke – loudly, confidently, smiling in anticipation of a joke he was about to make – Matthew realized he was Indian. He talked like someone accustomed to being the life of the party, making eye contact with Matthew, although he probably realized he had never laid eyes on Matthew before. Peter was laughing at the jokes and trying to match them with his own one-liners. The Indian man was trumping each one of those with his own lines, better ones. Matthew waited for Peter to turn and acknowledge him, but Peter didn't. Might as well get a bagel, Matthew thought.

'I'm Amy,' said the girl he had met earlier, coming up behind him as he slathered cream cheese on his bagel.

'Matthew.'

'Hey Matthew,' said Amy, picking up a bagel, then putting it back and picking up another one. 'Where's the light cream cheese?'

'Who's that guy?' asked Matthew, once the light cream cheese had been located and spread. They sat on a sofa in a spacious atrium outside the seminar hall. Through the glass walls they could see the large university parking lot, an expanse of tarmac spreading outward, its white striped markings reflecting the forenoon sun.

'Which guy?' asked Amy.

'The guy with the braids?'

'You don't know Bala? God, where have you been? The guy is like the most prolific researcher ever. He's got more than two hundred entries in DBLP, in just ten or twelve years. He's published with everyone you can think of. He's a total machine, just churning them out.'

'Where does he work?'

'He's from everywhere and nowhere,' said Amy, biting into her bagel. 'Vame zhe pashe heezh bee thay.'

Matthew smiled despite himself. 'What?'

'Name the place,' said Amy, swallowing the cream cheese and bagel, 'and he's been there. Last year he came to my department and gave a job talk. They offered him a job, and he accepted it. But then, in the fall, he didn't show up. No explanation. And the professors just laughed it off. That's Bala for you, they said. He's like a subatomic particle. The moment you pin him down in one place, he's already gone.'

'That's disgusting,' said Matthew.

'Disgusting?'

'Yes, irresponsible and disrespectful.'

'Calm down,' said Amy. 'You don't even know him.'

'That's true,' said Matthew, struggling to control himself. 'Very true.'

'So, what's your story?' asked Amy, regarding him quizzically, her eyes clear, her face – tilted to one side – very still.

The sight of people returning to the auditorium rescued Matthew. 'Bernard Levinson's talking next,' he said. 'It should be interesting.'

Levinson's talk felt like a dream Matthew had dreamt before. He anticipated the figures before the slides went up. The equations threw him into a reverie, and made him feel like he was back in his bedroom late at night, the lamp shining down on the printout and his eyes glazing over. He struggled to focus on the question he had thought he would ask, repeating it in his head, repeatedly losing the thread of the argument. By the time the session chair rose and called for questions, Matthew was badly in need of a cigarette. He rose from his seat. 'Yes,' said the session chair, pointing to him. Matthew waved his hand no, and turned and hurried through the row, knees banging against the upturned seats as he went.

'Matthew? Matthew Fleischer?' It was Ankush, standing by the doors.

'Ankush,' said Matthew, desperate now to push open the doors and gain the safety of the atrium outside. 'I need a smoke. You coming?'

Ankush smiled sheepishly. 'I kind of quit. But okay.'

Outside, once they had lit up, Matthew said: 'Nice talk.'

'Thanks.'

'And congratulations on getting that best paper award.'

'Just luck, man,' said Ankush, grinning widely. 'So where are you now?'

'I'm in Baltimore,' said Matthew. 'Financial consulting.'

'Baltimore,' said Ankush. 'In Maryland? I've driven past it a few times, but never turned in. They do financial consulting there?'

'Yes,' said Matthew, smiling. 'They do.'

'Cool,' said Ankush. 'But if you're in consulting, then . . .'

What am I doing here? thought Matthew. 'For old times' sake,' he said, bringing the cigarette up to his lips.

'Those were good times, dude,' said Ankush, remembering to drag on his own cigarette. 'It's been a while.'

Through the glass walls, Matthew saw Bala walk by. He saw his eyes light on Ankush.

'You know, I was thinking of you the other day,' said Ankush. 'I read this book about Rwanda. It was also written by a guy called Fleischer. John or James or something.'

'Joshua,' said Matthew. 'He's my brother.'

'Awesome book, man,' said Ankush. 'He knows a lot, and he has really good insights.'

'Hey smokers,' said Bala, stepping out, the doors swinging shut behind him.

'Hey Bala,' said Ankush.

'Would you like one?' asked Matthew, pointing the pack at him.

'No, thanks,' said Bala, looking greedily at the cigarettes. 'I quit. By the way, I'm Bala.'

'Matthew.'

'His brother wrote a great book about Rwanda,' said Ankush.

'Hey, you read books,' said Bala. 'That's great. I like books too. Sometimes I'll just go to a bookstore and pick up some books. Some weeks back I read this book about this English mathematician. It's fiction. So, this guy decides one day that he's going to work on the Riemann Hypothesis. It's difficult and he may not make it, but if he does, he'll be famous. He starts working on it. It's a secret, he doesn't tell anyone. He works and works and works and he comes up with an interesting conjecture. If it's true, he has a major breakthrough. But he can't prove the conjecture, nor can he disprove it. It's driving him crazy and he can't talk to anyone about it. In those days Ramanujan is in England, so finally, our friend decides to break the secrecy a little and just go and ask him. He won't tell him the reason or the significance, he thinks, just the conjecture. He goes to Ramanujan and he tells him the conjecture. Ramanujan thinks about it for two minutes and then he says, you know what he says?'

'What?' asked Ankush.

'It's probably not true for large numbers,' said Bala, slapping his hands together.

Matthew watched as the two of them dissolved into uncontrollable laughter. Ankush's cigarette fell from his hand. 'Not true for large numbers,' he said, gasping as he bent down to pick up the cigarette.

'Who would know more about large numbers than Ramanujan?' asked Bala, his hilarity picking up in intensity.

Behind his façade of polite laughter, Matthew found himself wondering how the fictional English mathematician must have felt, upstaged in his own country by the Indian genius.

After the last session finished, Matthew walked out of the room as quickly as he could. There was coffee laid out in the atrium. I do need coffee, he thought. He had been needing it for a while. What the hell, let me just get a quick coffee.

'Hey Matthew!' It was Amy.

'Hey.'

'You heading out?'

'Yeah.'

'Are you going to be here tomorrow or are you leaving tonight?' she asked, picking up a cup.

'I don't know.'

'I've been here since yesterday,' she said. 'I was really bored last night. There's no one from my department here.'

'Hmmm,' said Matthew, sipping his coffee.

'Do you want to hang out tonight?' she asked.

Matthew looked up at her. Her cheekbones were high and rounded, he noticed. Her glasses hid them somewhat. It's an innocent proposal, he thought. What am I going to do back in Baltimore tonight anyway?

'Sure,' he said. 'Where are you staying?'

It was almost ten when the doorbell finally rang, two hours since Kamran had called and said he wanted to come over.

'Kay?' asked Kamran, his face partially obscured by the dark metal of the grille door. She realized that with the porch light on outside, he couldn't see her face.

'Hey,' she said, her hand reaching for the doorknob. Her fingers touched the metal, felt around its rounded form, but did not grip the knob.

'I'm sorry,' said Kamran. 'I'm really sorry for what happened.'

Kay focused her mind on the knob and her recalcitrant hand did the simple job it had been assigned. The door swung open, Kamran stepping back to give it room.

'Come in,' she said.

'Hey,' he said, coming in. His arms began to spread out, his torso moved forward, as if to hug her. But she stiffened at the movement, so Kamran pulled back. 'Hey,' he said again.

'I'm going out for a smoke,' said Kay.

'Okay,' said Kamran, turning.

'No, not here. Upstairs.' She shut the doors and turned the bolts. Then she climbed the stairs, the sound of him trudging up behind her loud in her ears.

Outside, on the fire escape, she lit her cigarette while Kamran wriggled through the window. She looked across at Jeevan's backyard, neat and spare, the blueberry bushes settled in for the night. A trapezoid of light projected out of what she figured was Jeevan's room, illuminating a patch of earth. Kay wondered if Sunita was with him right now, in his room. What were they talking about? She wanted – a sudden pang, a rending desire – to be there with them, chatting, making jokes, basking in the serene glow of what the two of them shared. Matthew, she thought. Why aren't you here, Matthew?

'I don't know what I was thinking,' said Kamran, and Kay realized with a start that she had forgotten he was there.

'Do you want a cigarette?' she asked.

'No.'

His face was barely visible in the darkness but Kay could sense the contrition on it. Poor guy, poor confused guy.

'What we're doing is important,' he said, encouraged by her turning towards him. 'I shouldn't have dragged my own shit into it.'

'It's okay,' said Kay, bringing the cigarette to her mouth with her right hand and reaching out to him with her left.

'I'm sorry,' he said, taking her hand in both of his. 'I'm really, really sorry.'

'It's okay.'

'It's just that I'm so, so, you know, so confused,' he said, bringing her hand up to his face. 'I meet all these people who seem to know what they want. They know where they're coming from. Their families appreciate what they're doing, what they want to do. For me, it's like I'm on my own, totally on my own. I mean, my parents care for me, they do, but it's not like they know who I am. It's not like I can tell them what I want to do and expect them to understand. They've worked hard all their lives for me, but sometimes I think they don't really care for me, for what I am, what I want to be. They're stuck in some idea of what they think is best for me.'

'Families are like that,' said Kay. 'My mom is like that.'

Kamran opened her palm and ran his fingers along it. He moved his lips down to her wrist.

'You're doing good, though,' said Kay. 'I mean, this stuff you've found out, it's great. If this block can be saved because of what you've discovered, that would be something, wouldn't it?'

'I forgot to tell you the other day,' said Kamran, moving her hand away from his face but not letting go of it, 'this is the only one of the seven projects that got built.'

'Which seven projects?'

'I told you, right, that Rankin had planned seven commemorative blocks near the railtracks. Well, this was the first one, like a pilot, I guess. But they had real trouble selling the houses. And then the Depression hit, real estate plummeted. So they abandoned the other projects.'

'Wow,' said Kay. 'That nails the argument, doesn't it?'

'I think so,' said Kamran, raising her hand and gently pressing it to his chest. 'This place is unique.'

Kay stubbed her cigarette against the railing and threw it into the backyard. 'Come,' she said, gently moving her hand back but not pulling it away from him. 'Let's go in.'

The hallway inside was dark. Light from the lamp downstairs found one corner of it, but that only served to make the darkness deeper where Kay stood waiting for Kamran to climb in. He stumbled as he came, his foot catching the window frame.

'Easy there,' said Kay, putting her hand out.

'I'm okay.'

She took his hand in hers and led him down the hallway. Pausing in front of a door, she turned. Kamran could see, from the shape her hair took in the dark, that she was facing him. But unseen by Kamran, or by anyone else, Kay was looking at Kamran's form – a silhouette, immediate and warm, framed against the window and the night outside it. She opened the door and drew him into the room.

'Ow,' yelped Kamran, his shin hitting something hard as he walked into the darkened room. 'Shit.'

'That desk sticks out a bit,' said Kay, pulling him further in. 'Sorry.'

'Can we put a light on?'

Kay paused. 'Do you need a light?' she asked.

'It's okay,' said Kamran. 'I'm cool.'

Lying down on the bed, Kay pulled him towards her. He fell on her, his face landing on her breasts. Taking a button between his teeth, he pulled. It snapped and her shirt opened. Nuzzling his face into her shirt, he took the cup of her bra between his lips and pulled it back. His nose brushed a nipple. He took it into his mouth with a ferocity that made Kay cry out. Kicking his shoes off, he clambered onto the bed, his mouth never leaving her nipple, his tongue licking, his teeth nipping, then biting. He lined his body up against hers and ground his crotch into her thighs. Kay's hands went around his head and pulled it further into her chest, flattening her breast, squeezing his nose till he grew breathless. She reached under him and tried to unbutton his shirt, but there was no space between their bodies. 'Wait,' she said, pushing against his chest. 'Get up.'

Naked, bent over the bed, Kay waited for him to find his way into her. The smooth head of his penis poked and slid along her wet vagina. His hands gripped her waist, his fingers clawing at her flesh. 'Fuck me,' she said. 'Fuck me.' She twisted and turned, trying to help him in. He reached down with his hand, one finger searching in the dark for the place the rest of him could enter. 'Come on,' she said. 'Fuck me.'

'I'm trying,' said Kamran, his rasping voice cutting through the rustling of clothes and the creaking of the bed. Finally he found the spot he was looking for and lunged forward to fill it.

'Oh god,' said Kay as he entered her, the feeling filling her with a release, like the first drag of a cigarette hurriedly lit outside the airport after a long flight.

As he began to move within her, she clenched her muscles around his penis, trying to pull it further and further in. He pulled out, then pushed in again, harder. Her body went slack, her elbows buckled.

Fragments of memory came unhinged from their moorings with every thrust: Slipping on her cheerleader's skirt before a practice, bikers riding down Thayer Street late in the Providence night, a sailboat out to sea, off the coast of Monterey on a sunny day, her third-grade teacher smiling at her in the schoolyard, Henry pushing his walker down the street. Her mind – escaping through a chink in the fence of sensation that encircled her body – ran free.

Later, lying in bed next to Kay, Kamran reached out and switched on the bedside lamp. An undulating pattern of light and shade brought the room into view. On a hook behind the door hung a pair of jeans, the back pocket frayed all the way through. Matthew, thought Kamran, Matthew's pants. He looked over to Kay. Her eyes were shut. She was breathing evenly. Her breasts – pale-skinned, pink-nippled, bruised red from his handling – rose and fell with each breath. Kamran reached out and caressed them. Kay turned onto her side, her back to him.

'You awake?' Kamran said.

'I think you should go now,' Kay said, not turning.

Kamran sat up, a feeling of dread pushing at his chest. 'Go?'

'Yes,' said Kay. 'Go. Leave.'

Getting out of bed, Kamran walked around to her side of the bed. 'Kay,' he said. 'What's wrong?'

'Nothing,' said Kay, her eyes shut. 'I want you to go away.'

'Hey, what happened?' said Kamran, touching her shoulder.

Kay flinched at his touch. Her eyes flicked open. She removed his hand, then sat up in bed.

'Kay, don't push me away,' Kamran said. His right thigh was shaking as he spoke.

'Look, Kamran,' said Kay, her voice – to Kamran's relief – losing something of the hard edge it had taken on, 'what's happened has happened. And it's not as if I dislike you as a person. But after this … you have to understand.'

'Understand what?' said Kamran, the softening of her tone allowing a righteous anger to develop within him. 'That you have been playing with me? Is that what you want me to understand?'

'I'm sorry,' said Kay. 'I shouldn't have. I am sorry. Really. But I want you to leave now. I can't handle your being here right now.'

Kamran turned away in disgust. He walked to where his pants lay and started pulling them on, mumbling and snorting all the while. When he had buttoned up, he turned to her again. 'Where was all this high and mighty shit when you dragged me in here?' he asked. 'You fucking threw yourself at me and now you're acting like somehow this is all my fault. I'm not the slut here, okay? You're the fucking slut who fucks around behind her husband's back.'

Kay stood up from the bed. Kamran stepped back, then stopped when he saw she wasn't coming towards him.

'Yes,' she said. 'I'm the slut who fucks around behind her husband's back. Who the fuck are you?'

'All your socks and underwear are on this shelf, and I have put all the shirts on hangers,' said Sunita, stepping back and surveying the open wardrobe. 'The heavy shirts are folded and kept on the topmost shelf. We can bring them down in winter and put them up there.'

'Okay,' said Jeevan, sitting on the bed.

'And now the other cupboard is empty, so there is enough space for my clothes. Some of my saris I'll leave in that room, but the ones I wear every day and my salwar kameezes and other things will easily fit here.'

'Okay,' said Jeevan.

'Now tell me,' said Sunita, shutting the wardrobe doors with a satisfied finality, 'which side of the bed do you sleep on?'

'Ummm,' said Jeevan, getting up from the bed that had unexpectedly come under discussion. 'Sometimes this side, sometimes that side.'

'Which side do you want to sleep on?' asked Sunita.

'I don't know,' said Jeevan, looking at the bed with new eyes.

'Okay, tell me,' said Sunita, 'do you go to the bathroom at night? How many times do you go?'

'Uhh, I, I, I mean, sometimes I go.'

'Then you sleep on this side,' said Sunita. 'It's closer to the door.'

Jeevan sat back on what was now his side of the bed. 'There is something I want to tell you,' he said.

'What?'

'Sit,' he said, patting the spot next to him.

Sunita sat down, her thigh touching his.

'This bed is quite big,' said Jeevan, smiling.

'Hmmpf,' said Sunita, shifting further towards him, her arm rubbing against his. 'What do you want to tell me?'

'It's about Miss Lucy's house,' said Jeevan. 'Henry told me that Shabbir bhai gave Miss Lucy's husband a loan. A loan he never repaid. The house was the surety for that loan. And now Shabbir wants to take the house.'

'Take the house?'

'Yes,' said Jeevan. 'He found out that he will get a better price if he sells all the houses on the block to the City. So he wants to take Miss Lucy's house.'

'So let him take it,' said Sunita. 'Rashida baji told me that Shabbir bhai has seen some houses in the county. She said that he has seen one for you and me which is large enough for Miss Lucy also.'

Jeevan turned sharply and looked at her.

Sunita met his gaze evenly, a quizzical look in her eyes. 'I can look after Miss Lucy,' she said. 'She pretends to be a fighter, but she is really a very soft and loving person.'

'She is,' said Jeevan, nodding.

'She is someone to you,' said Sunita, taking his hand. 'So she is someone to me. Looking after her is my duty.'

A troubled smile appeared on Jeevan's face. 'It is not that,' he said. 'I know you will look after her well, not just for my sake, but because ... because you will. But still, her house is her house. It should be her house.'

'But the City is going to take it from her anyway,' said

Sunita. 'What difference does it make if Shabbir bhai takes it from her first?'

'It makes a difference,' said Jeevan. 'The City is big, too big. But Shabbir bhai is not that big. He is just a man, he is not a whole city.'

Sunita stood up. Walking to the dresser, she straightened a comb, then looked up into the mirror. Behind her, she could see Jeevan looking at her. His deep-set eyes – kind, sad eyes – were fixed on her back. He has a broad forehead, she thought. His nose is funny, but that forehead is nice and broad. 'What do you want to do?' she asked.

His eyes met hers in the mirror. 'Repay the loan,' he said.

She turned and faced him. 'Repay the loan? How can you repay the loan? How much was the loan?'

'It was eight thousand dollars,' said Jeevan. 'At three per cent interest over twenty years, it amounts to fourteen thousand four hundred and forty-nine dollars.'

'Fourteen thousand dollars!'

'Yes,' said Jeevan.

'Where will you get fourteen thousand dollars?' asked Sunita.

'I have some money.'

'You have that much money?'

'I have never spent any money,' said Jeevan. 'I have never …' His head dropped, his hands came up to his forehead. 'I have never sent my parents any money.'

'Your parents? Your parents are alive?'

Jeevan nodded. The motion brought his face into his hands. He sat like that, his body bent, unmoving. Sunita went up to the bed, sat down next to him and ran her hand over his back.

'I'll take care of you,' said Jeevan, straightening up. 'Even if I give that money to Shabbir, I will make sure you have food to eat and clothes to wear.'

'I know you will,' said Sunita.

Jeevan turned towards her. On his face was an expression of undiluted gratitude, an expression that went straight through Sunita and made her feel like crying. He brought her face to his chest, his hands going around her head and pressing her to him. Sunita put her arms around him and squeezed his body to hers.

'Will he take the money?' asked Sunita when they parted.

'I don't know,' said Jeevan, running his hand over her hair. 'He has the deed to the property. If he refuses to give it, I don't know what we can do.'

'He has the property papers?'

'Yes, Mr Murray had to give them to him as surety.'

'But if you give him the money, why won't he give the papers?' asked Sunita.

'This is just fourteen, fifteen thousand dollars,' said Jeevan. 'The City will give him much more, more than two times the amount. Plus he will have the right to buy three properties in the new development. Fourteen thousand dollars is nothing compared to what he will make.'

'So he will just refuse to take the money from you.'

'Yes.'

'What if Miss Lucy gives him the money back?' asked Sunita.

'Maybe then he has to accept it,' said Jeevan. 'Maybe the law forces him to accept it. But even if it does, Miss Lucy will never take money from me and give it to him.'

'And she can't return the money herself?'

'No,' said Jeevan. 'Social security is all she has, and even with that sometimes it becomes difficult.'

'Shabbir bhai will not give that deed to you so easily,' said Sunita. 'He is a good man, but money is his weakness.'

'I know,' said Jeevan. 'But what can we do? We can only offer him the money and hope that his Allah tells him that he should take it.'

'Or,' said Sunita, forming her words slowly, 'we can take the deed without him knowing.'

'Without him knowing what?'

'Without him knowing we have taken it.'

'Steal it?' asked Jeevan.

Sunita's brow cleared. A broad, mischievous smile burst onto her lips. 'Why say it like that?' she said. 'It is Miss Lucy's house, so it is Miss Lucy's deed. That isn't stealing.'

Jeevan laughed, a lightness entering his chest. 'You are mad,' he said.

'And you of course are very sensible, happily giving fifteen thousand dollars to get back an old lady's house which the City will then take from her,' said Sunita.

'Okay, okay,' said Jeevan. 'But how can we steal it? I don't know where this deed is. I have searched through all the papers I have and some that Shabbir doesn't think I know about. I didn't find anything.'

Sunita stood up and put her hands on her hips. She tilted her face upward to a suitably heroic angle. 'Be it hidden at the bottom of the deepest ocean or on top of the highest mountain, your highness, your slave will find that wretched property deed and throw it at your feet, shackled and penitent.'

'Mad,' said Jeevan, laughing uncontrollably. 'You are completely mad.'

'You are forgetting, your highness,' said Sunita, her hands off her hips now, bending forward, her face inches from Jeevan's face, 'I have lived in Shabbir bhai's house. And I kept my eyes open while I was living there.'

'Six in the corner pocket,' said Matthew, pulling the cue stick back and taking aim.

'You'll never make that shot,' said Amy.

The stick glided forward and struck the white ball, sending it skidding, then rolling across the baize. It struck the six ball with a clean, soft sound and sent it gently towards the corner pocket.

'Stop ball, stop ball,' said Amy, putting her beer down and using the fingers of both her hands to transmit a hex. But the trajectory was true and the ball rolled silently to the edge of the pocket and dropped in.

'And now, the eight ball,' said Matthew, chalking his cue while calculating his angles on the table. 'In the side pocket.'

The room was buzzing with a late evening crowd. Big plaid-shirted men stood by the arcade games, holding their beers casually by their sides, like six-shooters out of their holsters. At the bar sat a mix of too large or too small women, their carefully applied makeup unable to mask the fact that they worked too hard for their money and drank too much for their own good. Between these populations swam shoals of proportionately built people, students from the university, casually dressed in anticipation of the affluence that would come later in life when they moved to some city like Boston or Boulder, making this place and the people stuck here a distant, charming memory.

'So,' said Amy, once the eight ball had been sunk and they were back in their booth nursing their beers, 'now tell me, what's your story?'

'Story, what story, there's no story,' said Matthew, energized by his successful turn at the pool table.

'Sure there's a story,' said Amy. 'Everyone has a story.'

'What do you want to know?' asked Matthew, bringing his beer to his mouth. It tasted cold and fresh, just right.

'Are you a grad student?'

'No.'

'Are you a professor?'

'No.'

'Why are you here then?'

'I love Jersey,' said Matthew, raising his bottle. 'Let's drink to Jersey.'

'To Jersey!' said Amy, clinking bottles with him.

'I used to be a grad student,' said Matthew. 'I told you that. At Brown. Peter Graham was my advisor.'

'But you didn't graduate?'

'Nope, didn't even get to the proposal.'

'Oh,' said Amy. 'I'm sorry.'

'Yeah,' said Matthew. 'Shit happens.'

'What do you do now?'

'I am a code-whore for a financial consultancy,' said Matthew.

'That's cool,' said Amy.

'It's cool for the big shots who come up with the financial

models,' said Matthew. 'The Ph.Ds. The rest of us are just programmers. We're called analysts. You know what they say, you can't spell analyst without spelling anal.'

'I didn't know they said that.'

'They probably don't,' said Matthew.

'You're funny.'

'Funny as in riding the short bus funny or funny as in ha ha funny?'

Amy laughed. 'Stop,' she said.

'And what's your story?' asked Matthew.

'Nothing much,' said Amy. 'It's my second year at Penn State. My advisor wants me to work in, like, randomized algorithms and expanders and other cool stuff, so I'm trying to get my graph theory and probability up to speed. There's some really super work on derandomizing random walks that I'm looking at. The idea is really cool, you start with a set of nodes ...'

'Please,' said Matthew, 'spare me.'

Leaning back from the table, Amy pursed her lips shut.

'That didn't come out right,' said Matthew. 'I'm sorry. Tell me, I really want to hear about this derandomization stuff.'

'Forget it.'

'I didn't mean to sound dismissive,' said Matthew. 'I shouldn't have said it that way.'

'Then why did you?'

'Look, I'm sorry,' said Matthew. 'It's just that I'm really confused right now. I'm not thinking right. Leaving grad school was hard for me, but there was no other option. It wasn't just that my time was running out, my confidence had already run out. So I left. But I guess it never really left me. A few weeks ago, I was wasting time on the Internet and I came across this paper solving a problem I had worked on. I started reading it, and I started thinking about it, and then I had some ideas and now I think maybe I can do it. Maybe it'll happen this time. But I have a good job, I have a life, so should I just quit all that and jump back into this thing? I don't know.'

'Wow,' said Amy. 'That's a hard call to make.'

'And it's so difficult to break back in,' said Matthew. 'I met Peter, my former advisor. He had come to Baltimore to give a talk. He doesn't take me seriously. In this business you have to be a star from day one, I guess. If you screw up once, you're always the screw-up. I mean, there are so many young guys throwing shit around like they were born with an advanced math degree. There's no time to catch up. There are the Indians, the Israelis, the East Europeans, they show up here fully made. I mean, good for them, and it's not just them, of course, there are our own natural born geniuses, and it's cool that they're so good, but it just means there are no second chances for people like me.'

'It's difficult,' said Amy. 'I went to the Grace Hopper conference, it's meant to help women computer scientists be, like, mentored and stuff. But it was all the senior women networking furiously with each other, and the rest of us just sat around watching.'

'Yeah,' said Matthew. 'Ambition, networking, doing what it takes to get ahead, totally cutting across gender. I can see that.'

'But you're going to try again?' asked Amy.

'I don't know,' said Matthew. 'I thought coming here would help make up my mind. But I'm still confused.'

Amy made as if to reach across the table, then retracted her hand. 'Maybe you just need to figure out what it is you want to be,' she said.

Matthew could see the sympathy in her eyes. He held her gaze for a moment, then looked down at his beer. 'You know, a funny thing happened to me once, when I was in grad school,' he said. 'There was this deck on the floor my office was on, and I was outside one day, smoking. I saw this plane, Continental or Delta or something, flying by, high up. It took a turn in the sky and the sun glinted off the edge of the wing. You know, the way it does in commercials for airlines. And suddenly I had a strong, strong urge to be one of those guys in a light blue shirt and black pants, sitting in an aisle seat, headphones on, with my laptop open on the tray table, a spreadsheet on the screen, the *Wall Street Journal* rolled up and stuffed into the seat pocket in front of me, flying out to Denver in the morning for a meeting, back by the evening flight. It totally took me by surprise. I'd never wanted to be one of those guys. I'd made fun of them all my life. I tried to shake off the feeling, but it stayed with me for days and days. And you know the funny thing?'

'What?'

'I'm one of those guys now.'

One look at Kay and Sunita hurriedly ushered her into the house and took her to the kitchen. She poured some tea into a mug and brought it to the table. Kay took a sip. 'It's nice,' she said, her sinuses opening with the steam rising from the hot liquid.

'Not too sweet?' asked Sunita.

'No,' said Kay, although it was much sweeter than anything she would make for herself. 'Is Jeevan home?'

'Yes,' said Sunita. 'He is upstairs. Should I call him?'

'No,' said Kay, her hand raised. 'No. Don't call him.'

'Okay,' said Sunita.

A light morning sun was entering the kitchen through the back door. In the yard, birds were making their way around the bushes, twittering and calling as they went.

'I'm a bad person,' said Kay, looking Sunita in the eye. 'I'm a bad, bad person.'

Sunita shifted her chair so that she was closer to Kay. 'What happened?'

'It's been happening for a long time,' said Kay. 'I don't know what to do about it, I don't know how to get out of it.'

Sunita put her hand on Kay's shoulder.

'It wasn't like this when I was in school,' said Kay. 'My mother forced me to become a cheerleader and there were always a lot of guys asking me out, but I wasn't interested in those kind of guys. I had a sweet boyfriend who was nice to me. He would borrow his dad's car and we would just drive up and down the highway, or hang out at the beach. We kissed, fooled around a little, he never asked for more.'

'Fooled around meaning?' asked Sunita.

'You know,' said Kay, waving her hand in the air, 'fooling around.'

'Oh,' said Sunita.

'Then in college I met this guy, another nice guy, Daniel,'

said Kay. 'We had a good time. He liked to party more than I did. I went along with it. We even lived together for a year after college. I started working as a pharmacist, he started an MBA program. Then he broke up with me. Nothing had happened, he just broke up with me one day. Actually, that's not true. I had seen it coming. I knew that he found me boring, although he was too nice a guy to say so. If you want to be a doctor, be a doctor, he used to say. Tell your mother to can it, and just go for it. I'll support you. But I never told my mother to can it and he left me.'

They heard the sound of footsteps coming down the stairs. Kay grew silent. Sunita got up.

'Hey Jeevan,' said Kay, when he finally reached the foot of the staircase.

'Kay?' said Jeevan. 'Hello.'

'Are you going to Eddie's now?' asked Sunita. 'We need milk. Also, the onions are finished and the laundry detergent.'

'Eddie's? Yes, yes, I am going to Eddie's. Have you asked Kay if she wants some tea? Oh, you already gave her tea. Okay, I'm going to Eddie's. What do we need?'

'Milk, onions and detergent,' said Sunita.

'Okay, okay,' said Jeevan. 'Bye, Kay.'

'See you later, Jeevan,' said Kay, and then, when the door had shut behind him, 'he's really sweet.'

'Yes,' said Sunita, smiling. She sat down and put her hand on Kay's forearm.

'I hadn't realized that I would take Daniel's leaving so hard,' said Kay. 'I was miserable. I didn't feel like doing anything. I missed days of work, just sat at home on the couch and watched TV till my head hurt. Then, one day, it struck me that I should leave California. I started driving. Called work from a payphone in Phoenix and told them I had quit. It was good, just driving east, not knowing where I was going to stop. But then, in Dallas, I stopped for the night at a motel and went to the bar that was next door in a strip mall. A guy started hitting on me, he was kind of funny looking, his hair was gelled back, his nose was pierced. I didn't pay much attention to him, but he was persistent and somehow by the end of the night, I guess I drank too much, I ended up going back to the motel with him.'

'To your room?'

'Yeah. And it was strange, really strange. I don't remember much of what happened, just that when the lights went out and he started, you know, doing it, I felt something that, I can't explain, just something that made me feel weightless – you understand weightless?'

'No,' said Sunita.

'Like I was floating. In the air.'

'You were floating in the air?'

'No,' said Kay, smiling. 'I just felt like that. In the morning, when I woke up, he was gone and I felt sick. My head was hurting, I felt like vomiting. I paid my bill and left, didn't even stop for coffee till lunch time.'

'Then what happened?' asked Sunita, her heart pounding with a sort of fear she hadn't felt before.

'I drove for a few days,' said Kay. 'Through the south, then up the coast. By the time I got to DC, it felt like I had shaken that feeling, that sickness. I stayed in some cheap hotel in DC. It had a bar. I knew I shouldn't go to the bar, but I went anyway. And again, it happened.'

'Again?'

'Yes,' said Kay. 'Again. And this time it was worse because I realized when I was lying there in the dark, with this guy whose face I can't even remember now, that I didn't want it. I stopped him, I told him to get off me and get out. I don't know how I got him out of the room.'

When Kay looked up, she saw Sunita's face was painted over with astonishment and disgust. 'I'm sorry,' she said. 'I shouldn't be telling you all this.'

'No,' said Sunita, rearranging her features with some effort. 'If you want to talk, you should talk.'

'Thank you,' said Kay, putting her hand over Sunita's.

'There's no need for thank you,' said Sunita. 'Do you want some more tea?'

Kay shook her head.

'When did you meet Matthew?' Sunita asked.

'I met him in Providence,' said Kay. 'That's where I stopped driving. I got a job as a waitress, just trying to figure out what I wanted to do with myself. He came in one day, then he came again and again, and we got to talking. Then we went out and, then, you know.'

'You got married?'

'Yes,' said Kay. 'He had his issues, he was struggling with grad school, he didn't know what he wanted to do. Then there was pressure on him to leave, so he took this job in Jersey and we moved there. In Jersey things went bad again.'

'Between Matthew and you?'

'No,' said Kay. 'For me. In Providence, Matthew was always around, even if he was moping or brooding, he was always around. In the new job, he started travelling a lot.

He'd be gone for two or three days at a time. They had an office in Houston that he would have to visit. Those days were awful for me. Not the days so much, because I'd got another job as a pharmacist, but the nights I was all alone. And after a few such trips, I started feeling like going out to a bar and hanging out. I didn't have any friends there, I just felt like going out on my own. Finally I did, once, then again. And each time, it ended the same way. Flat on my back in some sleazy hotel, my brains being fucked out by some random guy I had just met. And once, and once . . .' Her voice trembled. Sunita pressed down on her hand.

'Something really terrible happened, so terrible that I can't even bring myself to say it,' said Kay. 'I knew it would devastate Matthew, so I didn't tell him. Instead I told him about my two other encounters. I thought he would leave me, that he would be mad and he would throw me out or leave himself.'

'But he didn't,' said Sunita.

'He didn't. He was angry and hurt. He shouted and he cried and he didn't talk to me for a week. But then, when he did talk, he said he wanted us to try harder, he wanted us to make it work. He suggested we go into counseling and we even did that for a few months.'

'He is a good man,' said Sunita.

'He is,' said Kay, and as she said it, she felt her insides cave in and her head fell forward into her hands. 'He's such a good man, and I am so bad, so, so bad.'

'You are a good person too,' said Sunita, putting her arm around Kay. 'You are not a bad person.'

Kay wept till her tears stopped, then raised her head and looked at Sunita. 'Thanks,' she said.

'I'm also with a man who is not my husband,' said Sunita, with a solemnity that made Kay smile.

'This one is your real husband,' said Kay, taking Sunita's hand. 'This one is for real.'

Sunita blushed.

Kay let go of her hand and stood. 'Thanks for listening to me,' she said, walking to the door. 'I really needed that.'

'You can talk to me whenever you want to,' said Sunita. Just as Kay was opening the door, a thought struck Sunita. 'Kay,' she said, 'everything you told me happened long ago. Why are you unhappy about it today? Did something happen?'

'Yes,' said Kay, a tightness reclaiming her head. 'I slept with Kamran last night.'

The train swayed and jostled its way through Elizabeth, onward to Linden. Rahway, Metropark, Metuchen, Matthew said to himself a moment before the static crackle repeated the names, adding a few more to the list. Clearing the battered hutments of Elizabeth, the train picked up speed, pulling hard through the New Jersey plain. The houses became a little better kept, their yards a little larger.

It could have been that one, thought Matthew, spotting a grey slate roof some distance from the tracks. That could have been where we lived. It had a deck in the back, just like the house they had lived in. A deck just like the one where Kay had told him that she had cheated on him. He tried now to remember how he had felt that night, but all he could recall was that it was a very clear night, there were so many stars in the sky that he had stood outside with the light off to see them all clearly. He had been standing there looking up when she came home, he hadn't even heard her till she was outside. What exactly did she say? Was it 'I have something to tell you', or was it 'Baby, we need to talk'? What did he say?

A train passed by on the next track, a shock of compressed air followed by a rhythmic whooshing. Across the aisle, a young mother pointed to the window and her son took off his New York Yankees cap and waved it at the passing train. Matthew leaned back to give the boy a better view, but the train was gone even before his head hit the back of the seat.

Amy was nice, he thought. She understood what he was going through, what he had been through. But he shouldn't have gone back to her room with her. At first he had thought he would just walk her back to the hotel, then go to bed. But he didn't press the button for his floor in the elevator, and she hadn't asked which floor he was on. Another chance to leave came outside her door, but she had been saying something as she opened the door and he followed her in because he didn't want to interrupt. No, it wasn't that. He could have interrupted her. He could have said, Actually, I'm married, I should go to my own room now. But he hadn't.

Outside the window, a complex ringed with barbed wire loomed, big white domed cylinders its centerpiece, thick pipes running around the cylinders. On one side was a building that looked like an office. A wreath hung outside the door, dotted with red – ribbons, probably. Two cars,

Japanese imports whose numerous bumper stickers couldn't be read from this distance, stood outside the building.

But so what if he had gone into Amy's room? Nothing had happened. Nothing as bad as what Kay had done when they were in Jersey. The comparison startled him. He had never thought of what Kay had done as something that could be set right by revenge. She had betrayed him, she had hurt him. She had been a selfish bitch. He had been angry, and she had deserved his anger. But it was not like him to think of paying her back in the same way. You've been with me through a lot of shit, he had told her when his anger had subsided, I know you love me. We can get through this. That's what he had said. And that's how he had felt. It was Jersey, lonely suburban Jersey, the boredom of her job that had driven her to it. And that's why, when the opportunity at Hopkins came her way, he had jumped at the idea. The shit he did in Jersey, he could do in Baltimore. It wasn't easy to find a job in Baltimore, but finally one had come up. It involved a pay cut and a profile he didn't really care for, but that was a small price to pay to make Kay happy. He had felt like he was doing the right thing by her, he was behaving in the way a real man should. Deal with the hurt, work on the marriage. Then why had that thought come, not just here in the train but even last night, standing outside Amy's room in the hotel: this is not half as bad as what Kay did.

And then, inside Amy's room, first grappling with her and pulling at her clothes, then pushing her onto the bed, he realized he wasn't getting hard. She tried, pulling his penis out, taking it in her mouth, rubbing her breasts in his face, but nothing worked. I can go down on you, he had said. No, forget it, she had said. It's okay, it happens. It happens to all men. But why was it happening? He could see she was attractive, he liked her as a person. And he was turned on, he wanted her, he wanted to want her. But his penis – did it know more about him than he knew about himself? – refused to come alive. The strange thing was that when they finally settled into bed, he didn't feel inadequate or unmanly; he was only relieved at not having to fuck her.

The soothing motion of the train lulled Matthew to sleep. In his dreams he saw himself at home, in his bedroom on 26th Street, naked with Kay in bed, the afternoon streaming in through the window. Waking with a start in Philadelphia's 33rd Street Station, he realized that he and Kay had not slept together once since moving to Baltimore. And he realized, shifting in his seat, that he had a hard, throbbing erection.

Late at night, on the corner of Calvert and 25th Street, a group of women are laughing and calling to each other and to people in cars passing by. Two of them cross the street, balanced precariously on six inches of heels, their shorts very short, their handbags swinging as they walk. Behind them on a stoop, another girl cups her breasts and pushes them up, looking down as she makes the adjustments. She straightens her shoulders, then wipes sweat down a line that starts on her neck and goes through her cleavage, down to her solar plexus. Cars swish by on Calvert Street, occasionally slowing as they pass, then speeding up and moving on.

The light changes and the cars back up three deep. Winding

her way to a silver Chevy, one of the girls bends deep at the driver's window. Words are exchanged. Her head moves from side to side as she speaks, her eyebrows bouncing. She digs her tongue into her cheek and pokes it outward repeatedly, lifting one hand off the car and bringing it to her mouth in a half-made fist. The driver-side window glides up, pushing her fingers off, leaving her staring at her own reflection in the darkened glass.

Further up Calvert Street, a four-by-four is idling in a side alley, its lights down. A plump woman in a dark skirt is standing beside it, on the passenger side, her leopard-skin patterned top pulled tight against her large drooping breasts. Her nipples are cutting a pattern into the front of the top. She nods her head in response to something conveyed from within the car and turns and walks in front of it. Her back to the windscreen, she bends down and begins to lift her skirt. The headlights come on, turning their harsh glare on what she is displaying. Then they blink down. She turns and looks through the windscreen, then bows her head and walks to the passenger door. It is being held open for her.

8

WHEN THEY ENTERED THE ALLEY THAT LED BACK TO 26TH street, Jeevan and Sunita heard the organ playing in the distance. Its jerky, discordant notes made Jeevan's heart race. His step quickened.

'It's a nice house,' Sunita said. 'And the lawn in the back is much bigger than ours. We can grow vegetables in it.'

'Yes, yes,' said Jeevan, striding harder.

'What happened?' Sunita asked, struggling to keep pace.

'I don't know,' said Jeevan. 'But something has happened.'

When they turned the corner – the organ louder and harsher as they got to the block – they saw Kay sitting on her stoop with her face in her hands. Henry stood near her, wagging a finger at Oscar, who was yowling with his head in the air. As they got nearer, Jeevan saw that Henry had a rapidly darkening bruise under one eye.

'What happened?' asked Jeevan.

'Where the hell were you?' Henry's voice was hoarse. 'Oscar, will you shut it now.'

'We had gone to see the house Shabbir bhai wants to buy for us,' said Sunita, cupping her mouth and yelling to be heard over the organ. 'Rashida baji took us there.'

'What happened?' asked Jeevan again.

Henry pointed up at the house.

Jeevan and Sunita turned to look. 'What is it, Henry?' Jeevan asked.

'Are you blind, Jeevan?' Henry shouted.

'The trains,' said Jeevan. 'Where are the trains?'

'They're gone,' said Kay, her voice cracking, her body shaking. 'The bastards scraped them off.'

There were traces of rubble on the sidewalk, Jeevan noticed now. He looked beyond Kay at her house and saw that the grille was gone, the white wood door stood exposed and ugly. He ran up the stoop and saw that the decorations above and below the windows had been covered with tiles. Picking at the edge of one of the tiles, he tried to pull it off, but the plaster had begun to set and it did not move.

'It's no use, Jeevan,' yelled Henry. 'They've filed away the engravings.'

Jeevan looked over to his house. He sprinted down the stairs.

'Forget it,' said Henry. 'They're all gone.'

The organ fell silent. Oscar was quiet too, sitting on his haunches and contemplating Kay, who was bent over again, her head on her knees.

'Who did this?' asked Jeevan.

'Who do you think did it?' snorted Henry.

'Shabbir?'

'When I came round the corner, I saw the men working,'

said Henry. 'Shabbir was standing there with them. When he saw me, he turned and walked away. I called out to him but he didn't turn, just hotfooted it down the alley.'

'That is why he didn't come with us,' said Sunita. 'Rashida baji said he had some work so he couldn't come.'

'He's a clever one, isn't he?' said Henry.

'And how did you get this?' asked Jeevan, pointing to the bruise below Henry's eye.

'Yessir,' said Henry. 'How did I get this? I got to thinking I could take on one of Shabbir's hired guns. I got a little crazy. Ten years ago I would have taken that no-good sonofabitch. But this walker slowed me down and he got one in before I could.'

'Did you put some medicine on it?' asked Sunita.

'Don't worry your head about it,' said Henry. 'Henry's seen worse.'

'But why did Shabbir bhai do this?' asked Sunita, turning to Jeevan.

'They were hoping to save this block from demolition by saying it is historic,' said Jeevan, indicating Kay with his hand. 'But now the evidence of it being historic is gone.'

'They?'

'Kamran and I,' said Kay, raising her head. 'What a stupid idea. What a stupid, stupid thing to want.'

Sunita sat down on the stoop next to Kay and put one arm around her. Kay turned towards her, another fit of weeping racking her body.

'I didn't know anything about this,' said Sunita. 'Rashida baji didn't tell me anything. How did Shabbir bhai find out about it?'

'Kamran must have told him,' said Jeevan. 'No one else would have told him.'

'What a fool,' said Henry. 'Where is he, anyway?'

'He went back to New York yesterday,' said Sunita quietly, tightening her grip on Kay's shoulders. 'Rashida baji told me.'

Kay raised her head. 'He told Shabbir on purpose,' she said, removing Sunita's hand. 'That fucking loser went running to his dad and told him on purpose so that he could ruin our plans.'

'Why would he do that?' asked Henry. 'Wasn't he the one who did the legwork for all this in the first place?'

Sunita looked away. Jeevan met Henry's questioning look with an impassive, inscrutable face.

'Are you folks hiding something from me?' asked Henry.

'I fucked him,' said Kay, the anger falling out of her voice. 'I fucked him and told him to leave. That's why he told Shabbir.'

The organ started up again, a slow, beautiful progression of notes, each one held down as if by heavy fingers. The sonorous music expanded outwards from Miss Lucy's house and, untrameled by the walls of a church, it spread beyond the street, beyond the block, beyond the tracks, covering everyone and everything it met like a thick mist descending on the city.

'It's a beautiful song,' said Sunita.

'Swing low, sweet chariot,' said Henry. 'Coming for to carry me home.'

'What does it mean?'

'It's a prayer,' said Jeevan. 'She is asking God's vehicle to come closer to the earth and carry her and take her home.'

'To her real home,' said Sunita, pointing upward.

'Yes,' said Jeevan.

'This fake home is gone,' said Kay, standing up. 'Where else will she go?'

'She will stay with us,' said Sunita. 'Shabbir bhai has found us a nice house in Pikesville. It has a big bedroom on the ground floor. Miss Lucy and her organ can both live there comfortably. We will look after her.'

Kay smiled. She squeezed Sunita's arm. 'I'm sure you will,' she said.

'That Mary Symcox showed me a couple of places up on Harford Road,' said Henry. 'Decent places.'

'Did Oscar like them?' asked Jeevan, going down on his haunches and taking the dog's ears in his hands.

A slow smile spread across Henry's face. 'Sharma, you don't miss a thing, do you?' he said. 'Oscar refused to go into either one of them. Lord knows how this dumb beast knew.'

Oscar licked Jeevan's face lovingly. Jeevan rested his head on the dog's head. His eyes closed for a moment, then he opened them and stood up again. 'He will go when the time comes,' he said.

'He will go,' said Henry. 'He's a good dog.'

'And where will I go?' asked Kay, her voice thick and anguished.

Jeevan, Sunita and Henry turned to look at her. Eyes red, her hair ragged, she stood there – the late afternoon sun shining dully off the red brick of the block – waiting for an answer.

'Hey there, people,' a voice called from down the street.

233

Matthew was walking towards them, his bookbag slung over his shoulder, waving at them.

Jeevan waved back at him. Matthew opened his hands in question. His mouth formed some words but they were lost in the music. Jeevan saw him glance up as he walked, then stop in his tracks, his cheery expression dissolving in an instant. He broke into a run, heading towards them.

'The trains,' he said, as he reached them. 'What happened to the trains?'

Henry took hold of his walker and started turning around. 'Come on, Oscar,' he said. 'Time to go home.'

'Is there a game today?' asked Jeevan.

'Yeah,' said Henry, bending down to pick up Oscar's leash. 'Got to feed this boy before it starts.'

'Is Cal playing?'

'He better,' said Henry, his back to them now, slowly moving up the street. 'Today of all days, he better be playing.'

Kay flopped down on the sofa, her head back, her eyes open wide and looking at the ceiling. Matthew put his bag away and came and sat next to her. 'You okay?' he asked.

'No,' she said.

'Do you want coffee?'

'No,' she said. 'But you get yours.'

'I'll just be back,' said Matthew, getting up.

When he returned to the living room, Kay was still sitting with her head back. A single tear rolled down her right cheek. Matthew went up to her, put his coffee down on the table, and took her hand. 'Baby,' he said, 'talk to me.'

'There's nothing to talk about,' she said. 'It's over.'

'Come on, Kay,' said Matthew. 'It was always a long shot. I mean, even if this hadn't happened, it's complicated trying to get a property designated historic. There are so many things that have to be in place. Like a hundred different things that are not in your control.'

'I guess,' said Kay.

'And you tried your best,' said Matthew. 'You and Kamran really got to the bottom of it. That's worth something.'

'But we couldn't save Miss Lucy's house,' said Kay.

'You tried,' said Matthew. 'You tried really hard for something that wouldn't benefit you any. Who does that? I'm really proud of you for even trying.'

Kay turned her face towards him and smiled weakly. 'Matt,' she said, 'you're so good to me, Matt.'

'The City's giving these people a good deal,' said Matthew. 'It really is. Miss Lucy will get a good house, they'll help her. I know they shouldn't be taking her house in the first place, but for all that, what they're giving in return will be good.'

'Sunita said that Shabbir has found her and Jeevan a house,' said Kay. 'They have enough space for Miss Lucy. And the organ. Sunita said she'll look after Miss Lucy.'

'She will,' said Matthew. 'They're good people. And Jeevan loves Miss Lucy like she's his mother.'

'Sunita said Miss Lucy is the mother-in-law she never had,' said Kay, a smile breaking through her gloom, a quick spasm of laughter, almost a cough, erupting from her chest.

'They're something else, those two,' said Matthew. 'It's really cool.'

Kay sat up and put her arms around Matthew. He brought

his mouth to hers and kissed her lips gently. Her mouth fell open and he moved further in, taking her lower lip between his lips and mashing down on it.

'It's odd though,' said Matthew, when they separated. 'Didn't Kamran know that Shabbir was going to do this? And if he did, why didn't he try to stop him? Where is Kamran, anyway?'

It felt like he had thrown a bucket of cold water in Kay's face. Her shoulders sagged. Something seemed to be clutching at and releasing the inside of her stomach. She stood up, a little unsteady, and walked across the room. 'There's something I have to tell you,' she said.

Matthew rose slowly to his feet. He knew what was coming, his intuition had been telling him what Kay was about to tell him for days now. He had tried to ready himself for the moment that he knew was upon him, but he had known even then that there was no way of preparing for it. He hadn't been prepared the first time it had happened, and he had thought that was because he had been taken by surprise. But now he knew that surprise was the least of it, there was no way of preparing for this. 'You slept with Kamran,' he said.

'I'm so sorry, Matt,' she said. 'I'm so, so sorry.'

'While I was in Jersey,' said Matthew, sitting down again.

'Yes,' said Kay. 'But just once. And I told him it would never happen again. That's why he went away. That's why he told Shabbir. That's why all this happened. It's all my fault, it's all my fucking fault.'

Tears rolled down her face as she spoke. She reached out to support herself and her hand fell on Matthew's bookbag.

When she turned and saw what it was she had touched, it felt like the pain would wash her away. She put both hands on the bag, then bent her head over it and wept. 'Oh Matt,' she said, over and over. 'I'm so sorry, Matt.'

Matthew came over to where she stood and ran his hand over her back. 'Kay,' he said. 'It's okay, Kay. Look at me. Listen to me.'

She looked up at him.

'Come here,' he said, leading her towards the couch. 'Sit down.'

Sitting next to her, he took both her hands in his. 'Baby,' he said, 'it's okay. If you have some kind of problem, we can work on it, we can go and see someone, you can get some help.'

'This isn't just my problem,' she said, anger rising within her.

'You're right,' he said. 'Totally. We can go together, we can see a marriage counselor of some sort. They know how these things work. They can help us.'

'I don't think anyone can help us, Matt,' said Kay.

Matthew let go of her hands. He sat back. 'I know it's happened like three times now,' he said. 'And I know it can happen again. But I want to fight this fight. It's like a medical problem, we can work on it.'

'I can't hurt you like this again and again,' said Kay. 'I can't, I just can't.'

'Listen to me,' said Matthew. 'If I'm the one getting hurt here, shouldn't what I'm saying count for something? We can do this together. I can get over this.'

'But I can't,' said Kay.

Matthew's mind was racing now with anxiety. Somewhere within him he knew that she was right, it was probably better to end it here. The thought of endless rounds of counseling – the darkness and frustration it would bring, the hours spent in rooms whose cheeriness somehow made them seem all the more depressing – daunted him. But, on the other side, there was a deep dark cavern and he couldn't turn his head and look into it.

'What can I do?' said Matthew. 'Tell me what I can do.'

'There's nothing you can do,' said Kay.

'Is it this Ph.D thing?' asked Matthew. 'Forget about it. It's a pie in the sky anyway. I'll totally forget about it. I can, I know I can. I've got a job, I make good money. And, more than all that, I've got you. That's all I need. What more do I need?'

Kay shook her head.

'And look,' said Matthew. 'We're here, you're at Hopkins. You're already taking organic chemistry. A few more classes and you're good for med school. Wherever you want to go, wherever they take you, I'll be totally cool with moving. I mean, I can find a job, I can pay the tuition. I make enough for that. You won't have to take a loan. And I'll be with you.'

'No, Matt,' said Kay, standing up. 'It's over. It really is. We had our chance.'

'You mean, I had my chance,' said Matthew. 'And I screwed up my chance. I really did screw it up, didn't I? Always traveling. Living in my head when I was with you. Obsessed with this bullshit research stuff. I did screw it up, Kay. But I know I did. I know now. I know what's worth something and what's worth shit. I need one more chance. Can't you give me one more chance?'

'You remember the time Joshua visited us in Jersey?' asked Kay. 'A couple of weeks before I told you the first time about, about ...'

'Yes,' said Matthew, standing up now. 'What about it?'

'You remember you came back from Denver the day after he arrived?'

'Yes,' said Matthew. 'I remember he was saying, forget about grad school, make it in the consulting business. He's so full of shit.'

'That night when you were in Denver,' said Kay, 'something happened.'

'What?'

'Joshua and I ...'

Matthew took a step back. The sofa hit him in the calf and he sat down with a bump. He got up with an effort, pushing down on the couch with both hands and, without another look at Kay, turned and left the room.

Shabbir was sitting behind the counter, running a pencil over an open ledger, when Jeevan entered Food Point. The tables were empty, their chairs tucked in neatly. The Urdu papers sat carefully stacked on a table, next to an inverted pillar of Styrofoam glasses. Through the open windows, the last of the evening's light suffused the room. From the kitchen, an aroma of cooking streamed out. Jeevan's stomach gurgled at the smell. 'Assalaam aleikum, Shabbir bhai,' he said.

'Waleikum assalaam, Jeevan,' said Shabbir, pointing to a table with his left hand. 'Sit. I'll just come.'

As Jeevan waited, a feeling of calm descended on him, dispelling the agitation that had accompanied him on the way over. He touched his right pocket and was reassured by the crackle of paper, the folded sheet he had put in there. Behind the counter, Shabbir was engrossed in what he was doing. Jeevan looked at him. Shabbir's hair was greyer than when they had first met, his face a little more pockmarked. Some more of the tightness had gone out of his skin. And, despite what he had come to do, Jeevan felt something like love for this man he had known for so long, this man who had taken him in – perhaps out of self-interest – and given him a job and a house, something like a family and, of course, Sunita. But could it really be called giving? Didn't Shabbir have to own all those things to be able to give them? He owned the house, perhaps, though the City was going to take that from him. But the other things, could he claim to own them, or even control them? What does it mean to own, to own in such a way that when you give, it can be called giving?

'Now tell me, Jeevan bhai,' said Shabbir, putting the pencil down and standing up. 'What is the news?'

'I saw what happened,' said Jeevan.

'What happened?'

'To the houses,' said Jeevan. 'I saw what you did.'

'They're looking better now, aren't they?' said Shabbir, sitting down across the table from Jeevan. 'Did you see the new tiling around the windows? Absolutely top class. I told Wicentowski to use the best tiles. That useless fellow sometimes says something and does something else.'

The sound of onions splashing into hot oil came around the corner, followed by the agitated sizzle of frying. Jeevan's nose twitched as the sharp odor entered it. 'I know why you did it, Shabbir bhai,' he said.

'Of course,' said Shabbir. 'All that old, blackened stuff was making the whole block look bad. Now it looks much better. We can claim a better valuation.'

'You knew they were planning to ask the State to make it a historic block,' said Jeevan. 'You knew you wouldn't get any compensation if that happened.'

Shabbir laughed. 'Okay, okay,' he said. 'I knew. Kamran told me what they were up to. That boy is young, he doesn't think. And he is stubborn, like his father. So, I thought, let us get rid of the problem before it becomes too big. Once the State gets involved, it becomes difficult. You remember what Shahzaib bhai went through in Washington.'

'Yes,' said Jeevan. 'I remember.'

'If there is no bamboo,' said Shabbir, 'no one can play the flute.'

'But what about the history?' said Jeevan. 'That block had historic value.'

'Arre, let it be, Jeevan bhai,' said Shabbir. 'What history? Whose history? If this history was so important, why was it rotting here for so many years? This is not your history or my history. Our history is that we came to this country and we worked hard and fed our families. That is our history. And that history is safe with me. What nonsense people talk! History! Useless.'

'Just because they don't care for it,' said Jeevan, 'that doesn't make this history useless.'

The door swung open and a short African man wearing a

Cleveland Indians cap came in. 'Assalaam aleikum,' he called. 'Anything to eat here for a hungry man?'

'In half an hour, Amadou,' said Shabbir. 'The cooking is not over yet.'

'Come on, Shabbir man,' said Amadou, taking his cap off and sitting down at the table with him. 'There must be something. Sharma, you tell him.'

'Okay, wait,' said Shabbir, getting up. He went into the kitchen and came out a few minutes later with a bowl of curry and some rice. 'Here,' he said. 'Eat.'

'Thanks, Shabbir,' said Amadou, drawing the tray towards himself and digging in without further discussion.

'We can talk later,' said Shabbir to Jeevan in Urdu.

'I think we should talk now,' said Jeevan.

'What is there to talk about?' asked Shabbir.

'You guys talking about me?' asked Amadou, his lips stained yellow, a grain of rice sticking to one of them.

'No, no,' said Shabbir. Then, in Urdu, he said: 'Okay, come inside.'

It was a small crowded room past the kitchen, with a framed photo of Rashida holding baby Kamran on one wall and a poster-sized illustration of the holy Ka'aba in Mecca on another. Shabbir had put a desk in the middle, behind which sat a metal safe with its key in the lock. He went and sat behind his desk. Jeevan took the chair in front, his usual place.

'What are you worried about, Jeevan?' asked Shabbir. 'You and Sunita are taken care of. You saw the house in Pikesville, didn't you? Isn't it big enough for you?'

'It is.'

'And your precious Miss Lucy,' said Shabbir. 'Did you see the room downstairs? She can live the rest of her days there in peace. What is the problem? Your Sunita will look after her, you are also there. And we will also be there, next door. It is much better than this prison. Don't you agree?'

'Yes,' said Jeevan.

'Then what is there to talk about?' asked Shabbir.

'I want to repay the loan,' said Jeevan.

'Which loan?'

'The loan Mr Murray took from you.'

Shabbir's brow knitted in puzzlement. Then it cleared, and he chuckled. 'Arre Sharma, yaar,' he said. 'You are too much. Repay the black man's loan. You have gone mad.'

'With interest it comes to fourteen thousand four hundred and forty-nine dollars,' said Jeevan. 'I calculated it at three per cent for twenty years.'

'And where will you get these fourteen thousand dollars?' asked Shabbir, smiling.

'I have some money,' said Jeevan.

'Have you talked to Sunita about this?'

'Yes.'

'Okay,' said Shabbir. 'Suppose I take your fourteen thousand dollars, do you know how much I will lose?'

'No,' said Jeevan.

'Firstly, I lose the payment for the house, maybe twenty thousand dollars,' said Shabbir. 'Then I lose the extra compensation for selling an entire block, that will be about ten thousand dollars. So, that's thirty minus your fourteen. I lose sixteen thousand dollars just now. Then, later, I will not be allowed to buy a house in exchange for that house in the new development. In fact, if I sell a whole block, I might be able to buy a whole commercial strip later. The rent for that, the value of that, can you imagine what it will be? My wife stands in front of a stove all day in a hot kitchen so that we can eat, and so that my son can have a future. Will your fourteen thousand dollars bring her out of that kitchen?'

As if on cue, Rashida entered. 'Jeevan bhai,' she said. 'When did you come?'

'Go back to the kitchen,' said Shabbir.

'Why?' said Rashida, putting her hands on her hips.

'Just go,' said Shabbir, and his voice held such a threat that Rashida turned on her heels and left. 'Keep your fourteen thousand dollars,' he said, turning back to Jeevan. 'I'm not taking it.'

'You have to,' said Jeevan, reaching into his pocket and bringing out a folded piece of paper. He unfolded it and handed it across the table to Shabbir.

Shabbir picked up his reading glasses and put them on. He peered down at the paper, then stood up. 'This is a Xerox,' he said.

'I have the original,' said Jeevan.

Shabbir turned and opened the safe. He reached into the lower shelf and pulled out a bunch of papers. Rifling through them, he brought out a folder. It was empty. 'You bastard,' he said, throwing the folder across the room.

Jeevan stood up. Shabbir came around the desk and grabbed Jeevan by the throat. He pushed him back against the wall. Jeevan's head hit a corner of the framed photograph. A stinging pain ran along his scalp.

'You thief,' said Shabbir, pushing his fist up Jeevan's jaw.

'I fed you and clothed you, you snake. Is this how you repay me?'

Jeevan's neck was hurting in Shabbir's grip. His breath was running short. But he didn't say anything. He could see the anger streaking Shabbir's eyes red. But he felt no fear. Instead, he felt a kind of release. He felt ready for whatever was to come.

'I trusted you,' said Shabbir, tightening his grip.

'She is an old woman,' said Jeevan, his gasping, halting voice still laced with an unnatural calm. 'This house is all she has.'

'I knew you would bite me one day,' said Shabbir. He held on to Jeevan's neck with one hand and slapped him with the other. Then he slapped him again, and again.

'That widow's husband took you home,' said Jeevan, forming his words between blows. 'He told her to feed you.'

'So what should I do?' shouted Shabbir, nursing the hand he had been hitting Jeevan with. 'Keep thanking her all my life?'

'All thanks are due to Allah,' said Jeevan in Arabic. 'The lord of everything, the generous, the merciful.'

Shabbir's grip went loose. He looked left and right, confused, like he was looking for something. Then he turned and went back to his desk. He sat down on his chair, his face in his hands. Jeevan stood with his back to the wall.

'I have organized all your business papers, the ones I had,' said Jeevan. 'They are packed properly. I have put notes on each file explaining what the papers are for and what further action is needed.'

Shabbir looked up at Jeevan. He looked like a boy trying to follow a lesson he did not understand.

'Sunita has packed her clothes,' said Jeevan. 'And my things are also ready. We can leave first thing tomorrow morning. Or even tonight if you want.'

'Where will you go?' asked Shabbir.

'I don't know,' said Jeevan. 'But I will inform you when I know my address. If there is any problem in any of the papers, you, or whoever else, can contact me.'

Shabbir nodded.

'And Shabbir bhai,' said Jeevan. 'I will never mention anything I have seen in your papers to anyone.'

Standing up, Shabbir turned to the poster of Mecca on the wall. He looked at it for a while, then he reached out with his right hand and touched one corner. Bowing his head, he repeated the prayer. Then he turned and came out from behind the desk and stood in front of Jeevan, his hands slack by his side.

'Jeevan bhai,' he said, his voice quivering as he spoke. 'Unpack the papers you have packed. And unpack your clothes.'

By the time Jeevan returned home, night had fallen. Matthew was sitting on his stoop, backpack on his shoulders, two suitcases lined up on the sidewalk below him. He was hunched over, looking down at the bags, and slowly, repeatedly, bringing a lit cigarette to his lips. Jeevan stopped in front of his own stoop, but before he could decide whether to go up or not, Matthew had turned and seen him.

'Hello,' said Jeevan, walking up to Matthew.

'Hey Jeevan,' said Matthew.

Jeevan looked at the suitcases and the backpack. There was another, narrower bag standing on its side at the top of the stairs, probably a laptop.

'You are going for a long time,' Jeevan said.

'Yeah,' said Matthew.

Jeevan nodded. 'Where will you go?' he asked.

'I was thinking Providence,' said Matthew.

'Do you know people there?' asked Jeevan.

'Some,' said Matthew. 'I used to be in grad school there.'

'Okay,' said Jeevan. 'By train?'

'Yes,' said Matthew. 'I hate flying.'

'Will there be a train at this time?' asked Jeevan.

'Maybe the last one,' said Matthew.

'If you miss it, you can stay at my house tonight,' said Jeevan.

Matthew looked up at Jeevan. He knows, thought Matthew. I wonder how long he has known. 'Thanks,' he said.

'No problem,' said Jeevan.

'You know,' said Matthew, 'I know I've been here only a few weeks, but, you know, I really liked it here.'

'It's a nice place,' said Jeevan.

'It is,' said Matthew. 'I was sitting here thinking I'd like to come back here someday and see you and Henry and Miss Lucy. But then …'

'This place will not be here in a few months' time,' said Jeevan.

'And all of you will be in all the places you'll be in,' said Matthew.

'Yes,' said Jeevan, smiling. 'We will.'

Matthew smiled too. 'I guess this is really a going away, then,' he said. 'A real real going away.'

A yellow taxi turned the corner from Howard Street and cruised slowly towards them. The driver leaned out the window, trying to read the house numbers.

'Here,' hailed Matthew, rising from the stoop.

'You called a cab, man?' asked the driver. 'Penn Station?'

'Yes,' said Matthew, slinging the laptop bag onto his shoulder.

'Hey Sharma,' said the cabbie, spotting Jeevan. 'What're you doing here, man?'

'I live here,' said Jeevan.

The driver and Jeevan helped Matthew load his luggage into the boot. When it was loaded, Matthew turned to Jeevan, made as if he were going to hug him, then put his hand out. Jeevan shook his hand and stepped back onto the sidewalk. He stood there watching as the cab slowly made its way down 26th Street and turned right onto Maryland Avenue, on its way downtown.

Sunita slipped her hand into Jeevan's as they walked down the street. A breeze started blowing, and up in the blue sky clouds moved in their stately way, exposing the sun, its rays bending around their puffy white edges and forming cones of light that shone down on the city like a benediction. Away to the south, the land sank downward and then, across the river, rose upward again to Bolton Hill, the very top of which was marked by the gentle round dome of a place of worship. Jeevan pointed to it and Sunita drew in her breath at the sight, seen every day and every day as beautiful as it was today.

They turned the corner onto Howard Street and walked a block, passing a parking lot half full of Bell Atlantic vans, antennas mounted atop them, resting between jobs, or perhaps retired and awaiting their destiny. Further away, the car wash was empty. Puddles of sudsy water lay on the floor; a curtain of rubber flaps sat idle, suspended from the ceiling. The drive-in's driveway was vacant, its red microphone mounted at an angle, awaiting the orders of customers who were yet to arrive. Outside the body shop, a display of casually piled-up tires took the sun at an angle that made them seem superannuated and tired. Sunita swung her arm as she walked, taking Jeevan's hand with hers. Jeevan smiled.

At the gas station, Sunita paused. 'The milk is finished,' she said. 'Shall I get it from here?'

'Okay,' said Jeevan, disengaging his hand from hers.

She went into the convenience store. Jeevan stood with his back to the door, looking out at the gas pumps and the street beyond them.

A car turned off Howard Street and pulled up into the gas station. A tall man in a white T-shirt and a baseball cap got out and walked around to the pump. There was something familiar about him. Jeevan's eyes scrunched up as he tried to catch a glimpse of the man's face. The man swiped his credit card and, when he turned to put the nozzle into his car, Jeevan saw his face. Is it him? thought Jeevan. What is he doing here? He walked forward, and stopped a few paces away from the car.

'Excuse me,' Jeevan said.

The man looked up. His eyes were light-colored and piercing. He looked over his shoulder, then at the pump's display where the numbers were running up, not rapidly enough. This was not the kind of neighborhood where he wanted to be accosted by a stranger.

'I'm sorry to disturb you,' said Jeevan. 'But, are you Cal Ripken?'

'Yes,' said the man.

'I'm honored to meet you, Mr Ripken,' said Jeevan, quickly turning to look at the door of the convenience store. Should he run in and call Sunita, or would Cal leave by the time he came out? Did he have the time to run to Henry's house and call him? Could he ask Cal to wait?

'Thanks,' said Cal.

'I don't know much about baseball,' said Jeevan, 'but my neighbor Henry has always said very good things about you.'

'That's great,' said Cal.

'Henry and you have something in common,' said Jeevan.

'What's that?' asked Cal, taking the nozzle out of his car and putting the tank's cap back on.

'He also never missed a day of work,' said Jeevan.

Cal looked up at Jeevan and smiled. 'Is that right?'

'Yes,' said Jeevan. 'He's retired now. But when he was working, he never missed a day of work. His leg was broken in the war, but he limped through work every day.'

'Listen!' Sunita's voice came from behind him. Jeevan turned.

'Do you want ice cream?' asked Sunita.

'Yes,' said Jeevan hurriedly. 'Vanilla.'

When Jeevan turned, Cal was still there, standing by his car. 'One second,' he said. 'I think I might have something for your friend Henry.'

He opened the back door of the car and leant in, coming out with a baseball and a pen. He wrote something on the baseball and walked towards Jeevan with it. 'Here,' he said. 'Maybe Henry would like to have this.'

Jeevan looked down at the ball. Scrawled in small letters were the words: 'Henry, thanks for going to work every day, Cal.'

Looking up at the man who would play two thousand six hundred and thirty-two games in a row over seventeen years before finally taking a break, Jeevan found he didn't have the words to say what he wanted to say. He nodded at him and smiled. Cal put his hand out. 'And you are?'

'I'm Jeevan Sharma,' said Jeevan, putting his hand in Cal Ripken's and shaking it.

Acknowledgements

THE FIRST DEBT IS TO TOM CHALKLEY, WHOSE PIECE ON Baltimore's geology inspired me, and whose early encouragement helped me tremendously. The writer and film-maker Charles Cohen, Johns W. Hopkins of Baltimore Heritage Inc., Professor Raymond Wimbush of Morgan State University and Charles Rutheiser of the Annie E. Casey Foundation were kind enough to shed light on various aspects of redevelopment in Baltimore. Special thanks are due to Helen Szablya, Arlene Conn, Karen Johnson and LaShea Hunter at East Baltimore Development Inc. for patiently answering my questions about the relocation process.

Conversations with Bushra Rehman and Melanie Allred were critical in the early development of this book. Ashok Chopra and Hay House provided crucial support in the writing. Stephen Alter and Woodstock School also gave their support to the process. Andre Bernard was very helpful in the early stages of getting this book to publication.

Thanks are also due to Shruti Debi at Aitken Alexander and the entire team at HarperCollins India.

Finally, I want to thank Tripurari Singh, who picked me up from the airport when I first landed in Baltimore, Amitabh Chaudhary, who flew out with me when I left, and Sameer Jadhav, who walked with me to every point we could walk to from our place in Charles Village while I lived there.